# RIDERS ON THE STORM

## RICHARD SPARACINO

Copyright © 2016 by Richard Sparacino

All rights reserved. This book or any portion thereof may not be reproduced or used in any manner whatsoever without the express written permission of the publisher except for the use of brief quotations in a book review@

Cover Design and Internal Layouts by the Scarlett Rugers Book Design Agency

www.scarlettrugers.com

Printed in the United States of America

ISBN 978-0-692-75258-6

*This book is dedicated to my family. You are indeed the most important thing in my life.*

## Acknowledgements

Thanks to my wife, Mari, for her patience and understanding during the many rounds of rewrites.

A big thank you to Jacqueline Forster, for her gracious help, support and encouragement when I needed it most.

Praise for my editor, Shannon Roberts, and all those at The Editorial Department for their excellent advice and service.

Kudos to my daughters, Serena and Marissa, for their inspiration and keen insights

Thanks to my daughter, Dayna, for her unwavering compassion for others.

And thanks to my son, Joseph, for being a real life example of true courage

# PROLOGUE

The afternoon sun shone brightly over the dome of St. Peter's Basilica as the young man carrying a day pack strolled through the crowd toward the Egyptian obelisk at the center of the plaza.

When he reached the monument, he sat on a bench and gazed about the square. Several children were chasing each other around the obelisk, bumping into tourists attempting to take pictures. A mother called after her two sons.

The young man glanced at his watch, slid the pack off his shoulder, and pushed it under the bench.

Then he stood up and walked away.

A short distance from the square, an ex-Marine in the traditional uniform of the Swiss Papal Guard stood beside the entrance to the secret archives of the Vatican Library.

Drakin gazed through the eyes of his host and pursed the mercenary's lips into a crooked smile. *Right on time.*

BOOM!

The explosion was deafening. Black smoke billowed high into the air as the obelisk came crashing down in a blaze of fire.

In the ensuing chaos, Drakin rode the ex-Marine through the Via di Porta Angelica and stopped at the entrance to the archives.

Two guards stood at attention.

"There's been an explosion in the piazza," he said. "We've been ordered to evacuate."

"We can't leave our post," one of the guards said. "You should know that."

The other guard gave him a curious look. "I've not seen you before."

"You see me now." He made as if to turn away but then pulled out a pistol and shot them both between the eyes.

The mercenary climbed the narrow winding staircase past barred windows and tiny paneled chambers. At the top of the Tower of the Winds, he entered a great room crammed with tens of thousands of ancient tomes.

Drakin peered through the man's eyes. Books didn't interest him. He was here for only one thing: the staff.

He walked past row after row, searching for the room that housed the artifacts. Finally, in one of the alcoves to his right, he saw a locked door.

He pulled back his leg and with one swift movement kicked it in.

Drakin spent several minutes searching, certain he'd sense its location. But he felt nothing. "Where the hell is it?"

"What are you doing in here?" A man with a gray beard and spectacles, hunched with age, glared at him.

"Are you deaf, old man?" the mercenary said. "There's been an explosion in the plaza. Are you the curator here?"

"Yes." The old man glanced at the shattered door in confusion.

Drakin took advantage, slipping out of the mind of the mercenary and sliding into the curator's. He wasn't interested in manipulating the old man—he needed information.

After a few moments of probing, he found what he wanted and felt a surge of anger.

The staff had been moved—to New York City.

No matter. Drakin had mastered the art of adaptation centuries ago. Even in the face of disappointment, he tried to maintain a fluid attitude. Besides, the most vital elements of his plan were still on track.

He returned to the mind of the mercenary and retraced his steps out of the building and toward the plaza.

The scent of blood and anguish was thick in the air. Dozens were dead. Many more were seriously wounded. Drakin unraveled himself from the mercenary's mind and floated over what remained of the obelisk, letting the negative energy wash over him. He tingled with excitement.

This would be a feast.

He watched the light flicker and die in the eyes of the fatally wounded, drinking in the fear, the pain, the horror. Soon, his hunger was satisfied. Despite the turn of events, today had still been a glorious day.

Now it was time to visit New York.

Drakin rose up, floated over St. Peter's Basilica, and disappeared into the sky.

# CHAPTER 1

### DECEMBER 1, 2015

The elevator doors opened and a bald man with bloodshot eyes walked out. Detective Anthony Santini stepped past him into the elevator and pushed the button for the 102nd floor. There was a jolt as the car began its ascent. When it stopped and the doors slid open, he walked out onto the observatory platform of the Empire State Building.

He looked around. It was dark and he was alone.

The wind and rain hammered his body as he walked toward the railing. Shivering, he gazed out into the distance, straining to see the Manhattan skyline.

But there was no skyline—only fire. Everywhere he looked.

Buildings and bridges were gone, collapsed into piles of rubble. Hot embers rained down, and black smoke billowed in the sky.

He smelled the pungent odor of burning flesh as a crash of lightning lit the night, revealing a mass grave as far as the eye could see.

Then he heard it—quietly at first and gradually escalating into a frenzy of anguished screams. He covered his ears, but the screams wouldn't stop.

From behind, a blast of cold wind slammed his body against the railing. He turned and braced himself, trying to resist, but the wind overcame his effort and he toppled over the side. As he fell, he managed to grab the railing with one hand. He dangled there, muscles straining, a hundred stories above the ground, as the wind howled and shrieked. Then his hand slipped and he plunged through the air, his own screams now joining the others.

Santini jolted upright in bed, beads of sweat sliding down his temples. He opened his eyes. For a moment he felt like he was still falling.

He reached over, turned on the lamp, and looked at the clock. It was 3:00 a.m.

Sleep would be impossible now, so he went into the bathroom and splashed cold water onto his face. He looked into the mirror. Little bags hung from beneath red eyes, and his black hair was matted with sweat. He took a deep breath.

The dream was always the same. A man he'd never seen before would leave the elevator. Santini would ride to the top and look out over an apocalyptic scene. Then the screaming would start, and the wind would push him over the edge. He always woke up before he hit the ground.

He'd only ever had one other recurring nightmare in his entire life: his father's murder. But this was new, with a clarity and intensity that was totally different.

He rubbed his throbbing temples. As a homicide detective, he'd spent his life analyzing clues. It was a long shot, but last week during his off time, he had a sketch artist reproduce the bald man from his dream and run the resulting image through the computerized facial-recognition program. No results. Nothing in the data base at least. Maybe the man didn't even exist. All Santini knew was that there was something very unsettling about him.

Thunder rumbled in the distance. Santini was exhausted and needed to clear his head. He glanced over at his running shoes in the corner of the bedroom. It was still dark, but it wasn't raining yet. Maybe he could get in a run before the clouds broke loose. He pulled on his shoes, threw on some clothes, and locked the door of his Brooklyn brownstone behind him. He took a familiar route down Graham Avenue and turned right onto Bushwick. It was hard to catch his breath in the cold, damp air, but his lungs eventually settled down.

The streets were deserted. All the shops were still dark at this hour. The only dim lights came from Joe's Bakery. He smelled fresh Italian bread and pastries as he jogged past. Maybe he'd stop there on the way back.

As he ran, the snap of a cold wind against his face reminded him of the treacherous wind in last night's dream.

His subconscious was trying to tell him something, and as he picked up his pace and sprinted further into the night, he was determined to figure out what it was.

# CHAPTER 2

Detective John Salvo leaned over the victim and scraped some fingernail residue into an evidence bag as the wind outside rattled the windows of the apartment.

"Same as the other two," Santini said. "Strapped to a chair. Gagged. A hypodermic protruding from each arm." He slowly walked around the body. "But this one has a needle thrust into his heart."

Salvo rifled through the victim's wallet. "Looks like cash was taken again."

"This wasn't a robbery," Santini said. "This was personal."

"Somebody has it in for heroin dealers," Salvo said. "Drug paraphernalia everywhere. We'll probably find a hidden stash, just like the other two."

Santini closed his eyes and called up the images of the previous crime scenes. He had a clear picture: gray bodies strapped and gagged. Dangling hypodermics. Vacuous eyes.

He opened his eyes. Salvo was staring at him.

"You're giving me that look again," Santini said.

"The one where I'm not sure if I should open my mouth because my partner goes into a daydream?"

"You should be used to it by now."

"I should be, but I'm not." He sighed. "Anything?"

Santini frowned. "I should have caught this one sooner."

"You always say that."

"There's a kid, maybe eight or ten years old. No father, just him and his mom. She's a heroin addict. He's used to taking care of her. He comes home one day and finds her face-down in her own vomit—an overdose. He's shuffled from foster home to foster home, and his anger festers until he's old enough to take revenge."

"I'll call Marissa at headquarters," Salvo said. "Have her search the past ten to fifteen years for a heroin-overdose victim, female, who left behind a young boy."

"Probably wasn't far from this neighborhood," Santini said. "You find him, you've found our killer."

Salvo stepped out of the room and made the call. When he returned, Santini could feel Salvo's eyes staring at him again.

"What now?" Santini said.

"Don't you think it's time you did something about this?"

"I just told you—"

"I'm talking about your insomnia."

Santini shrugged.

"Seriously," Salvo said. "You look like shit. When was the last time you slept—I mean *really* slept?"

Santini closed his eyes and rubbed his temples. The images from his nightmare surfaced. In the distance he could hear the thunder rumbling like an oncoming train inside his head. "I don't know," he said eventually. "Five, maybe six weeks ago."

Salvo, who'd bent back down to study the body, glanced up. "Let me know when you start hallucinating. I don't want to be mistaken for a perp."

Santini walked over to the window and looked out at the darkening sky. "You think my performance is slipping?"

"Not yet," Salvo said. "But you're not at the top of your game."

"I wouldn't know."

"Twenty years you've been looking at this crap. When was the last time you had a vacation? You know, sandy beach, blazing sunset, a Mai Tai in each hand."

"Bad guys don't take vacations."

Salvo rolled his eyes. "That's not the point. You need a break. Especially from this." Salvo gestured toward the victim. "Why don't you come over for dinner tonight? My kids miss their godfather."

Santini shook his head. "Thanks, but I'll take a rain check."

For a few minutes, they stared each other down, until Salvo crossed his arms.

"You're going back up there tonight, aren't you?" He frowned. "What the hell do you think you're going to find?"

"I don't know," Santini said. "A clue, some insight . . . There's got to be a reason I'm having this nightmare."

"You really think you're the only cop that has nightmares?" Salvo sighed. "Look, we've been friends a long time, so maybe you won't slug me for saying this, but you should really go see Dr. Jordan."

Santini glared at his partner. "You know how I feel about shrinks."

"She knows cops. Say you'll at least consider it."

Santini pulled on his long black overcoat and wrapped a gray scarf around his neck. "I'll think about it."

"And I'm going up there with you tonight."

"I don't need anybody to hold my hand," he said. "I just need to gather my thoughts. Alone."

"Fine. I'll have the uniforms canvas the apartment complex." Salvo gave him a look. "Guess I'm stuck doing the paperwork."

"That's what partners are for."

Santini stole another glance at the victim before putting on his black cap and walking out the door.

Maybe he did need a vacation.

# CHAPTER 3

Santini walked toward the railing that surrounded the observation deck of the Empire State Building. As he peered over the edge, he felt a wave of vertigo. He thought about his dream and backed away.

A cold relentless wind hammered the deck. Low-hanging clouds obscured the Manhattan skyline, though occasionally one would blow past and dissipate, giving him a momentary glimpse of the city below. The city he had devoted his life to trying to protect.

Since the skyscraper's construction in 1931, thirty-four people had hurled themselves to their deaths from this building. He'd investigated one himself a while back. It had been considered a potential homicide, but it turned out she'd jumped willingly.

What the hell could make a person think life was more painful than a hundred-story plunge onto cold hard concrete?

There were only a handful of people up here tonight, and he had the north side of the skyscraper to himself. This was the spot from his dream, where the wind had pushed him over.

He forced himself back toward the railing.

He'd been up here three times this week already, and he'd walked the platform every time, noting every nook and cranny, studying the city from every possible vantage point. He had no idea what he was looking for, what he was hoping to find.

Maybe Salvo was right. Everybody has nightmares.

He watched black clouds race across the sky.

For the last two decades, he'd tracked down some of the worst predators to walk the face of the Earth. He'd brought justice to the victims and taken solace in that. But was it enough? For every killer caught, two more took their place. What had he really accomplished?

A bolt of lightning lit the sky, triggering a steady downpour, and a cold wind wormed its way through his body. He rubbed his hands together, but the chill only seemed to get worse.

"*Santini.*"

He spun around. There was no one.

Shivering, he inhaled. *Must be the lack of sleep.*

"*Santini.*"

This time there was no mistaking the sound of his name.

"Who's calling me?" he yelled over the wind.

A buzzing filled his head, barely audible at first and then growing in intensity. Deep fatigue flooded every muscle. Pressure squeezed his temples as the noise grew louder, making it hard to think.

Just when he thought his brain would explode, he heard a voice.

"You want to end the nightmares?" It was in his head, deep and hissing, but it wasn't him. "Then jump."

Santini looked around and clutched the railing, knuckles white. There was no one else there, but the cold was getting worse.

"Come, Detective. You deserve a rest." The voice sounded so . . . reasonable. "Just climb the rails and you can soar like an eagle."

"No!" Santini cried. But then he heard another voice—a more familiar voice.

"Anthony?" It was his father. "Come home, Anthony. Your mother and I are waiting for you. Just one more step, son."

Santini clamped his hands over his ears, but his father's voice wouldn't be stifled. The wind seemed to push him forward.

"Just one more step, son. One more step and you'll be free. *Fly home to us, son.*"

Santini's whole body trembled. Time stood still as the wind screeched and screamed around him. Thunder crashed as the voices clamored for him to jump.

Eyes shut tight, he thought of his father's funeral, remembered standing over the coffin.

*I swear I'll find who did this.* He'd made a promise.

Summoning all his strength, Santini hurled his body backward, against the wind and away from the railing, and landed with a smack on the observatory platform.

As he lay there, a fresh torrent of icy rain pelted his face. Squinting through watery eyes, he saw another flash of lightning.

The bald man stood over him, eyes bloodshot, smiling.

He tried to leap to his feet, but his body was cold and slow to respond. By the time he made it upright, the man was gone.

> *"Man is made or unmade by himself,*
> *In the armory of thought, he forges the weapons*
> *By which he destroys himself,*
> *He also fashions the tools with which he builds for himself*
> *Heavenly mansions of joy, strength and peace."*
> *—James Allen*

# CHAPTER 4

Drakin rode the bald man in much the same way that the man now rode the subway from Fifth Avenue to Grand Central Station. But though he was a passenger, he was certainly not a passive one.

Drakin's essence coiled around the man's brain, encapsulating it like a spider's web, enabling him to observe the entire mental and emotional landscape of his mind: every thought, every feeling, every memory.

He was surprised to find the detective snooping around on the observatory deck again. His suspicion aroused, he entered the mind of the man as he looked out over the city and discovered that the detective was having some very interesting dreams. Quite an unusual ability for a human. So, as a precaution, he'd tried to kill him. Unfortunately, he couldn't get him to jump. He would have simply used the bald man to do the job, but this man was not wired for that level of violence. Drakin could plant suggestions and push the envelope, but he couldn't force a human to do anything not in his or her character.

Most were no challenge. Most were weak fools. Once he recognized the negative mental patterns and the violent tendencies within a mind, entry was easy. And once he was inside, all it took was a thought planted here, an idea amplified there, and the puppet show would begin.

Drakin was not accustomed to being repelled, and his energy field had been weakened by his clash with the detective's mind. Usually, he took the time to assess the viability of a new host. Entering Santini had been a spontaneous act of curiosity.

No harm done. But it was time to replenish himself, and since the bald man had been compromised, it was time for a new host. One with fewer scruples.

When the man got off the train to retrieve his car, Drakin interceded.

*I could use a stiff drink right about now,* the man thought. So he walked into the nearest bar.

An hour later, Drakin could hear the bartender as he leaned over the counter.

"You've had enough for one night, Mac. How about I call you a cab?"

The man's face folded into a scowl. "I'm fine. One more for the road."

The bartender grabbed his empty glass. "The road doesn't want one more. You've had enough."

"What? The hell with you!" He turned and stumbled out the front door into the wind and rain.

Drakin watched through the man's eyes as he looked around for his car. When he finally found it—a Ford pickup—he tried several times to insert the key into the lock.

"Ah, shit. I should call a cab."

As soon as Drakin felt resistance, he increased the pressure. A buzzing filled the man's head, and then another line of reasoning took off.

*Come on, concentrate. You can do it. A real man can hold his liquor. Just focus.*

He licked his lips with determination, slipped the key into the lock, and climbed inside. Forgetting his seat belt, he cranked the engine.

The pickup weaved its way down Fifth Street, zigzagging from one side of the road to the other, clipping parked cars as it passed.

He thought about his last day of work and heard his boss's voice.

"You're fired, Slater. Security! Escort him out of the building. Now!"

He gripped the steering wheel tighter and clenched his jaws. "Who the hell does he think he is?" he shouted.

Drakin sensed another opportunity, so he triggered the man's memory.

"You pathetic excuse for a husband. I'm sick of your empty promises."

He pushed down on the accelerator, and the truck lurched forward. The speed gave him a sense of power and exhilaration.

Drakin felt the tension mounting in the man's mind. The wipers slammed furiously back and forth, and another flurry of voices jockeyed for attention:

"I can't believe I married such a weak, sniveling excuse for a man."

"You're fired, Slater."

"My mother was right. You're a loser."

"I'll show them," he said.

With a defiant grin on his face and eyes that blazed a fiery red, the bald man's foot slammed the gas pedal to the floor.

The truck shot forward, the engine roared, and tires screeched as the vehicle sliced through the wind and rain.

Drakin fled the man's mind just before his skull found glass and metal at eighty mph. It was always prudent for him to evacuate before things got messy.

Orchestrating accidents was a simple task, but one that generated large amounts of negative energy. And it was this that sustained him.

A tremendous crack of thunder and lightning lit up what was left of the red Mustang and the twisted faces of the four teens crushed against its metal. The two in the front seat were already dead, their heads pummeled by the force of the impact. The two in the backseat, their bodies mangled and broken, shuddering and bleeding, were not yet dead. They would do nicely.

The haunting voices in the wind howled and shrieked.

He descended on the first female and slipped his invisible tentacles deep into her mind so he could absorb the energy of fear, pain, and anguish.

As Drakin held firm, he felt each tendril pulsate with an undulation of energy. With each surge, the voices on the wind responded and wailed in a roaring frenzy. With each negative emotion extracted, the storm reacted with ever greater crashes of thunder and lightning until a haunting symphony seemed to play out between the feeding entity and the elements of the storm.

Drakin sensed that she could feel his tentacles writhing through her mind and that she knew she was dying. He saw the horror in her eyes as the light within them slowly flickered and went out.

Drakin shuddered and let out a long deep moan, like the howl of a wolf, that ripped through the storm.

He considered waiting for the arrival of the police and firefighters. They could always be counted on to radiate negative emotions, and he always enjoyed watching their minds as they tried to puzzle together what had happened.

But he was done here. This was a mere diversion, something to pass the time and quell his appetite for energy, while the elements of his next, more ambitious project began to take shape.

The world had changed in his favor. He could feel it in the tips of his tendrils. He could sense it in the willing nature of the minds he pushed. Humanity had taken a major step in his direction, and he had more allies and more strength than ever.

Although content, he reminded himself that he'd have to deal with the detective.

Drakin had learned to never leave anything to chance. Especially when it came to humans. For now, the detective was just a confused and troubled man haunted by a nightmare. But he was also persistent and strong-willed.

Now that Drakin had penetrated the man's mind, he knew everything about him. Everything. He had discovered the technique for accessing memory centuries ago. It was no small feat, requiring the application of his own energy into certain circuits of a human's brain that would light up those neurons and display the memories. So he knew more about Detective Anthony Santini than the man knew about himself. By the time Drakin was finished with him, he'd wish he had jumped when given the chance.

Drakin pulsated with satisfaction and coalesced above the crushed car. He slowly drifted down Fairfax Avenue, rose into the sky, and disappeared into the night.

*If you keep looking back, the past
will eventually catch up with you.*

# CHAPTER 5

By the time Santini made it home, he was exhausted. The rain was pouring in a steady cadence, and the thunder from the escalating storm seemed to be hovering directly over his brownstone.

He traded his wet clothes for jeans and a T-shirt and poured himself a glass of scotch. The warm glow of the drink was comforting as he leaned back into the soft leather couch. Finally his body stopped shaking.

He'd tried to find the man he thought he'd seen, running to the elevator, searching the lobby, looking up and down Fifth Avenue in the pouring rain. But the man had vanished into thin air.

Santini considered himself a rational, analytical type, not given to flights of fancy. He'd used his intuition throughout his career, but it was intuition born of facts, and reason had always been the cornerstone of how his mind operated. It was the nature of detective work. But now he was hearing voices and seeing phantoms from his dream.

Maybe his lack of sleep had finally given way to hallucinations, like Salvo had implied. But the voices and the man's face seemed all too real. He took another gulp of his drink.

And there was something else. The voices that encouraged his suicide seemed to originate from his own mind, which was disturbing enough, but what had really shaken him was to hear his father's voice.

He glanced up at the framed photo of his father in uniform holding his son on his lap. His father had loved him. At least that much he was certain of tonight. So he couldn't accept that his own subconscious would use his father's voice against him. But it had happened.

Maybe the insomnia, the nightmares, the voices were all signs of a more deeply rooted problem. He knew his career had taken its toll. His most recent case had consumed him—a serial killer who enjoyed torching his victims. He could still see the charred, smoldering bodies. Four innocent people had died horrific deaths before he and Salvo tracked the maniac down. But they'd been three victims too late.

He listened to the sound of thunder rumbling overhead and the battering of the rain on his windows. There was something about this storm that gnawed at him like a knife probing inside his head. And these new nightmares and lack of sleep were leaving him exhausted, as if he weren't quite plugged into his body.

As he stared out the window, an overwhelming loneliness washed over him. It was like a deep ache in the pit of his stomach.

He drained the rest of the scotch, leaned back and closed his eyes.

For the first time in his life, he felt like he was losing it.

The next morning, Santini paced in Dr. Kelly Jordan's waiting room and wondered if he'd made the right decision.

A few years ago he'd undergone counseling to salvage what was left of his marriage, but that had failed miserably. He wasn't thrilled about the idea of someone prying into his head again.

It was a small room, brightly painted in red and yellow, with several landscape and ocean pictures on the walls. *Scenes to soothe the troubled mind*, he thought.

There were just a few chairs. Usually, not much waiting was done here. Shrinks kept tight control over their schedules. When your hour was up, you were out the door.

He glanced over at the receptionist, wondering how much longer he would have to endure this wait.

She noticed his nervousness. "Sorry, Mr. Santini. Patients have been late due to the storm, so the doctor is running behind."

He continued pacing.

"They say the storm might last several more days," she said, "and could be one of the worst in decades."

He said nothing but stopped pacing to stare out the window.

"Already there's flooding," she said, "and power outages all over."

As if on cue, the office lights flickered as the backup generators kicked in.

Santini turned toward the receptionist. "You should be on the six o'clock news. Are you trying to cheer me up with a weather report?"

She laughed. "Did it work?"

Santini couldn't help smiling.

Finally the door to Dr. Jordan's office swung open. A young girl stood there.

"The doctor can see you now, Mr. Santini."

He had the sudden urge to turn and run, but somehow his body moved toward the open door. When he stepped inside, the doctor immediately walked over and shook his hand.

"Good morning, Detective Santini. I'm Dr. Kelly Jordan."

He was tongue-tied. He didn't expect a shrink to be as attractive as the woman who stood there smiling. She had dark brown hair, tied back, and soft brown eyes that immediately grabbed his attention. He could tell she was athletic, and she moved with an air of confidence that he found reassuring. She motioned toward one of two high-back leather chairs facing each other.

"Please have a seat."

He looked around the room. "What, no couch?"

She laughed. "I save that for the more serious cases."

He grabbed a chair.

"I've studied your file," she said. "It seems you're very good at what you do. Quite a distinguished career, with several cases attracting national attention."

"I don't like the spotlight," he said. "I'm a private person. But my partner makes up for it."

She leaned forward. "So why are you here, Detective?"

"I'm not sleeping well. Maybe you can prescribe something?"

"You know it's not going to be as easy as that."

He shrugged. "It was worth a try."

"Why are you having difficulty sleeping?"

The images from his dream surfaced and he tried to push them out. "It's the nightmares."

"Tell me about them."

He looked down and thought for a minute. "There's one I've been having for a while now."

"Describe the dream."

She looked intently into Santini's eyes in a way he found encouraging. He tried not to think about how attractive she was. Finally, he closed his eyes and proceeded to recount the dream on the observatory platform.

"Why this particular location?" she said. "Does it hold any significance for you?"

He opened his eyes. "Don't think so. When I was a kid, my parents brought me there a few times."

"Were those fond memories?"

"Yeah, sure." Santini closed his eyes. "I remember running out onto the platform, arms outstretched, pretending to be an eagle flying over the city."

She smiled. "That sounds like a happy moment."

He shrugged. "I was a kid. Unaware of the violence on the streets below."

She nodded. "What other times have you been there?"

"A while back, investigating a suicide. A woman jumped to her death."

He noticed that this caught her attention.

"Cases like that must be difficult," she said.

"Suicides trouble me. But if I let every case rattle me, I'd have been in here a long time ago."

"In your dream, you say you fell from the skyscraper."

"Yeah, but I didn't jump."

"Could it be this suicide investigation triggered your nightmare?"

He paused to think. "That investigation was over a year ago. It can't be related."

Dr. Jordan leaned back in her chair. "So what made you decide to become a homicide detective? Was it something you always wanted to do?"

Santini hesitated. "Is this where I tell you about my childhood and you shake your head while taking prodigious notes?"

She held out her open hands. He couldn't help noticing there was no ring on the left hand. "As you can see, I don't take notes, nor do I record sessions. I've been blessed with an excellent memory, so I remember everything you tell me."

He raised an eyebrow. "I don't know if that's such a great thing . . . for you, I mean. You must have quite a collection of stories in your head."

Dr. Jordan smiled. "Are you avoiding the question, Detective?"

After hesitating, he lifted the gold chain that hung around his neck and pulled out the badge suspended from it. "This was my father's. I always carry it with me."

"And what happened to your father?"

"He was a police officer, shot while off duty. I was there."

"Your father was shot in front of you?" She shook her head. "I'm so sorry."

Santini was skilled at reading faces and could see the sincerity in her eyes. "Yeah. Since then I've dreamed about it."

"Tell me about this dream."

He'd known this was coming. He took a deep breath and closed his eyes. "It was the summer of 1982. We were going to Yankee Stadium. I'd turned twelve that day. The tickets to the game were my birthday present. I don't think I've ever been more excited. The dream begins when we stop at the bake shop for doughnuts. The owner goes to the back of the store. My father turns to tell me Tommy John was pitching for the Yankees. Several loud cracks fill the air and cause me to jump. My father goes down. I see a circle of bright red spreading across his chest. I cry, begging him not to leave me, but he dies instantly. Then I wake up." Santini sighed. "He was a smart cop. Had one of the best records in the NYPD. But he didn't have a chance. Never saw it coming. The man just walked up, shot him, and looted the register."

He turned the badge over in his hand.

"Only the day before we were practicing in the park. I'd just become strong enough to swing my father's bat. It was an old Louisville Slugger. But he always said I swung too hard." His eyes watered. " 'Don't try to kill the ball,' he'd say. 'Swing easy. And remember, it's the curve balls that can throw off your timing. You never know when they're coming.' "

Santini paused and looked down at his hands.

"He got that right. I keep his bat leaning against my bookcase at home. When I grip the bat, it feels warm, as if I can feel my father's energy." He stopped abruptly, as if wanting to take back what he'd just said. "Maybe that sounds nuts."

"No, it doesn't, Detective." Dr. Jordan smiled. "Not at all."

Santini appreciated her response. "Have you ever had something like that happen to you? One moment the world is all good, then suddenly it's upside down?"

She was pensive for a moment. "Nothing in my life compares to witnessing the murder of a loved one, Detective, but my world has been turned upside down once or twice. What's important is how we process these events so we can eventually move on."

Santini nodded.

"It must have been difficult for you and your mother afterward," she said.

"There were good people in the neighborhood back then. People took care of each other."

"Did she ever remarry?"

"She had the good sense to wait till I was older, so it was just the two of us until I was eighteen and I entered the academy. Then she met Tom and eventually got married."

"Did you get along with your stepfather?"

"He was all right. Took care of my mother. Always treated me good. But I'm afraid I gave him a hard time."

"Why was that?"

"It's not easy to see another man with your mom, living in the same house where my father lived." He sighed. "As soon as I could, I moved out."

"And where is your mother now?"

Santini looked down. "Died. Five years ago. Cancer."

"And your stepfather."

"Moved down to Florida to be with his kids. He sends me a card now and then."

"Do you have any other family, Detective?"

"Just my partner and the precinct."

They both remained quiet for a few moments.

"So you became a police officer because of what happened to your father?"

Santini looked at his father's badge. "At the funeral they gave me this. I remember how it glittered in the morning sun. Just before they lowered him into the ground, I placed my hand on his coffin and made a promise."

"And what was it you promised?"

"That I'd find the man who did this. That I'd make him pay, and that I'd devote my life to putting human garbage like him behind bars. Now you know what motivates me."

"That's an enormous undertaking for a twelve-year-old."

Santini shrugged. "Like I said, my partner and I have a pretty good record. But . . ."

"But what, Detective?"

He looked down, a defeated expression on his face.

"He's still out there. My father's killer. A lowlife who would kill a man for pocket change. Just vanished into thin air. There's not a day goes by I don't think about it."

Dr. Jordan nodded. "Let's get back to your dream of the observatory. Is the man in the elevator always the same?"

"Yes."

"Someone you know?

"Never seen him before."

"A victim maybe, or a perpetrator?"

"No. Believe me, I'm trained to remember faces and I've racked my memory."

"In your dream, the city was destroyed and people were killed. As difficult as it is, do you feel as if you've adequately protected the people in New York?"

His eyes widened. "You're kidding, right? Do you think this dream is about guilt? My partner and I have done the best we could. Better than most. Hell, it's an insane world out there and you of all people should know that."

"Of course, Detective. I'm sorry, but we're just trying to decipher the symbolism of you dream and explore all possible meanings."

He relaxed, his annoyance softened by her sincerity.

"And you say you were pushed off the building?" she said.

"By the wind."

"Have you ever had suicidal thoughts?"

He fidgeted. *She's probing again.* He thought about the voices that demanded he jump. *But they weren't my thoughts.* And he'd fought against them. "I'd never take my own life. It's not how I'm wired."

Dr. Jordan gazed intently at him. He could tell she was trying to determine the truthfulness of his last answer.

"As you said, it's a hard world we live in, and most people have periods in their lives when they struggle with sadness. Because of the nature of your work, it's common for police officers to suffer from depression. Have you noticed any emotional changes recently that might hint of that possibility?"

Santini hesitated. *Probing, probing.* It was always hard for him to admit to weakness. Talking to a stranger about his emotions was difficult. When his father died, his life had been about surviving. At the time, happiness was an indulgence he couldn't afford. He thought about his failed marriage.

"I don't know." he said. "I suppose I'm not exactly a barrel of laughs."

"You were married once?"

"For three years."

"What was her name?"

He realized it had been a long time since he'd spoken her name. "Casey."

"What happened?"

"Like I said, I'm not exactly a barrel of laughs."

Dr. Jordan paused, and he sensed she was processing his remarks.

"You said not a day goes by you don't think about your father's murder. Unresolved issues like that have a tendency to fester in the subconscious. And often those issues manifest as recurring dreams. Hopefully, we can discover their symbolism."

"I just want to be able to sleep again."

"And you will," she said. "Come again this week. Keep a pad by your bedside. When you awaken from a dream, write down the details immediately. I'm going to prescribe a light sedative that will help you sleep but won't interfere with your dreams. There's still much we can learn from them."

Santini stood up. "Did we accomplish anything?"

"This will take time. It's like peeling layers off an onion to get to the core. There are images buried deep in your subconscious mind that are starting to surface into your dreams and cause trouble. Police officers often compartmentalize gruesome images from crime scenes. It's a smart psychological strategy, but given the right triggers, these images eventually escape their cages."

"Is that what you think is happening?" he asked. "Crime scenes coming back to haunt me?"

"Yes. And I can help you deal with these images." Then her expression turned serious. "But you must be patient, and most importantly, you must be completely honest with me. Then I'll be able to help you."

He shook her hand. "Thank you."

As Santini walked out, he wished he could be as confident as she seemed to be.

# CHAPTER 6

The 109th Precinct was relatively quiet today. The loudest sound was that of the pounding rain on the old roof of the building. Several leaks splattered water onto the floor, and the janitor scurried about with a mop and a few buckets.

Santini walked into the cold-case evidence room in the windowless basement beneath the main office of the precinct. It was dark, dreary, and musty, as if a brighter ambience would disturb the dead victims each box represented.

Sergeant Jacobs, custodian of records, popped his head up from his desk. Jacobs was very happy with his administrative position, but he was never happy when he had to get up from his desk and carry around his excess fifty pounds.

"Haven't seen you in a while," Jacobs said. "What can I do for you, Detective?"

Santini had seen as many as seven or eight faces behind this counter over the years. Some looked older than the case files stored here. When they first started out, they tried to be encouraging, hoping each box they hauled out to be reviewed would shed new light on a case and bring some closure for the victims and their families. Eventually, they came to realize that the odds of that happening were very small.

"Case file 1742," Santini said.

Jacobs frowned. "You always seem to want the files stored in the other side of the building. All right, give me a minute."

Santini watched as the man slowly disappeared down a long aisle of stacked boxes, some of which had sagged and turned yellow with age. A few minutes later the Sergeant returned and Santini signed the release. He brought the box back to his desk.

A year ago, he and Salvo had investigated the shooting of a schoolteacher by a gang member. The evidence was thin and they'd never found the murder weapon, but a neighbor finally came forward claiming she'd seen a young man running from the victim's house on the night she was killed. Apparently, she was afraid and had kept her mouth shut. Until today.

Salvo was taking the woman's statement in the interrogation room. A sketch artist was with them.

*He'll be a while yet*, Santini thought, so he turned around and headed back downstairs to the evidence room.

"Forget something, Detective?" Sergeant Jacobs asked.

Santini hesitated. "Case file 0189."

The sergeant stared at him. "Again?"

"Yeah, again," he said.

Jacobs turned and walked down one of the aisles, grumbling.

Santini dropped the second box onto his desk. He could feel his heart race. He opened the box and emptied the contents one at a time, laying the objects out neatly in a row.

The photos of his father lying in a pool of blood were still painful to look at, and though he'd trained himself to be an objective observer, they always rattled him. And the pictures always triggered his memory.

He closed his eyes. He's twelve, standing with his father in the bakery. In the corner of his eye, he sees an outstretched arm, and then the gunshots. His father goes down.

Someone tapped his shoulder. Santini's eyes flew open. He turned to see Salvo standing behind him. His partner glanced at the photos on the desk.

"What happened to the Rosen file?"

"It's right here."

Salvo shook his head. "It's been a long time since you've looked at this ... Why now? And don't tell me it's because we've missed something."

Santini shrugged. "I thought it was just time."

"This is about your dreams, isn't it?"

"Do you always have to play detective with me?"

"Yeah, because that's the only way I can find out what's going on inside that skull of yours."

"Isn't it odd after a lifetime of dreaming about my father's murder, it stops?" Santini snapped his fingers. "Just like that."

"The upside is you won't have to watch your father being shot every night."

Santini began collecting the items on his desk and placing them back in the box. "If I'd only turned around, I would have seen the man. I was an eyewitness. A useless one. It was all a blur. I don't remember seeing a damn thing."

Salvo glanced at the framed photo of his two sons on his desk. His eldest was the same age Santini had been when his father was shot. "You were just a kid. In shock. If you'd turned around, you'd probably be dead."

"I know what you're going to tell me. Let it go."

"I wish you would. I wish you'd give yourself a break and stop obsessing about it. There's nothing more you can do."

Santini remained silent as he picked up the box.

"And how was your last trip up to the observatory?" Salvo asked.

Santini sighed. He decided then not to share the details of his last episode on the Empire State Building with his partner. It was all still a confused jumble. "It was a waste of time."

But Santini could sense that Salvo knew he was holding something back.

Salvo stared at him. "Look, we try to be honest with each other, right? That's why we've survived as partners for as long as we have. But lately, I don't know what the hell is going on with you."

Santini nodded. "You're right. The problem is, I don't know what the hell's going on either."

There was a long silence.

"Any progress with Dr. Jordan?" Salvo asked.

"I don't know. She said it's like peeling layers off an onion. Whatever that means."

"Give her a chance."

"You could have warned me."

"Warned you about what?"

"That she was a babe."

Salvo grinned. "Would you have preferred a Dr. Ruth type, or maybe a bearded man with a cigar?"

"It's distracting."

"Damn. Don't tell me you have a thing for her. That's not good. Patient-doctor relationship ethics, remember. It won't work out well."

"I know, I know." Santini stared at his partner. "How do you do it?"

"What?"

"Mary, the kids, keeping it all together. Despite the crap we see."

Salvo looked pensive for a moment. "If it wasn't for Mary and the boys, I'd have been in Jordan's office a long time ago. They ground me. They pull me out of the dark places my mind slips into. Just the sound of the kids' laughter snaps me back."

Santini turned somber. "I miss her."

"I know."

"I won't make the same mistake again."

"I know you won't," Salvo said.

A fresh torrent of wind and rain hammered the roof, and an explosion of thunder rocked the old building.

Santini shook his head. "Could be I've slipped into a dark place."

"Dr. Jordan will pull you out," Salvo said.

"I don't know. I hope so."

Salvo placed his hand on Santini's shoulder. "She will, partner."

# CHAPTER 7

Santini opened his eyes and sat at the edge of the bed. It was dark. Rain pelted the roof and thunder crashed. He reached over to turn on his bedside lamp but couldn't seem to locate it. He stood up and walked toward the doorway, feeling for the light switch. He turned it on.

This wasn't his bedroom.

He walked down a hallway and turned into a kitchen, where he opened a drawer and grabbed a long knife. He walked back down the hallway to his parents' bedroom.

No, not his parents'. Someone else's.

In the darkness of the bedroom he could see two people asleep. A bolt of lightning lit the room, and in the flash of light he could see his shadow—no, someone else's shadow—cast against the wall with the knife held high in the air.

He tried to stop the arm from swinging downward. He tried to warn them, screaming for them to wake up. But his screams were soundless, and he watched in horror as the knife plunged repeatedly into them.

He walked back down the hallway to the bedroom and sat on the edge of the bed. He looked down at bloodied hands—then the knife turned inward. He could see the glint of the sharp blade lit by another bolt of lightning. He tried to turn the knife away, but it wouldn't move. *No, don't do it!*

The knife reared back and plunged into his stomach.

Santini shot upright in bed, droplets of sweat rolling down his temples. He leaned over and flicked on the lamp. It was his bedroom. He glanced down at his hands. No blood. He rubbed his abdomen, half-expecting a grimace of pain. Nothing.

*What the hell was that?*

He glanced at the clock. Two a.m. *Forget sleep.* He dragged himself out of bed. His hands were still shaking and he was breathing heavily.

He couldn't decide whether it was too early or too late for a drink. He finally decided he didn't care, so he got dressed and poured himself a scotch.

Replaying the dream in his head, he didn't know what to make of it. He didn't know what to make of any of these dreams lately. He glanced over at the notepad on his night table. He didn't need to write anything down. The details of this nightmare were not something he was likely to forget.

He walked over to the window. He hadn't seen a storm like this in a long time. The windows rattled as if the wind would break through at any second and present him with a front-row seat to the torrential rain, and the trees swayed as if their roots would be pulled up at any moment.

There was something off about this storm. He couldn't quite put his finger on what it was, but he wished it would end.

It was six o'clock when he dozed off. It was seven when his cell phone rang.

"Santini here."

"It's Salvo. Just got a call. Frost Street. CSI is already there. I'll pick you up in a half hour."

"Right."

He took a cold shower to wake himself up. He was glad to have a case to work on, hoping it would take his mind off the dreams. He was tired and needed a distraction.

The blue unmarked Crown Victoria pulled up in front of Santini's brownstone, and he climbed in.

Salvo scrutinized his partner. "I don't suppose you slept last night."

Santini suppressed a yawn. "Two or three hours."

"When do you see the doc again?"

"Thursday. I can't wait."

"Give her a chance." Salvo sniffed the air. "And self-medicating isn't the answer."

Santini glanced at his partner.

The rain began pouring as they continued down Bushwick Avenue and then turned onto Frost Street. They stopped in front of a house where three police cars, a crime scene van, and an ambulance were parked.

Santini and Salvo walked past the crime scene tape and were met by Officer Manny Menendez. He looked tired and was soaked through.

"What do we have, Manny?" Santini asked.

"We have a mess, that's what. And he's one of our own. Retired."

"Who called it in?" Salvo asked.

"Cleaning lady. She starts early every other Tuesday. She's pretty shaken up."

"She touch anything?" Santini asked.

"Nope. Ran right out of the house and called 911."

"All right, Manny," Salvo said. "Let's get out of the rain."

They filed into the house, and Santini felt a flutter in the pit of his stomach.

The rooms smelled of stale cigar smoke. The furniture was dated but well kept. A recliner and a couch were centered on a large flat-screen TV. There were family photos scattered around the living room, several of a man in police uniform. Santini stopped to look at one of the photos.

"John Gorman," Manny said. "Seventy-fifth Precinct in Staten Island. Thirty-five years on the force. Only five years retired. A damn shame."

Manny led them down the hallway and turned into one of the bedrooms. Santini and Salvo trailed. Two CSI officers were collecting evidence and taking photographs.

"Looks like their son was the perpetrator," Manny said. "Jason Gorman. Now, that's not an easy way to kill yourself. Looks like a murder-suicide."

Santini stared at the body of the young man on the bed. A long knife protruded from his bloodied abdomen. He blinked several times and for a moment couldn't breathe.

"You know this kid?" Salvo asked him.

Santini didn't answer. "Where are the parents?"

Manny led them down the hallway to another bedroom.

Salvo walked in while Santini peered in from the doorway. He looked around the room and then turned and went back down the hallway to the kitchen. He opened one of the drawers and went back to the first bedroom.

"I need a time of death, Higgins," Santini said.

The CSI officer looked up.

"Based on temperature and lividity, it's been about three hours. The M.E should be able to nail it down, but that's pretty accurate."

Santini made a quick calculation. "So time of death would be between 4:00 and 5:00 a.m."

"That's about right, Detective."

Santini turned and walked out of the house. Standing on the front steps, he inhaled deeply. The cold rain pelted his face, but he took no notice.

"What the hell is going on?" Salvo was standing next to him with a puzzled expression.

Santini wiped the rain from his eyes. "It's like Manny said. A murder-suicide."

"Don't you think processing the scene would be a good idea? Just on the off chance we may need some details to corroborate our report?"

"I'm sorry." Santini glanced at his partner and could see the confusion in his eyes. "Take over the investigation."

"What!"

"I need to walk. I'll find my way home."

"Santini. Where the hell are you going? . . . Santini!"

He started down the street and disappeared into the gloom of the early morning.

# CHAPTER 8

The next day, Santini sat in Dr. Jordan's waiting room wondering if he should have come back.

He'd been struggling to come to terms with his dream. He'd gone over it a hundred times. The details of the dream, the details of the crime scene. The two were identical. Except for the time line.

He knew he shouldn't have left Salvo like that, but he'd been rattled. Who wouldn't have been?

"You must be honest with me," Dr. Jordan had said.

So far he hadn't been. He was reluctant to mention the voices he'd heard on the platform of the observatory for obvious reasons. Still, he was reaching the end of his rope and wanted all of this to end.

And now he'd dreamed of a murder before it occurred. He'd talked to the medical examiner, and the exact time of the deaths had been placed at 4:30 a.m. He'd awoken from his dream at 2:00 a.m.

He was called in to see Dr. Jordan. Despite his sullen mood, he couldn't help noticing her brightly colored blouse and reassuring smile. He decided to be as truthful as possible.

"So how did you sleep since I saw you last, Detective?"

"Not well."

"Did you try the light sedative I prescribed?"

Santini shook his head. "Doesn't mix well with the scotch."

"Do you drink every night?"

"I have one or two drinks to unwind at the end of the day."

"Do you ever have more than that?"

He hesitated. "Sometimes."

Dr. Jordan remained silent.

"Was it the same nightmare on the observatory that disturbed your sleep?"

"No. It was different." He thought about the knife plunging into his stomach.

"Tell me about this dream."

"Can I ask you a question first?"

Dr. Jordan leaned back in her chair. "Sure."

"What's your professional opinion of precognitive dreams?"

Her eyes widened. There was a long silence.

"You mean dreams that can foretell future events?"

"Yeah."

She pressed the fingertips of both hands together. "I've never come across an actual case to convince me precognitive dreams were real. There are too many charlatans claiming psychic abilities preying on the gullible. And they're difficult to substantiate. Most are the result of coincidence." She stared intently at Santini. "Is this the type of dream you think you had?"

Santini's brow furrowed. After her skeptical response, his mind was filled with uncertainty. *Be honest.* Finally, he gave it up.

"Two nights ago I dreamed of a murder . . . before it happened."

She sat gazing at Santini.

"You're certain there's no other explanation?"

"I'm certain." He could tell this had taken her by surprise.

"Okay, let's discuss this dream."

He closed his eyes. "On the night of November the twenty-second, I dreamed I woke up in a strange bedroom. In my dream I was seeing through the eyes of a young man. He got up, walked into a kitchen, opened a drawer, pulled out a knife, and crept into his parents' bedroom. I tried to warn them, screaming for them to wake up, but my screams were soundless as I watched him stab both parents. Then he walked back into his bedroom, sat on the bed, and turned the knife on himself." Santini paused, the memory of the dream still raw in his mind. "When I felt the searing pain of the blade, I woke up."

"I assume it was you who was called to the crime scene?" she said.

He nodded. "From the moment my partner and I walked into the house, it was déjà vu. Everything looked familiar. But I brushed it off to lack of sleep. Then when I saw the bodies, the wounds, the murder weapon, the faces of the parents, I knew it was my dream. The medical examiner placed the time of the deaths at 4:30 a.m. When I awakened from the dream it was 2:00 a.m."

There was a long silence.

"Often our dreams reflect events that occurred in the past. Maybe you simply dreamed of a past crime scene that resembles this one?"

He shook his head vigorously. "No. I thought about that. A pitfall of crime detection is to force the evidence, and I've always been wary of this." He could tell she seemed unconvinced. "That's *not* what this is."

She stared at him. "What else can you tell me about this dream?"

"You don't believe me."

"What makes you think I don't—"

"Like you, I read people every day in my line of work," he said.

"What's important is what you believe. The subconscious mind is shrewd and can play tricks on us."

"I'm telling you, I dreamed of this before it happened."

Dr. Jordan shook her head. "Your subconscious has convinced you of this, Detective. And your rational approach to events is being clouded by exhaustion. The nightmares are disrupting your sleep, so let's run some tests to rule out any physical problems."

He gave her a skeptical look. "What kind of tests?"

"Routine but thorough. Blood work, EEG . . . I'd like you to stay for three nights under my supervision at Blackthorne for evaluation."

Santini jumped out of his chair. "I'm not crazy."

"Of course not," she said. "The west wing is the mental hospital. The new east wing of Blackthorne has one of the top sleep clinics in the world. As part of my private practice, I have access to the sleep clinic. You'd be there voluntarily."

Dr. Jordan's soothing voice calmed him down. "Voluntarily?"

"That's right. We'll monitor your brain wave patterns through the various levels of sleep, including the dream state. And we can continue our conversations."

"And I can leave any time I want?"

"You can leave at any time."

He stopped holding his breath. "I'll have to think about it."

"Please, Detective Santini, if you will sit back down . . ."

He dropped down onto the chair. She was quiet for several moments, and he could tell her wheels were spinning.

Dr. Jordan leaned forward in her chair. "Many officers are troubled by gruesome crime scenes to the point where they can't get the images out of their heads. Has that ever happened? Do you see many of the victims' faces in your mind, Detective?"

He stared down at his hands, trying to decide what to say next. Then he looked up.

"When I first made detective, a seven-year-old girl was brutally raped and murdered. We found her body tossed onto the side of the road, lying in the mud. I lost it at the crime scene."

"How so?"

"I was green at the time." He hesitated, feeling somewhat embarrassed. "I cried. Right there, at the scene. I wanted to run, turn in my badge."

"But you didn't. Why not?"

"Because I realized the only thing I could do for this kid was to find the monster that killed her. Stephanie was his fourth victim."

"Was this the only time you lost it at a crime scene?"

"Like that, yes. Now I try not to let my emotions cloud my thinking."

"Do you think about this little girl?"

"Stephanie Winchester. She'd be twenty-seven now. Sometimes I try to imagine what she would look like today."

"Have you had dreams about her?"

"Sporadically, maybe three or four times a year. But always on the day she was murdered."

"What do you dream about?"

He sighed. "I see the little body, the flowered white dress bloodied and torn, the lifeless eyes staring up at the sky." He paused. "Like she was looking up to demand accountability from a God who would allow such innocence to be violated."

"Did you find the child's killer?"

"Damned right I did."

"And what happened when you found him?"

Santini closed his eyes. "I remember how I seethed with anger when I slammed the grinning scumbag facedown and cuffed him." He paused and opened his eyes. "It was the first time I ever thought about putting a bullet in the back of a man's head."

"But you didn't."

"No."

"Did finding the murderer make you feel any better?"

"The fact he's roasting in hell right now is some consolation. But Stephanie is just as dead."

Dr. Jordan nodded. "You've spent your life chasing evil people, haven't you, Detective?"

"Yes."

"What's that like?"

Santini thought for a moment. "It's the smart ones that are hardest to catch. They're like ghosts. They leave no clues behind. So I've spent my life trying to think like them. Trying to see the world through their eyes. That's the reason I'm so successful at what I do."

"Give me an example of how you do this."

"A serial killer develops patterns of behavior." he said. "I spent every waking moment thinking about the man that killed little Stephanie Winchester. What's he eating? How does he dress? What are his triggers? What are his weaknesses? What are his talents? What does he feel when he kills? What does he look like? I'd even pick up the surgical knife which was deemed his weapon of choice and try to reproduce his movements in my imagination." Santini closed his eyes. "I try to visualize all of this and I immerse myself in the crime scenes. Every detail." He opened his eyes. "My partner thinks I take it too far. Eventually I reach a point where I'm beginning to think like them."

"That could be very disturbing," said Dr. Jordan. "What's that like?"

Santini rubbed his temples. "Honestly, it's like being dipped in shit and not being able to get rid of the smell . . . But in this case, it's what eventually helped me track down the bastard."

Dr. Jordan nodded. "Actors sometimes delve so deeply into their characters that they lose their sense of self." She paused and leaned forward. "Have you ever felt that way? Like you were losing yourself?"

He was silent as he shifted uncomfortably in his chair. "What's important are the results."

"But at what price? This process must take an enormous emotional toll."

"Maybe. Would you rather Stephanie's killer was still out there?"

"Of course not." She leaned forward. "Is there anything else, even the most seemingly insignificant detail about your dreams?"

Santini looked straight past Dr. Jordan for a moment. He started to speak, but then he hesitated. Finally, he looked at her and shook his head in resignation. "There's something else."

"What?"

"This is all confidential. Correct?"

"Of course, Detective. Doctor-patient confidentiality."

He closed his eyes. "There's something recently in my dreams. It has no face. No form. It's more like a feeling, a presence, a dark shadow."

"And what kind of a feeling does this presence elicit?"

"A feeling of dread. I can sense its evil intent." This seemed to grab her attention.

"Do you feel threatened by it?"

"Recently, yes."

"Why? What has happened recently to make you feel threatened?"

Santini hesitated, unsure if he should continue. He finally let it out. "It spoke to me."

"And what did it say?"

" 'Jump' . . . over and over. It tried to get me to jump."

"Jump where, Detective?"

"Off the Empire State Building."

"And in your dream, did you jump?"

Santini shook his head vigorously. "No! You don't understand. This happened three nights ago. I was visiting the observatory of the Empire State Building. And I was as wide awake as I am right now."

*"It is necessary for the perfection of human society that there should be men who devote their lives to contemplation."*
—St. Thomas Aquinas

# CHAPTER 9

The wind and rain slammed against the stained glass windows of St. Patrick's Cathedral as if attempting to shatter the celestial scenes into tiny shards.

In the semi-darkness of the confessional box, Father Timothy O'Brian slid the little wooden door across the small partition to reveal the shadow of a gray-haired woman.

"Bless me, Father, for I have sinned. It has been two months since my last confession."

There was a long pause. O'Brian waited for the next line in the ritual, "and these are my sins," but the words didn't come. Instead, small sobs broke the silence.

"There, there, my child. Here you can open your heart to God's mercy and forgiveness. Tell Him what you have come to confess."

The sobbing continued as she tried to speak.

"You know me well, Father. For ten years I've been a faithful parishioner and a devout Christian. I've given my life over to God."

O'Brian turned to look into the shadow of the confessional and recognized Anna Renaldo. Since her husband died five years ago, she'd come to Mass just about every day. And every Sunday she'd help serve Communion, not only at Mass but also in the homes of those who couldn't travel.

"Please help me, Father. I don't know what to confess. I don't know what sin I have committed. But I know it must be something terrible."

Of all his parishioners, Anna was the last person whom he would deem capable of doing something terrible.

"Tell me what it is you think you might have done."

"I don't know. But I've fallen out of grace with God."

"And what would make you think such a thing?"

"Father, I've prayed most of my life, and it has always been a blessing . . . a sanctuary. And many times I've felt God's presence, his love." She started to sob again. "But now when I pray, I swear I can hear voices. Blasphemous voices. I'm so afraid, Father. I don't understand. Am I being punished?"

The priest closed his eyes as a shiver of fear ran up his spine. Anna was the fourth parishioner this week with the same story.

"God does not punish us for our prayers," he said, struggling to keep his voice calm and reassuring. "Don't be frightened. Fear is what Satan hopes for. It is his ally. And he relishes in tempting the most godly among us. Be strong. I cannot think of one more grounded in God's grace and love as Anna Renaldo. Drown out these voices by reciting the Lord's Prayer. And I'll pray for you also, my child. You're not alone. Let's recite the Lord's Prayer right now, together."

When the prayer ended, the sobbing stopped and there was silence. "Thank you, Father. I will do as you say."

Father O'Brian listened as the old woman stood up and the door to the confessional creaked open and then closed. He took a deep breath and walked out into the church.

The air was colder and damper than at any time he could remember in the ten years he'd been here. There were about a dozen people in the pews praying, a small fraction of the normal number, the storm deterring even the most faithful.

He watched the flashes of lightning illuminate the stained glass scenes, but there was something strange about the expressions on the saints' faces, almost as if they were grimacing. He attributed this to his mood and the effect of the lightning.

When the first two parishioners had come to him about the voices, he didn't know what to think, so he referred them to Dr. Jordan, a psychiatrist he trusted.

Now he was hearing the voices as well.

He slowly walked toward the altar, his seventy-five-year-old body aching in the cold damp air, his heart heavy.

Kneeling at the altar, he folded his hands and began to pray. The storm seemed to anticipate this, the thunder crashed with a growing frenzy. He spoke his prayers aloud, trying to overcome the elements of the storm, but the clamorous thunder and whipping wind that rattled the old church became more ferocious in proportion to his incantations.

After a few minutes he gave up. It was just as Anna and the others had said.

When the disturbance had first begun, the voices were faint, barely noticeable. Now they were louder, stronger. They hissed and cursed. They spoke of agony and despair. They spoke with a venomous hatred for God and religion and declared both to be lies. They spoke of death, destruction, and torture. They mocked all that was good and righteous in the world.

He walked across the church and through a side door that led to his apartment. It was a modest dwelling that looked more like a cozy library. O'Brian loved books, and his collections ranged from Catholic mysticism to theological philosophy. He also had numerous books on the Eastern and Oriental religions and particularly enjoyed the practicality of the Buddhist writings. Shivering, he poured himself some hot tea, hoping to thaw the deep chill that had settled into his bones.

Ever since he'd returned to New York from the Vatican, he sensed there was something unnatural about this storm. Behind the rumbling thunder, he could hear voices filled with menace. The same disturbances that had interfered with his prayers and meditations. The same voices now haunting his most devout parishioners.

O'Brian had been a priest now for over forty years, and in all those forty years his faith had never wavered. Until now.

It was not just global events that underscored the violence and hatred that seemed to be growing at an accelerated rate but a deep sense that God was losing the battle for humanity's soul. He tried to not believe this, to ignore what was happening around him, and to believe that things would get better. But he was getting old and tired. On his last visit to Rome, he'd announced his retirement. He took a sip of tea and closed his eyes.

His friend Pope Augustine had been made aware of what was happening here. Tomorrow, he'd speak to him.

He just wished he had something better to report.

The next day Father O'Brian sat at his computer with the image of Pope Augustine on his screen.

The pope smiled. "I would attempt one last effort to change your mind, but I know it would be senseless. I will miss your wise council and your friendship, Timothy."

"I'm honored, Your Holiness. But you know I'll always remain available to you."

The pope nodded. "You must write and tell me what retired life is like. I may never get the chance to find out."

"Your predecessor broke tradition and stepped down voluntarily," O'Brian said. "So you do have options. Although I think you will not follow his lead. You're too attached to your collection of hats. I notice how your face lights up when you don your *galero*."

The pope laughed. "It is my favorite. And it does add a little flair to my appearance. Though I did not know I was so transparent. But then again, not many know me as well as you, Timothy."

"And that has been my honor."

"You and I are alike. We live only to serve. And you have served God and your Church well, my friend." The pope's expression took a serious turn. "Is there news on the disturbance?"

"It has gotten worse. But still confined to those who practice deep contemplation and meditation."

"Unfortunately, since we last spoke of this, I've received similar reports from monks everywhere. The Carmelites, the Benedictines, even those outside the faith."

O'Brian sighed. "The problem is growing."

"Yesterday I received a communication from the Dalai Lama. He's hoping the disturbances are the result of frustration and anxiety among religious leaders. A kind of group nervousness."

"Unfortunately, there's ample evidence for his reasoning."

"Exactly," the pope said. "There's widespread moral and spiritual decline. Hence, we're distracted, troubled. We're like shepherds whose flock has gone astray. But the puzzling thing is, from everything I've heard, it's most noticeable in your city."

"Many of my parishioners are frightened and will no longer pray," O'Brian said. "As for me, I find no peace in meditation and prayer."

The pope's face turned grim. "There are some men, not given to exaggeration, who declare it is the coming of the Anti-Christ. We must not let these groundless claims loose upon the world."

"I agree. There's much we still don't know."

"I'll continue to seek council with spiritual leaders from around the world. But there's one fact in this mystery that's undeniable. There is the scent of evil in the air, my friend. Though you are retiring, God may deem otherwise and may still have further use of your faithful service."

"It is what I live for," O'Brian said.

"Keep me apprised, Timothy."

"I will do as you ask, Your Holiness."

Father O'Brian shut down his computer. As he reached for his tea, he felt his body begin to shiver again. He shuffled over to his file cabinet and unlocked one of the drawers and pulled out a book.

It was one of the many rare books gifted to him from the pope's private library. But this particular book was given to him not so much in the spirit of a gift but more as out of the pope's desire to get rid of it.

He carried the book to his desk. It seemed heavier tonight.

Vatican scholars had puzzled over the origin and dating of the book. It was written in an archaic yet translatable dialect of Latin and seemed to dwell on a catastrophic global event. There was one particular passage O'Brian had bookmarked. He turned to the page and read it again;

> *When the Souls of Men have been Corrupted in Sufficient Numbers,*
> *And Love Withers at its Roots,*
> *When the Collective Mind of Man has turned away from the Light,*
> *And in its Stead there foments Hate, Fear, and Violence,*
> *It is Then the Portal will Open,*
> *And They will Ride Through,*
> *Propelled by an epoch storm,*
> *Thrusting Humankind into a Darkness so complete,*
> *That there Shall be no Escape from Hell on Earth.*

Father O'Brian closed his eyes and listened to the howl of the wind.

For the first time, in a very long time, the old priest was afraid. Very afraid.

# CHAPTER 10

Torrents of rain pelted the old roof and windows of the 109th Precinct. The janitor could barely keep up with the leaks that seemed to be sprouting anew from the ceiling, and the detectives had to tread carefully lest they slip and fall.

"We're lucky the damn roof hasn't collapsed," Salvo said as he read a newspaper.

Santini looked over at him. "Why do you read that crap? Don't you and I see enough bad news every day?"

Salvo slapped the newspaper onto his desk, and Santini caught a headline: "Drunk Driver Kills Four Teens in Deadly Crash."

"My nephew knew one of the kids," Salvo said. "They were buddies. My sister says he's pretty shaken up."

"I'm sorry."

Salvo sighed. "She wants me to come over and talk with him. His father's useless."

"I thought he was out of the picture," Santini said.

"He is now, after he and I had a little friendly chat."

"What about the drunk driver?"

"The bastard was dead on the scene. Saves the city some money. Maybe then they can afford to fix our roof."

Santini's eye caught sight of the photo of the drunk driver. His face turned white. He picked up the newspaper and dropped down into his chair.

"You know this guy?" Salvo asked.

Santini glared at his partner.

"Well?" Salvo persisted.

Santini lowered his voice to a whisper. "You said earlier the reason our partnership works is because we're honest with each other. Well, I was honest with you yesterday when I told you I dreamed about that kid killing his parents. But you didn't believe me."

Salvo stared at his partner. "Look, I don't deny your instincts are extraordinary, but this is different. Am I supposed to believe you've become psychic overnight? And you just walked away from a crime scene."

"For that I apologize. But you don't believe me, so why should I continue to confide in you?"

"You're kidding, right? Because I'm all you've got. That and, despite all of this recent bullshit, I still believe you're a brilliant detective. So I've learned to know when to keep my mouth shut. But now is not one of those times. So tell me who the hell this is."

Santini opened a drawer and pulled out a sheet of paper and handed it to Salvo. "A few weeks ago our sketch artist tried to re-create the man in my dreams. But there were no hits in the data bank."

Salvo stared unblinking at his partner and then at the drawing. "The drunk SOB that killed these four kids is the man in your dream?"

"I'm certain."

"What do you know about him?"

Santini picked up the paper again and looked intently at the photo. "Absolutely nothing."

Salvo stared at his partner again. "At least now we have a name." He picked up the newspaper and walked over to the desk of Marissa Bianco, the precinct's computer whiz.

"Can you do me a favor, Marissa."

She batted her eyes. "Anything for you, Johnny."

Salvo's face turned pink. "I need everything you can find on this man, Jerry Slater." He handed her the newspaper. "Everything."

"I'm on it, Detective."

When Salvo returned to his desk, Santini managed a small smile. "Johnny?"

"Let it go, Santini." Salvo stared at the newspaper. "Maybe you've seen him somewhere before but don't remember."

"But why would he be in my dream night after night?"

"Let's see what Marissa turns up. By the time she's done, we'll know what this guy had for lunch in the third grade."

Suddenly, they heard shouting coming from Captain Johnson's office.

"I haven't heard him that pissed off since that prostitute accused him of cheating her out of her fee," Salvo said. "Even after she confessed to lying about the whole thing."

"Wonder what's got him in a twist," Santini said.

Inside the office, the captain's voice escalated.

"Based on what? . . . Look, Doc, I know the man and I don't believe that for a second . . . I don't like this . . . I sure hope you know what you're doing."

When the conversation ended, Captain Johnson appeared in the doorway wearing a grim expression.

"Santini. I need to speak with you."

Santini and Salvo exchanged puzzled looks before Santini got up and went into his office.

"Shut the door, Santini."

"What's this about, Captain?"

Johnson was pacing, trying to calm himself down. He wasn't successful.

Johnson was an excellent commander and had clawed his way to the top with hard work, loyalty, and a passion for justice. Many times he'd diffused the heat from Internal Affairs when they tried to steamroll one of his detectives, so he had a reputation for watching his officers' backs. He stopped pacing and turned to Santini.

"Look, Santini. You know how I feel about your work. You're one of my best detectives. But it's policy. I can't go against the medical review."

"What are you talking about?"

"Dr. Jordan. She seems to think you need a break."

*"Are you suspending me?"*

"Let's consider it sick leave, Santini."

"Sick leave? I feel fine."

Johnson frowned and shook his head. "You know I don't like doing this, and hopefully we can get this cleared up in short order. But I'm going to need your badge and your gun."

Santini stared at Johnson in disbelief. "I went to her voluntarily. Is this what happens when a cop tries to get help coping with this fucking job?"

He slammed his gun onto the captain's desk, tossed his badge into the air and stormed out of his office.

He stopped at Salvo's desk. "Thanks for the referral, partner."

Then he turned and walked out of the building.

# CHAPTER 11

Four-year-old Amy Tyler pressed her nose against the cold glass of the window as the rain and wind continued to pound against it. She'd been waiting patiently for the rain to subside, but the storm only seemed to be getting worse.

"I want to play with Melinda, Daddy. Can't the big black car take me to her house? Please? I'll bring my Minnie Mouse umbrella."

"Come over and sit on my lap, Amy." The little girl climbed onto her father's lap and nestled in his arms. He was a big man, a commanding six foot three inches, and the little girl almost disappeared in his embrace.

"I'm sorry, but the storm is very bad tonight. It's better if you stay inside where it's warm and dry. Your mom will read you a story."

"*The Cat in the Hat*!" she said excitedly.

"*The Cat in the Hat* it shall be," he said.

Rosalyn Tyler walked over to her daughter and stroked her hair. "If you want me to read to you, first you have to brush your teeth and get ready for bed. And kiss your father good night. He won't be here to tuck you in tonight."

"Okay, Mommy." She kissed her father and ran off.

Rosalyn stared through the window. "It's gotten worse, hasn't it?"

Reginald Tyler nodded. "It seems to be focused in the New England states, especially around the New York metropolitan area."

"More flooding?"

"I'm afraid so."

"So what's going on? Another symptom of climate change? I've never seen anything like this."

"Don't know. Hopefully, this meeting will shed some light on the matter."

She walked over and put her arms around him. "You're exhausted."

Tyler could see the worry lines creasing her forehead. "I'm fine, Rosalyn. Stop worrying." He kissed her and wondered how he would have made it through a second term without her.

There was a knock on the door.

"Come in."

Chief of Staff James Whitaker walked in.

"Good evening, Rosalyn."

"Hello, Jim."

"Everyone is assembled, Mr. President."

"Thank you, Whitaker. Has Beaumont from NASA arrived?"

"Yes, Mr. President."

"And Reynolds from FEMA?"

"Yes, sir. As I said, everyone is assembled."

Tyler smiled. "Sorry, Jim. This storm has me a little distracted."

"I think it has everyone a little on edge, Mr. President."

Tyler nodded. "All right then. Let's go."

Another bolt of lightning lit the room as the two men, wearing grim expressions, headed for the White House Situation Room.

President Reginald Tyler sat at the head of the long mahogany conference table surrounded by his advisers. His cool blue eyes were more intense than usual as he listened to scientist John Beaumont, the head of NASA, make an effort to explain the meteorological events of the last forty-eight hours.

Beaumont was a short robust man who wore his wire-rim spectacles low on the bridge of his nose. He was nicknamed "the professor" because whenever he spoke, he needed to translate what he'd just said.

"We've never seen anything like this before," he began. "The electromagnetic activity of the storm has fried many of our instruments, and the lightning strikes on the surface are ten times that of even the most severe storms on record. There have been twenty reported deaths already just in the last few days from these strikes."

"Any ideas as to what's causing this, Beaumont? Global warming?"

"The effects of global warming, according to most models, are gradual over time. We're doing our best to come up with some theories, Mr. President, but currently we're at a loss."

The president turned to Serena Morales, director of homeland security. "Is the National Guard in the New York City area yet?"

"Colonel Stuart has notified me they're in position just outside the metropolitan area," Morales said. "We're coordinating with FEMA on the possibility of having to close some tunnels and bridges and the potential suspension of all public transportation in New York City. The mayor and the governor have been informed. Evacuation plans are in place for some of the lower-lying areas."

"Is there any indication the rain and electrical activity of the storm might be letting up?" Tyler directed the question to Beaumont.

"Actually, just the opposite, Mr. President. All of our measurements show an increase in the intensity of electromagnetic activity."

The president looked around the table. "Is there anything else you can tell me, Beaumont?"

The head of NASA fidgeted. "There's one more thing, sir."

"Well, Beaumont?"

"We'd been focusing mostly on the electromagnetic characteristics of this storm, but one of our team thought to analyze its auditory qualities. We have sophisticated equipment that can screen out selected amplitudes of sound and isolate certain components of the storm's auditory spectrum." He hesitated.

"I'm waiting, Beaumont."

"Well, when we screen out the sound of thunder, rain, wind, and the overall static charge of the storm, we're left with a very weak noise that was very difficult to identify."

"Are there any guesses as to what this noise might be?"

"It's not a very clear signal, so we've had to amplify the sound exponentially." He hesitated once again. "As strange as the interpretation of the data might sound, most of our analysts are fairly certain."

President Tyler slapped his hand on the table. "This is like pulling teeth. Fairly certain of what? Out with it, Beaumont."

"Voices, Mr. President."

A total silence fell on the Situation Room. President Tyler stared at the NASA scientist with a bewildered look. "What?"

"It's voices, sir. Voices in the storm."

## CHAPTER 12

Santini paced outside the door to Dr. Jordan's office. So much for complete honesty. He never should have told her about the voices on the observatory.

"Dr. Jordan will see you now."

He stalked past the receptionist into the office and slammed the door shut. He remained standing, glaring at her.

"Is this your idea of therapy? Is this what I can expect for being honest? A goddamn suspension?"

Dr. Jordan stood up and folded her arms. "Put yourself in my position. An officer of the law tells me a subconscious entity from his dream has crossed over into his waking consciousness. He tells me he's hearing voices and these voices are telling him to commit suicide." She kept her voice calm, professional. "You realize none of this is good."

"You could have given me a heads up."

"I'm concerned about your safety, Detective, and I acted quickly. It may not seem so, but I'm on your side."

"Bullshit," he said. "If you really gave a damn and really listened to what I said, you would know how much my work means to me."

"I listen to everything my patients tell me, Detective, and I promise you I'm not about to make the same mistake twice."

Santini frowned. "What are you talking about?"

"Forget that." She took a deep breath. "It's . . . The important thing, the *most* important thing, Detective, is your mental health. Please, try to see this as a temporary measure, all right? You need a chance to decompress, which I'm guessing hasn't happened in a very long time."

"Fine." He forced his body to relax. "I'll take a couple of days off."

She shook her head. "I won't clear you to go back to work until I've completed a comprehensive evaluation."

"And exactly what does this 'comprehensive evaluation' entail?"

"Three nights at the Blackthorne Sleep Clinic."

His jaw clenched. "And what will that accomplish, exactly?"

She met his stare. "That depends on you, Detective."

He threw up his hands. Further confrontation wouldn't do a damn thing except extend his stay at Blackthorne. And maybe she was right about his needing a break.

He dropped down into the chair facing her.

"All right, Doc. We'll do it your way."

Santini stared at the ceiling, his mind churning.

Through the single tiny window in his room at the Blackthorne Sleep Clinic, he could still hear wind howling outside and rain battering the glass.

Except for the LED lights on the equipment and the faint glow of a monitor, the room was dark.

He didn't see the point of all this, but he didn't have much of a choice.

After several hours of lying there, he knew sleep was impossible. No matter which way he shifted, sensors taped to his head and chest irritated and pulled at his skin. There was no way to get comfortable.

So he lay there thinking, and he always came back to the same conclusion. It was far-fetched but one he had to consider.

The bald guy, Jerry Slater, was real. What if he *was* on the observatory platform that night? What if it *was* his voice he'd heard? He could have been hiding somewhere and then tried to persuade Santini to jump off the platform.

Why? What was their connection? And that still wouldn't explain his father's voice, or why he'd seen Jerry Slater in his dreams.

He was sure of one thing, though: he'd dreamed about the Gorman-family murder just before it happened. Which means he'd seen into the future. Was it a one-time event? What about his dream of the city destroyed? Was that the future? What if he'd been given a glimpse of it for a reason? And what if this Slater was somehow involved?

He decided he'd have to keep these thoughts to himself or he'd never get out of here. Maybe he could spin things a little so that Dr. Jordan wouldn't think he was a danger to himself.

After endless hours, a medical technician poked his head through the door.

"Still awake, Detective?"

"You could say that." He watched as the young man fiddled with the monitors, checking scrolls of graph paper and making notes.

"Your appointment is in one hour," he said. "Plenty of time to hit the cafeteria, grab a little breakfast."

"Not hungry," Santini said. "But coffee sounds great."

The young man unhooked the electrodes, leaving red marks on Santini's skin.

Santini stood and stretched, trying to work out the kinks in his spine, and then grabbed his clothes off the nearby dresser.

The young man scrutinized the printouts and shook his head. "The doc won't be happy."

"I'm not feeling too happy myself," Santini said.

He settled into the chair facing Dr. Jordan.

"According to the records, you hardly slept at all last night," she said.

"How can anyone sleep like that?"

"I'm sorry. I know it's difficult." She opened his file folder. "The good news is, all of your tests came back negative. EEG, EKG, C.T. scan, blood work, pulse and blood pressure . . . According to those you're perfectly healthy."

"So why am I on sick leave?"

"Please. Let's not rehash that."

Santini remained silent.

"We did find that your brain-wave patterns cycled through the REM level too quickly," she said. "That's why you've been so tired." She studied him. "Are you fighting sleep?"

"I don't look forward to the evening's entertainment."

Dr. Jordan nodded and leaned back in her chair. "Let's talk about those voices you heard on the observatory."

"I had a feeling you'd bring that up," he said. "But a sleepless night can sometimes provide an insight, because I think I've figured that out."

Dr. Jordan raised an eyebrow. "Oh?"

"Since our last meeting, I've learned the man in my dream is real." He'd brought a copy of the newspaper with him, and now he set it on the desk and tapped the photo of Jerry Slater. "I saw him the night I heard those voices. I'm guessing he was hiding somewhere on the observatory platform." He didn't mention hearing his father's voice.

Dr. Jordan studied the paper and frowned. "It seems odd that you'd have dreamed about him several times. Do you know him?"

"No, but we're running a background check as we speak. I've put a lot of people behind bars in the past twenty years. He could be the relative of a perp looking for revenge."

She eyed him. "And calling out to you from some hiding place for you to jump was his way of getting revenge."

"Look, he was obviously disturbed and drunk enough to kill four kids by ramming into their car with his truck." He held up the paper and waved it at her. "The important thing is, the voices were not in my head."

"And why do you think he was in your dreams?"

"Who knows?"

Dr. Jordan tapped her pen on the desk. "I asked you in our first meeting if you ever had suicidal thoughts. You were adamant that you hadn't." She caught his gaze and held it. "Is that true?"

"I have my down days," he said. "Everybody does. But I wasn't lying when I told you that's not how I'm wired."

Dr. Jordan remained quiet for a moment. "The next time we meet I'd like to discuss the recurring dream of your father's murder. The violent death of a loved one can create subconscious turmoil, especially when the issue remains unresolved in the mind of the patient."

Santini stared straight ahead. "I've never given up finding him. And I never will."

"And what is the likelihood you'll find this person?"

"I have no choice."

"You always have a choice, Detective."

Santini shook his head. "Look, I agree I have some issues to work out, but I'm not suicidal. Your instincts should tell you that. So when can I go back to work?"

There was a long pause. "You have two more nights here," she said. "Let's meet again tomorrow. I'll be curious about your dreams now that

Slater has been identified. Then we can discuss whether you should go back to work any time soon."

Santini abruptly stood and slapped the newspaper on his thigh. He began to protest but thought better of it and tried to calm down.

"All right, Doc. Two more nights to convince you I'm not crazy."

# CHAPTER 13

Santini stared out the little window of the Blackthorne east-wing sleep clinic. Frustrated, he pulled off the wires and sat on the only chair in the room.

The storm had grown angrier in the last twenty minutes. The rain pelted the glass, and the wind lashed out at the swaying branches of the trees. He could just barely make out the barbed steel fencing that encircled the perimeter of the complex. Beyond that he could see very little, and it created the illusion that beyond the fencing was a tumultuous sea whose waves could swallow the building at any minute

The parking lot was deserted. This was not a night for visitors, not that many came here anyway.

The west wing was home to a who's who of homicidal maniacs. Built by one of the esteemed asylum architects of the early 1920s, the haunting Victorian structure had survived three generations of lunatics.

*How ironic*, Santini thought. He'd probably been responsible for putting a lot of those loony tunes in there. He reminded himself he was in the east-wing sleep clinic. A temporary situation.

It was midnight, and so far he'd successfully battled the medication. Not that he didn't want to sleep. Not that he didn't yearn to close the eyelids that felt as heavy as bricks and were held up by sheer will. Sheer will and fear. Fear of the nightmares that were haunting him.

But he knew the monitors would register whether or not he'd slept, and if he didn't sleep, he might find himself in here for longer than he wanted to be.

His eyelids slowly began to close, but he caught them just in time. He thought about his last meeting with Dr. Jordan. He had to admit he liked her. All too often he'd witnessed the dark side of human nature, and when he met someone who displayed just the opposite, it was like seeing a lighthouse in a storm. She seemed genuine in her desire to help him, even though he knew his assertions about his dreams challenged her view of reality.

Unfortunately, since she was a psychiatrist, there was the distinct possibility that she thought he was unstable. Not the greatest way to begin a relationship.

He rubbed his aching temples and stared out the window at the growing storm. The howling of the wind filled his mind with unsettling thoughts and dark shadows that skittered at the edge of perception. Then a deep fatigue reached every muscle. He tried to force his body to get up, but there was no response.

Once again his eyelids closed, only this time the curtain fell. With his head cocked to one side and his body slumped down in the chair, consciousness slipped away from him.

It was dark. Rain hammered the roof, and somewhere outside a wind chime clanged, out of sync.

He was sitting on a sofa. His sofa? It felt different. A flash of lightning lit the room. He looked up, out the wide picture window, past great oak trees to a Tudor-style house across the street. *Where am I?*

Now he was walking down the hallway. He stopped, turned, opened the door, and peered into a child's bedroom.

He silently crept to the edge of the bed and sat beside her, watching her sweet face. The child stirred under his caresses and dreamily opened her eyes.

"Mommy, is that you?"

"Yes, sweetie, I'm here."

"I had a bad dream, Mommy."

"It's all right. You're safe and sound in your own room and in your own bed. Now close your eyes and go back to sleep, sweetie."

Then Santini could hear the woman's thoughts.

*The world is a frightening place, full of pain and suffering. Eventually, bad people corrupt your children and try to steal their purity. Why couldn't they stay like this forever . . . young, innocent, never having to see the world as it really is, never having to see the evil and feel the pain that's everywhere?*

She continued to caress the child's forehead until she finally drifted off to sleep. Then she kissed her lips. Slowly, so as not to disturb her slumber, she slid the pillow out from beneath her head and pressed it firmly over the child's face.

*No! Stop!* He felt the hands – that weren't his – pressing the pillow down harder as the child started to kick and the little arms came up to try to push away the pillow. Eventually the arms and legs grew weary and the little body became still.

Santini jerked upright in his chair. For a moment, he didn't know where he was. Droplets of sweat slid down his temples and his heart thrashed in his chest. Then, from within the darkness, the nightmare image of the dying child jumped out at him.

He placed his hands over his face.

*Why is this happening to me?*

When his heart finally stopped pounding, he knew it was time to change strategy. It was time to leave.

He found his clothes still hanging neatly in the closet, got dressed, opened the door to his room, and quickly began walking down the hallway, heading for the nearest exit.

He thought about the dream and came to a decision. He wasn't going to make the same mistake twice. He had to find the little girl. Fast.

But how? He thought about the details of the dream. There were some clues, but not many, and maybe not enough. Again, the image of the child lying under the pillow flashed before him.

He didn't know how much time he had, assuming he could even find her. But he knew he had to try.

When he made it outside, he pulled out his cell phone.

"Detective Salvo here."

"Salvo, I need you to pick me up in front of Blackthorne right away."

"Do you know what time it is? What about your treatment?"

"Treatment is over."

"What?!"

"No time to explain. With every second wasted, a child's life is at stake. Just get over here, Salvo. Now!"

# CHAPTER 14

Salvo shook his head in disbelief.

"So here we are in the middle of the night looking for a house you saw in a dream? I should be home, Santini, in a warm bed sleeping next to my wife."

"Turn right on the next street," Santini said. "And slow down, I can barely see." The rain and wind continued unabated as he squinted through the windshield.

"Marissa got back to me on Slater," Salvo said.

"And?"

"She didn't come up with much. A couple of DUIs, no other criminal charges. He was part of the maintenance crew at the Empire State Building. Seems he was fired recently for disappearing several times while on shift. Maybe you saw him there."

Santini shook his head. "I don't think so." He filed away the information on Slater. Right now he was preoccupied with finding the little girl's house.

Thankfully, in his dream, he recalled seeing large oak trees through the window, and a street sign rattling in the rain—Tindal Street.

Marissa had found three Tindal Streets in the New York City area, but only one Tindal Street was lined with oak trees—in Jamaica Estates, Queens.

They wound their way slowly through the neighborhood. Heavy black clouds hung low and made it almost impossible to see anything. As the storm intensified, Santini felt a growing sense of panic. He closed his eyes and desperately searched his memory for any piece of dream fragment that might help. He inhaled and tried to relax. A Tudor-style house with gray roof shingles flashed into his mind. He fought to call up the image again. Now he could see steep stone steps that wound their way to the front door.

The Crown Vic continued down Tindal Street as the seconds ticked slowly by. Santini was beginning to think the search was futile. Then a crash of lightning illuminated a house.

"Stop the car!"

Santini jumped out into the pouring rain and gazed at the house. It looked familiar. He wiped the water from his eyes and leaped up the stone steps to the front door with Salvo trailing behind.

It took several doorbell rings before the outside light flickered on.

"Who's there?" A man's voice grumbled from behind the door. "I have a big dog and he bites."

"It's the police, sir," Santini said. "Can we speak to you for a moment?"

The door eased open about three inches as the chain lock engaged and a gray-haired man in a blue robe peered warily through the opening.

Salvo flashed his badge as a little Terrier started yapping relentlessly in a high-pitched shrill.

"Sir, we've had a report of a dangerous criminal hiding in this area," Santini said. "We just want to make sure everyone is safe and keeps their doors and windows locked. Especially the children. Make sure their windows are locked also."

"What children? We don't have any children. It's just my wife and I and Scrubby here." The man eyed the detectives. "What's this all about?"

"Just make sure your windows and doors are locked," Santini said. "And call 911 if you see anything suspicious."

When they got back down to the car, Salvo shook his head.

"Report of a dangerous criminal? That would be you. What the hell's going on, Santini?"

But Santini wasn't paying attention. In his dream, he'd been looking out a picture window at the house where they'd just been. So this wasn't the right house at all. He stared intently at the house across the street and at one of the swaying tree branches. Dangling from a limb was a set of wind chimes that banged and rattled in the wind.

A light turned on and off in one of the rooms, and through the window—for an instant—he could just make out the faint figure of a woman walking slowly across the room.

"Quick, this way."

Santini dashed across the street to the front door of the house. He repeatedly pressed the doorbell—nothing. He pounded the door with his fist. Then he motioned to his partner.

"Shoulder the door!"

Salvo, who had just made it to the front door, looked at his friend questioningly.

"We can get into serious trouble for this. No warrant, no probable cause. Oh, I forgot, we have your dream as probable cause."

"I'll take full responsibility. Now break down the goddamn door!"

Salvo took a deep breath and slammed his shoulder into the door.

The door swung forward and crashed against the inside wall, making enough noise to awaken the entire neighborhood, but the house was silent.

Santini motioned his partner to go left as he quickly headed in the opposite direction to the room where he'd seen the woman through the window. Fleeting shadows loomed in the hallway. He stopped at a closed door. No sound emerged. When he opened the door, it was like stepping into his own nightmare.

A deafening crack of lightning lit the room and revealed the back of a dark-haired woman holding a pillow over a child's face. He sprinted across the room and came down on the woman, grabbing her shoulders in an attempt to throw her off. To his surprise, the woman didn't budge. He yanked at her arms, but they were locked like a vise onto the pillow. He saw Salvo standing behind him.

"Help me get her off!" Santini yelled.

Salvo leaped forward, and both men pulled at the woman, whose eyes stared unblinking into space. Finally, they pried her loose, and she and Santini fell to the floor with a thud

Santini lay on his back, stunned. Another bolt of lightning illuminated the room and revealed a twisted grin on the face of the woman. Then her body stiffened and she passed out.

At the same moment, a black shadow emerged from her body. Santini thought he heard laughter. Then an ice-cold chill wormed its way into his head, followed by a buzzing that escalated into a rant of voices.

Suddenly there was silence and a lone voice emerged.

"What a sorry excuse for a son. All these years and no justice. What happened to your promise? You swore on my coffin. You're a fraud and a failure."

"Santini?" Salvo was staring at his partner.

Then another voice surfaced, this one crying softly.

"All the heartache you put me through. Why? All those years. I was so lonely. It was always all about the job, never about me."

Santini placed his hands over his ears. "Casey? I'm so sorry."

"Santini?" Salvo edged toward the little girl's bedside.

"Get out!" Santini yelled. "Get out of my head!"

Abruptly the voices stopped.

After a few seconds, Santini opened his eyes. He concentrated and quickly hoisted himself off the floor, only to find himself staring into the barrel of his partner's gun.

"Salvo. What the hell are you doing?"

Salvo didn't respond. He just stared unblinking at his partner. Santini glanced over at the little girl lying motionless on the bed.

He turned toward Salvo, his partner's gun still pointed at him.

"Salvo. Drop the gun. It's me."

Salvo's arm trembled. He shook his head vigorously, as if trying to wake himself up, and then with a shriek he threw his gun against the far wall.

Santini watched his partner jerk forward and fall unconscious to the floor.

He quickly turned and began CPR on the girl. The seconds ticked slowly by, but eventually he was able to get a pulse.

Santini breathed a sigh of relief.

The wind and rain pounded the trees until a particularly large branch creaked and groaned and eventually snapped, ripping through a power line and leaving Jamaica Estates without electricity.

Neighbors awakened by the sirens peered out from their windows through the pouring rain at the kaleidoscope of colors created by the ambulance and the police cars that lined the once peaceful neighborhood.

Santini and Salvo stood side by side in the pouring rain. The lampposts cast a pale yellow light on their grim faces as they watched the two stretchers emerge from the house. The mother and her daughter were whisked away to the local emergency room. The boy was taken by child protective services.

"Hope the kid is okay," Santini said.

Salvo shook his head. "You saved her. That nut job tried to kill her own daughter." He rubbed his temples. "What the hell happened in there?"

Santini gazed into his friend's eyes. "How do you feel?"

"Like shit."

Santini placed his hand on his partner's shoulder. "Me, too. Come on, let's get out of the rain."

The two detectives sat in the Crown Victoria sipping hot coffee as faint signs of daylight began to lift the blackness that had settled over the neighborhood. The rain turned to hail, and from inside the car it sounded as if they were under heavy artillery fire.

Santini turned up the heat, but he couldn't shake the chill of the night's unusual turn of events.

"Headache still?" Santini asked.

Salvo nodded. Santini rummaged through the glove box and handed a packet of aspirin to his partner. Salvo swallowed the pills and washed them down with coffee.

"So are you going to tell me what the hell just happened?" Salvo said.

Santini nodded. "We saved that kid because I dreamed about her murder."

"That's impossible."

"That's what you said about the Gorman kid. How else could I have known?"

Salvo had no answer.

"Tell me what happened from the moment you entered the house." Santini said.

"It's all a fog. Give me a minute to think." Salvo closed his eyes. "We broke down the door. I turned left, down a long hallway. I entered a bedroom and saw a boy asleep. Then I ran to the bedroom where you were struggling with that crazy woman . . . I don't know what she was on, but I've never seen strength like that."

"What happened next?" Santini asked.

"We wrestled her to the floor . . . Then you were just lying there. I thought you hit your head because you started talking to Casey. Then you yelled for her to get out of your head. What was that all about?"

"Forget that," Santini said. "Then what happened?"

"And then . . ." Salvo stared straight ahead with a confused look. "Everything got cold. I heard your voice, but it was far away, as though you were at the end of a long tunnel." His voice faltered. "That's when I heard it."

"Heard what?"

Salvo shook his head. "You and I will have adjoining suites at Blackthorne after tonight. The nasty west wing I'm afraid."

"What did you hear?"

"At first a buzzing. Then a voice, inside my head. Telling me . . . telling me to shoot Joel Zimmerman before it's too late."

"*Joel Zimmerman?* The man you shot just before he tried to shoot his own wife?"

"He was there. Right where you were standing," Salvo said. "But it wasn't you. It was him. I could see Zimmerman's piercing black eyes and the grin on his face. 'Shoot,' the voice said . . . 'Don't hesitate, shoot now, save the wife.' But I knew something was wrong. I knew I'd shot the bastard years ago. That's when I tossed my gun away." Salvo paused and took another sip of coffee. "After that I don't remember a damn thing."

The hail had transformed back to its liquid counterpart. Dark, heavy clouds lingered over the large oak trees and rooftops and seemed to press down on the car as the detectives stared silently out through the water-strewn windshield.

Santini shook his head. "This confirms it."

"Confirms what?"

"Do you remember when you asked me how my last trip up to the observatory went?"

"Yeah, you said it was a waste of time."

"That wasn't completely accurate."

"I knew you were hiding something."

"I thought I was losing my mind. And since then I've groped for any other possible explanation. But something got inside my head and tried to get me to jump off that building. Thankfully, like you, I was able to resist."

"Resist what? A spirit or something?"

"I don't know what this thing is, but it can enter a person's mind, plant suggestions, and manipulate behavior. That's why it tapped into your memory of Zimmerman."

"And why did I pass out?"

Santini thought for a moment. "Maybe, in some instances, when it leaves a host the reaction causes a momentary loss of consciousness, like the shock from the recoil of a gun when the bullet exits. But the important thing is we both resisted, so it seems to have limitations."

"Limitations?" Salvo slapped the top of the dashboard. "I almost shot you because it tricked me into believing you were Zimmerman. What other tricks does this thing have up its sleeve?"

"Maybe it can only push a person's mind so far," Santini said. "Somehow we need to track this thing down."

Salvo gave Santini a look of bewilderment. "This is bullshit. How are we supposed to find something invisible? Even if we do manage to track it down, what then—blow fairy dust up its ass?"

Santini managed a slight smile, but it quickly fell. "This thing needs a human body to do its work. That may be its weakness."

Salvo abruptly got out of the car and slammed the door shut. Santini followed and stood next to his partner, the wind and rain pounding them.

"This is crazy," Salvo said.

Santini placed his hand on Salvo's shoulder. "I know."

"I can't believe this."

"Really, after everything that's happened, everything you've seen?"

Salvo covered his water streaked face with his hands.

"Evil is loose in the world," Santini said. "You know it. For years we've seen its handiwork. For years we've chased it. It's real. You felt it yourself."

Salvo dropped his hands and stared at Santini, an expression of disgust on his face. "It felt like worms crawling inside my head."

"It was the same thing that manipulated the Gorman kid and now this woman," Santini said. "And tonight it tried to trick you into shooting me."

"Lucky for you it didn't succeed."

"And you should be congratulated," Santini said, "because now I know you can be trusted."

"Trusted for what?"

"Trusted to be able to fend off another attack."

Salvo glared at his partner. "Another attack? What the fuck have you gotten me into?"

Santini frowned. "I really don't know, Salvo."

They both climbed back into the car and for several moments stared through the windshield, lost in thought.

"We need to pay a visit to our doctor friend," Santini said. "I need my badge and my gun back so I can function at full capacity."

"You can't do that. Your treatment requires you stay at Blackthorne until she gives the okay. There's no other way."

"I can't go back there, Salvo."

"For once stop trying to buck authority. Without your badge and gun you're hamstrung. We need all the resources of the NYPD to find this thing."

Santini sat in silence listening to the sound of the rain.

"I suppose you're right. But only one more night. That's it."

"I'll drive you back," Salvo said.

"We have to stop this thing," Santini said. "Before it tries to kill someone else . . . or worse."

## CHAPTER 15

The older and more infamous west wing of Blackthorne shook in the torrential wind and rain as the lights flickered and the backup generators kicked on.

Drakin's ethereal form floated through the dimly lit corridors, slipping silently through the security checkpoints, trailing alongside the guard like an invisible shadow.

His essence, though a form of energy, couldn't penetrate through non-biological matter. Skull and brain tissue wasn't a problem, but walls and doors posed somewhat of a challenge.

Drakin was furious that the two detectives had so rudely interrupted his nightly feeding. Apparently, there was more to Santini's dreams than just the premonition of a destroyed city. Apparently, the man's dreams were also tracking his actions. Quite unusual. This required immediate action.

Drakin could hear the intensity of the storm growing as he continued to float through the hallways. The dark energy of the west wing was palpable.

*The perfect place to recruit an accomplice,* he thought. *An entire building filled with minds pre-wired for violence. The cream of the human crop.*

There were some who were difficult to sway. The strong-willed. The righteous. Those whose strength of character would not allow the suggestions he planted to take root. His pal Anthony Santini, for example.

Unfortunately, a virtuous human mind required a greater expenditure of energy to enter, though at times it was unavoidable. And although Drakin was powerful, he did have his limitations.

He might find a way in, hitching onto a momentary thought of envy, greed, fear, or anger, but once a human mind rejected him, manipulation was difficult. Which is why most of the time he stalked his potential hosts to assess their suitability. Especially if they were vital to his plans.

But there was never a shortage of fertile minds. They were everywhere.

Being an opportunist, Drakin had slipped in and out of the guard's mind and discovered that the man loved to torture one inmate in particular, John Collins.

John Collins was a serial rapist and killer who specialized in young girls. So Drakin nudged the guard into performing his usual taunt.

The guard stopped at Collins's cell and peered through the little window. Seeing that he was asleep, he pulled out his baton and opened the door.

The first baton strike caught Collins in the back. The man fell off his cot and onto the floor howling in pain.

Drakin saw his opportunity and slipped into Collins's mind.

The guard slid his hand slowly over the baton. "Hurts, doesn't it?"

As he raised the baton high into the air, Drakin-Collins's leg swung out with surprising speed and knocked the guard off balance, toppling him to the floor.

A human host exhibited unusual strength and speed when occupied by Drakin, and in a flash, Drakin-Collins was on top of the man. He pried the baton loose from the guard's hand and with just one blow crushed the man's skull. Drakin-Collins grabbed the keys that hung from the man's belt and slipped the baton behind his back.

Silently, Drakin-Collins headed toward the east wing of Blackthorne to find—and put an end to—Anthony Santini.

Santini found himself once again staring at the ceiling, wires hanging from his chest and head, hoping for sleep that wouldn't come.

It had been a long night, and though the sun was still obscured, he could see faint signs of daylight. Finally, realizing it was a lost cause, he pulled the wires off his body, stood up and got dressed. He'd had enough. It was time to leave again.

As he walked down a dimly lit corridor, he thought about their recent battle with the entity. At least now he knew he wasn't crazy. Salvo had experienced it, too. He didn't know how or why he had the ability to see this thing when dreaming, but it was the only tool they had for finding it.

Lost in thought, he turned into another corridor and came to an abrupt stop. Standing motionless in the hallway was a man wearing what looked to be an inmate's jumpsuit.

Santini was a big man, wiry, strong, and skilled in several forms of self-defense, so he didn't frighten easily. But alarm bells rang inside his head.

The man was broad-shouldered and well over six feet. His head was bald except for patches of dark stubble and a jagged scar over his right temple. He had a wolfish grin on his face that exposed several missing teeth. His eyes were deeply set in their sockets, and his eyebrows were black, thick and unruly. His face showed several days of unshaven dark shadow. But the most striking thing about him was the tattoos. The arms were completely covered, a kaleidoscope of snakes, knives, and dragons. He stared at Santini with unblinking bloodshot eyes.

*Why isn't this man locked up?* He stepped forward to cautiously walk around him, and as he passed the man spoke.

"Poor Detective. Still haven't found Daddy's killer, have you?"

Santini stopped in his tracks.

"You really should have jumped," the man hissed. "I know you wanted to."

Santini turned to face the man. "Do I know you?"

The man's grin exploded into a burst of laughter that convulsed his entire body and echoed through the hallway. Eventually, the shudders of laughter subsided and he glared menacingly at Santini.

"Oh, you don't know me, but I know you." The man's eyes were blazing as he advanced toward Santini. "In fact, I know everything about you. Your nightmares, your failed marriage, your silly promise." He grinned. "I even know about your dead daddy's bat leaning neatly against your bookcase. How sentimental. But what I'm most curious about are your dreams."

Santini's eyes widened. "It was you on the observatory, wasn't it?"

The man flashed a wide grin. "In a sense, you and I are in the same line of work. We're both hunters. We hunt those that radiate negative energy. We hunt the worst of humanity."

"I'm nothing like you."

"Really? The hunt has given your life purpose. You would be lost without it. Your mind reeks of the evil men you chase. You've climbed into their heads one too many times and now you can't climb out. I know. I've seen the dark holes in your mind. The hopelessness. The despair. Growing like a cancer. Eating away at your soul."

Santini was speechless.

The man grinned. "You know I'm right. We *are* alike. That's why you dream about me. We are linked."

"I'm a threat to you, aren't I?"

The man advanced toward him, laughing. "I've dealt with much bigger fish than you, little man."

Santini backed away as another crack of thunder thrust the hallway into darkness. A howl of laughter emerged from the shadowy figure in front of him, and before he could react, he felt the tight grip of hands around his throat.

Both of Santini's arms flew up to break the hold, but as strong as Santini was, the vise-like grip only tightened. In the darkness, he could see the bright red glare of his assailant's eyes bearing down on him.

"Actually, I'll be doing you a big favor, Detective," he hissed. "You will not want to see what the world looks like when I'm finished with it."

Santini's lungs felt like they were about to burst. He knew that if he didn't breathe soon, he was finished.

With a final act of will, he summoned all his strength and shot his fist straight into the shadows and connected with his attacker's throat.

There was a deep grunt from within the darkness and the grip around Santini's throat released. He gasped as a rush of air filled his burning lungs. The lights flickered on. The man moved toward him again, only this time he was holding the guard's baton in his hand.

Santini's instincts told him he was no match for this man, especially now that he was brandishing a weapon, so he bolted down the hallway toward the nearest exit.

"Go ahead and run." A voice howled in anger. "There's nowhere you can hide from me, Detective."

Santini could hear cackles of laughter as he ran down the hallway. The lights flickered and he turned to look down the corridor from where he'd come, but there was no sign of the tattooed man.

When Santini made it outside, he stopped to catch his breath. He was rattled. His throat throbbed as if the man's cold hands were still wrapped around his neck.

His mind whirled in confusion. How did he know so much about Santini's past? And how the hell did he know about his father's baseball bat?

He thought about the voices at the top of the Empire State Building. *What the hell is going on here?*

He called the precinct.

"Doug, this is Santini. I want two patrol cars sent over to Blackthorne Sanitarium right away. There's an inmate running loose. Contact security over there and tell them to exercise caution. This guy is extremely dangerous." He turned and looked up at the barred windows of the east wing, shaking his head. "Some security."

A cold wind ripped through his body, but he didn't care. He was glad to be outside.

He called Salvo.

"Pick me up right away,"

"Are you trying to make me crazy? . . . Because if so, you're succeeding."

"It tried to kill me. Used one of the inmates."

"Shit. I'll be right there."

Santini was drenched and shivering by the time Salvo pulled up. He was glad to be sitting in the warmth of the car.

"It's time we pay a visit to Dr. Jordan," Santini said. "You'll help me convince her I'm not crazy."

Salvo frowned. "Great. Now we'll both lose our badges. Anyway, it's too late. She's not in her office."

"Then we go to her home."

"That's a bad idea," Salvo said. "Besides, we don't know where she lives."

"We're detectives, aren't we? We have to convince her. And I think I know how."

Salvo shook his head as he slapped the siren onto the roof of the car and tore out into the road. The tires skidded, struggling to find traction on the flooded street, but the car finally straightened as they sped away into the gloom of the night.

## CHAPTER 16

Santini rang the doorbell several times.

"I'm not gonna break down the door again," Salvo said.

Finally the door eased open and Dr. Jordan stood at the entrance.

"You'd better have a damn good reason for being here this time of night at my private residence, Detective."

Santini was tongue-tied once again. He couldn't help staring at this woman whom he'd seen only in professional attire. Her hair was down, and the long brown wavy curls brushed the tops of her shoulders. Her yellow robe fell to mid-thigh length and revealed shapely legs.

"I apologize for the intrusion, Doctor, but it's urgent we speak to you. I brought Salvo along to verify my story."

"And what story is that?"

"A story that will prove I'm not crazy," Santini said.

She glared at him. "Look, I know you're still angry about being suspended, but showing up here like this isn't the way to go about being reinstated."

"Please, just hear me out."

She crossed her arms. "No, you hear me out, Detective. You've suffered for years from recurring nightmares. You claim you dream of murders before they happen. You see shadows and hear voices in your dreams. And now you hear voices while awake telling you to commit suicide. I'm concerned about you. We need to get to the bottom of what's going on in your mind. So go back to Blackthorne."

"I can't do that," Santini said.

"Can't?" She moved closer to him and lowered her voice. "I thought we had an agreement, Detective."

"You would be placing him in danger if he went back there," Salvo said.

She stared at Salvo. "What are you talking about?"

"We can explain," Santini said. "If you'd just give us a few minutes."

"No!"

Almost on cue, a clap of thunder struck and the rain fell in a heavy downpour.

Santini moved closer to Jordan. "When you said to me in our last session that you won't make the same mistake twice, I wondered what you meant. Then it came to me. Officer Reilly was your patient when he shot himself, wasn't he?"

There was a long tense silence. "I can't discuss that."

"So you screwed up a case and now I have to pay the price?"

Jordan's face turned red. "I didn't screw up. I did what I thought was right. In his case and in yours. And any psychiatrist worth a damn would have done the same thing!"

He and Jordan stood motionless with eyes locked.

"But just maybe you're overreacting because of what happened to Reilly," Santini said. "Please. I've given twenty years of my life to this job. Just fifteen minutes of your time. Please."

Salvo shook his head as the detectives stood in the pouring rain.

She relented. "All right, fifteen minutes. But don't expect me to change my mind on this."

"Thank you," Santini said.

Salvo wiped the water from his eyes. "Any chance of some hot coffee, Doc?"

When they stepped inside, Dr. Jordan immediately found some towels and tossed them to the soaked detectives.

"There's a coat rack in the corner to hang your jackets," she said. "And take your shoes off. I don't want my carpet ruined."

Santini and Salvo glanced down at their shoes, which were puddling water onto the tile.

"There's a Keurig on the kitchen counter," she said. "The pods are in the drawer underneath. Mugs are in the closet just above. I drink my coffee black, so if you want cream you're out of luck."

The detectives just nodded.

"Oh, and sit on the towels, please."

They nodded again.

While Dr. Jordan dressed, Santini and Salvo waited in the living room sipping coffee. Santini looked around. The décor was of the Elizabethan era. The carpet was a rich mosaic of bright colors. The antique furniture was in impeccable condition and gave a warm rich feel to the rooms. Salvo sat in a classic Chesterfield brown leather sofa. Santini purposefully avoided the couch and sat in a hand-carved oak armchair with a red leather seat and ornately scrolled arms.

Santini studied the framed prints on the far wall, a few of which he recognized. Botticelli's *Madonna, Child, and Angel*, Monet's *Water Lily Pond*, and Edvard Munch's *The Scream*. Lately, Santini could relate to that one more than the others.

There were also photos of a young woman, maybe in her early twenties, whom Santini surmised was Jordan's daughter. He noted that there were no pictures of the father.

When Jordan returned, her visage hadn't softened. She poured herself some coffee, black, and sat across from the detectives.

"You've already used up five of your fifteen minutes," she said.

"This is off the record, right?" Salvo asked.

"If you want it to be," Jordan said.

Santini began. "Last night I dreamed of a little girl being smothered by her mother. With a few clues from my dream, Salvo and I were able to locate the house in question. When I walked into the bedroom, the mother was holding a pillow over the little girl's face. Salvo helped me pull her off and I administered CPR on the girl."

"Santini's dream saved that kid's life," Salvo said.

Dr. Jordan sat in silence. Finally she said, "Is that it?"

The detectives glanced at each other with puzzled expressions.

"Look, Detective Salvo," she said. "I've worked with law enforcement a long time, so I know how this works. Partners will do or say almost anything to protect each other."

"Come on, Doc," Salvo said. "If I thought Santini was a danger to himself, I wouldn't hesitate to get him help. It's the damn dreams. Why do you think I referred him to you in the first place?" Santini could see that Salvo was getting worked up. "I'd never lie to you about this. Everything Santini stated concerning that little girl happened. And there's something else." He hesitated and took a deep breath. "The last thing I want to do is sit here and tell a psychiatrist I heard voices. But while we were in that house, something came into my mind . . . and it tried to get me to shoot Santini."

"What?!" She shook her head rapidly. "You're experiencing some kind of shared delusion."

"Then how do you explain all this?" Santini said. "It's not chance we just happened to break into a house where a murder was being committed identical to the one I dreamed about. And Salvo doesn't have the imagination to make up such a bizarre story."

"Now wait just a minute," Salvo said.

"Dr. Jordan, you suspended me because you were concerned about my safety." Santini sat forward in his chair. "Last night there was a security breach at Blackthorne. You can call over there to verify this. An inmate from the west wing was loose and tried to kill me. We fought. I was just barely able to escape with my life. Coincidence that I was there? No. And I believe this entity, the same one that tried to get Salvo to shoot me, used this psychopath to try to kill me."

Dr. Jordan looked as if her head were spinning. "So now, besides precognitive dreams, you want me to believe in supernatural forces?"

"I know it seems impossible," Santini said, "and at first I thought I was losing my mind, but that's one of the ways this thing operates."

"I'm going to need more tangible proof, Detectives, before I alter my entire notion of reality."

"Let me ask you a question," Santini said. "In your professional experience, what are the main causes of sociopathic behavior?"

"I didn't know my clinical conclusions were going to be part of this conversation," she said.

"Humor me."

She shook her head. Santini could see her patience beginning to stretch thin.

"All right. Childhood abuse, psychological trauma, physical trauma, prolonged exposure to stress, brain-chemistry imbalance, genetics. Any combinations of the latter. What exactly does this have to do with anything, Detective?"

"Have you ever had a case where absolutely none of these factors were present?"

Dr. Jordan hesitated. Santini could see the answer in her eyes.

"All right," she said. "I admit there may have been a few cases like that."

"I've always suspected and am now convinced that evil is real," Santini said. "An external force, preying upon the vulnerable. Preying upon anyone with weakness."

"I don't believe in supernatural forces."

"Do you remember the Jeffrey Dahmer case?" Santini asked.

"What's the point of all this?"

"The maniac killed young boys and then had sex with their decomposing corpses. A real piece of work. The quintessential face of evil. And if you remember, the medical community petitioned the court to dissect his brain. But they found nothing. A normal brain inside the skull of one of the most callous, evil human beings to walk the face of the Earth."

"So his brain was normal. So what?" she said. "Did you expect the devil's calling card to be pinned to his frontal lobe?"

Santini shook his head. "Then I'll just have to convince you in another way."

"And what way is that, Detective?"

Santini looked over at the couch. "Put me to sleep."

"What?"

"Put me to sleep. Use any sleep-inducing techniques you'd like."

"And how will that convince me you're both not suffering from delusions?"

"Because I can prove my dreams are precognitive. And if I dream about this thing committing violence, you can do a ride-along."

Salvo shook his head. "I don't know about this idea. It places the doctor at risk."

"You and I will make sure Dr. Jordan is safe. It's the only way. I need my badge and gun back."

Dr. Jordan glanced from one detective to the other.

"So how about it, Doc?" Santini said. "Can you sing me a lullaby?"

She shook her head. "This is utter nonsense."

"Please," Santini said. "If nothing comes of it, I'll voluntarily continue treatment at Blackthorne, and we can have as many . . . conversations as you'd like."

She paused. "I still think you're deluding yourself. Maybe this exercise will confirm that."

Santini surprised himself and took her hand. "Thank you. I always knew you would get me onto the couch."

Jordan smiled for the first time. "So it seems, Detective."

# CHAPTER 17

Drakin smiled through the gleaming teeth of the bearded man as he walked slowly and confidently through the lobby of the Waldorf Astoria Hotel. He strode over to the concierge.

The man behind the desk jumped into a standing posture as if his chair had just caught fire.

"Good evening, Mr. Shahid," he said. "A pleasure to see you again."

"You can dispense with the pleasantries," Shahid said. "I expect the suite has been cleaned spotless. The last time I was here there was a stain on the carpet. A disgrace."

The man fidgeted. "I personally inspected the rooms this morning, Mr. Shahid. Everything should be to your satisfaction."

Shahid held the man's gaze. "And remember, I want the white gold caviar, not the gray shit you tried to poison me with last time."

The man nodded profusely. "The bottles of Champagne are chilling as we speak, Mr. Shahid, and the caviar is on its way."

Shahid grinned, enjoying the man's nervousness. "Good. You can sit down now."

Josef Shahid had learned that the best way not to attract attention was to go out of his way to attract attention. So he was flamboyant in everything he did. With his booming voice, his Middle Eastern garb, his twenty-four karat ring and his diamond-studded Rolex watch, he spread money around as if it had no limits. And it didn't. The oil coffers of ISIS were virtually unlimited. And his impeccably prefabricated bio as a rich eccentric Saudi business tycoon traveling with an entourage of bodyguards had managed to keep him off the government's radar.

Drakin was intrigued by the workings of this man's mind. His hatred for America was visceral. Although Drakin himself was the undisputed master of deception and manipulation, this man did have talent. Some humans still managed to entertain him.

Drakin-Shahid took the VIP elevator to the thirty-fifth floor of the Towers. When he reached the door to the Presidential Suite, he slid his card through the lock entry and entered. His eyes swept the room. Then he laughed.

It was humorous that he'd be conducting business where so many American presidents had slept. He walked over to the rocking chair and sat in it. It had belonged to Kennedy. The suite contained many such personal items contributed by the presidents to add to the mystique of the room.

Drakin thought back to 1962. He had come so close, but Kennedy and Khrushchev wouldn't launch the missiles. What a shame. But he smiled, remembering how he'd exacted his revenge on the man.

While he awaited the arrival of his guest, he called a special number for two of the most expensive prostitutes he could find. Drakin found base sexual energy to be akin to negative energy, provided it was free of any form of affection. It didn't have the same power as fear, anger, or hatred, but he still found it invigorating.

He walked to the large floor-to-ceiling windows that lined the entire suite and gazed out at the city, listening intently, his senses keenly aware of the voices in the storm. The negative energy was growing. The canopy of fear, anger, and violence that shrouded the planet was expanding. His plan was working.

In the last fifty years, he'd upset the balance that, until now, had kept the planet safe. It had been a slow process, but through the centuries he'd been patient.

With a little help from Drakin, human nature had taken its true course. Wars were widespread, and thousands of violent acts spawned a cumulative negative energy that rose and mushroomed into black clouds that pitched and undulated over land and sea.

Now his efforts were culminating. This storm was evidence of his success. All that was needed now was a catastrophic event that would trigger an avalanche of negative energy and rip the barrier that protected humanity. Just one more of his little dominoes needed to be pushed.

But there was one more annoying detail he had to deal with.

Apparently, Detective Santini was not only having precognitive dreams about the bomb but was also dreaming about Drakin's movements. An unusual occurrence. He'd have to make allowances for the detective's precognitive abilities, since his attempts to kill the man had failed.

There was a knock on the door. A broad man in a fine silk suit entered, with eyes dark as coal and a black mustache that dangled low in the corners of his mouth. His eyes quickly scanned the room, seemingly suspicious of his surroundings. Finally, he turned to Drakin-Shahid and smiled.

"Not bad, my friend. The Presidential Suite. The irony is almost too much."

The two men shook hands and sat across from each other. Drakin-Shahid handed the man a glass of Champagne.

"So, Sarkozy, how much longer?" Drakin-Shahid asked.

The man smiled through his black mustache. "The last piece was smuggled in three weeks ago across the Lukeville-Sonoita border and into Tucson, Arizona," Sarkozy said, his Russian accent subtle but still noticeable. "All parts shipped through the Southwestern border over the last year are being assembled as we speak."

"And what of the plutonium?"

"The plutonium is being flown in from Canada tomorrow. The weapon should be fully assembled and ready for you by the end of the week."

"Excellent," Shahid said.

"This transaction will be the *Mona Lisa* of my career," Sarkozy said. "As you know, a weapon such as this, of this magnitude, has never before been created."

"Your team of disaffected Russian scientists exceeded our expectations," Shahid said.

"Russians can be resourceful," Sarkozy said, "when the right price motivates them. With your payment, which I expect on delivery as agreed, I'll live like a prince. And as an added bonus, I get to stick it to the West one more time. For Mother Russia."

Drakin-Shahid smiled and raised his glass. "Here is to Prince Sarkozy and to Mother Russia."

The two clinked glasses.

"To Mother Russia," Sarkozy said.

Drakin-Shahid then thought about Detective Santini. "There's something more I need from you, Ivan."

"And what's that?"

"A facsimile."

"What do you mean?"

"A replica. Similar in every way to the nuclear device but devoid of the plutonium. Maybe you can load it with C4 explosives. But I'll need a bomb made to look like a nuclear device."

Sarkozy's smile faded. "I don't understand why you would want a non-functioning replica unless you plan on scamming someone, and in that case I don't want my name associated with that transaction. I have a reputation to uphold."

Drakin-Shahid smiled. "Don't worry about that. Your name won't be mentioned to anyone. As far as the replica, that's my business. I'll pay you an additional one million dollars for it, and I'll have your final payment when both items are delivered."

Sarkozy nodded. "This shouldn't be a problem." Then he leaned in closer to Drakin-Shahid, a mischievous grin sliding across his face. "So tell me, my friend, what is the target?"

Shahid filled Sarkozy's glass. "Sorry. Not possible. Just don't linger too long in this country after you've been paid." He raised his Champagne glass. "You and I are about to make history." They clinked glasses once again.

There was a knock on the door. Drakin-Shahid walked over and opened it. Two beautiful young girls entered the suite.

Sarkozy smiled. "You're full of surprises, Shahid."

"Ten thousand dollars for these gems," Shahid said.

"You are indeed very generous, my friend." He walked over and handed a glass of Champagne to the brunette.

"Generous?" Shahid shook his head. "This is coming out of your payment, Sarkozy."

Sarkozy's smile quickly evaporated. Then Drakin-Shahid burst into a fit of laughter. Slowly, Sarkozy caught on and they both howled with delight.

Drakin-Shahid's cell phone rang.

"Yes, yes. He has clearance. Send him up right away."

A few moments later there was another knock on the door. When Shahid opened it, one of his men stood there with a submissive look on his face.

"Pardon the interruption, sir, but I thought you would want to hear of this news immediately."

Drakin-Shahid glared at the man. "What is it, Obed, that couldn't wait?"

"Sir. We've found the staff!"

Drakin-Shahid dragged the man off to the other side of the room. "*Where?*"

"A priest. Here in the city."

"You have a name?"

"Yes, Shahid."

"Excellent. Your bonus will be doubled."

"Shall I procure the staff, Shahid?"

Drakin-Shahid shook his head. This splinter of wood had caused him trouble once before, and he was not about to let that happen again.

"No. I'll handle this personally."

Drakin's tentacles tingled with excitement as the man turned and walked away.

# CHAPTER 18

The taxi dropped off Father O'Brian in front of St. Patrick's Cathedral. He slowly climbed the stone steps that led to the front doors of the church, his umbrella fighting the wind that tried its best to rip it apart. He finally made it to the top, pushed on the heavy oak doors, and walked inside.

It was midnight and the church was empty. Its usual ambience of nighttime peace and stillness was disturbed by the howling of the wind and the rattling of the stained glass windows.

O'Brian was exhausted. He had just come from the hospital to give last rites to a child whose battle with leukemia had ended. He sighed deeply, walked over to the prayer candles, and lit one for the young boy. The little flame flickered to life, joining the hundreds of other candles that cast long shadows on the far wall.

O'Brian said a prayer, ignoring the voices, and walked back toward the door of his apartment.

Then he stopped.

The door and the lock were shattered. He listened for any sounds from within, but all he could hear was the wind and the rain. He cautiously stepped inside and switched on the light.

Broken furniture and shattered lamps and dishes were scattered everywhere. Bookcases were knocked down, couches torn up, the heating vents pried loose.

He called 911.

In less than ten minutes, Sergeant Sean Cassidy was standing beside him carefully taking notes.

"Can you think of anyone who has a grudge against you or the Church, Father?"

The priest shrugged. "There are a lot of people who don't like the doctrines of the Church."

"Have you had any altercations recently?"

"No."

"Any parishioners acting strange lately?"

O'Brian hesitated before answering. "No. I don't know anyone who would do this, Sean."

The officer looked around. "Seems like they were looking for something. Do you keep valuables here, Father?"

"Not really. I have some old books, but they're not something that can easily be turned into cash."

"Is there anything missing, either here or in the church?"

"Not that I can tell. The church itself doesn't seem to have been vandalized. They targeted my apartment."

"I'll have the place dusted for fingerprints. See if anything shows up in our records. Is there anywhere you can spend the night? We have an extra room at our place if not."

"Thanks, Sean, but I'll manage. If you could just help me turn my bed back over."

When they were finished, Cassidy called his precinct.

"I'm having a patrol car stationed outside the church tonight, Father."

"Thanks Sean."

Cassidy looked around again. "I'll have two of my off-duty guys come over tomorrow, help you put this place back together."

"Thank you. I'd appreciate that."

Cassidy started to leave but then turned. "Don't worry. We'll find the son of a bitch who did this." He quickly put his hand over his mouth. "Sorry, Father."

"It's all right, Sean. Just say three Hail Mary prayers on your way home."

Cassidy smiled and walked out.

O'Brian shivered. The chill in the air seemed to be getting worse as the rain continued its assault. He dug through the rubble on the floor and managed to find an unbroken cup and a tea bag. Before long the teapot was whistling.

He turned over one of the kitchen chairs, sat down, and took a sip of tea.

O'Brian didn't like the implications of this. He was hoping it had been just a mindless act of vandalism, but his gut told him otherwise.

The wind howled outside with a distinctly higher pitch, as if it were angry that it couldn't break through the windows. He took a last sip of tea and lay on his bed, listening intently to the storm and thinking about the voices that were disturbing his prayers.

He was convinced the two were related. The storm seemed to be fueling the voices. Or was it the other way around?

As he pondered this, a deep fatigue settled into his body. He closed his eyes and fell asleep.

He was standing in the midst of devastation. Buildings had been reduced to rubble. The sky was thick with smoke and ash. Fires erupted everywhere.

In the distance he noticed a black mist. It drifted toward him, a swirling orb of tentacles that pulsated with energy. When it stopped, its tentacles reached out for him.

From the corner of his eye he could see a man approaching.

The man walked slowly and carried a staff. As the man came closer, the staff ignited, shimmering and gleaming and lighting up the black sky like the morning sun.

When the creature turned to face the approaching man, it let out a deafening shriek and charged—tentacles whipping, teeth chattering, tongue darting, eyes blazing red with anger.

At the same instant, the man lifted the staff and drove it into the heart of the creature. A tremendous explosion of light and sound filled the air. The priest shielded his eyes, and when he finally was able to look, both the creature and the man were gone.

O'Brian woke up and sat at the edge of his bed. His face was damp with sweat. He took a deep breath and replayed the dream in his head.

He walked into the church. He counted off twenty-seven pews and stopped. He leaned over, undid the latch hidden underneath, and lifted the seat. Then he removed the false bottom, fabricated per his instructions, and pulled out a long object.

He didn't know why, but his instincts told him to hide it somewhere else.

He walked behind an alcove and climbed the old wooden stairs that led to the organ. Of the two organs at St. Patrick's, the Gallery Organ, hand-carved and adorned with angels and Latin inscriptions, was his favorite. It had one of the most beautiful wood facades in all the world.

He walked around the side of the organ and lifted one of the smaller side panels that enclosed the organ's eight thousand pipes. O'Brian slid the object out from the purple silk cloth and cradled the wooden staff in his hands. Maybe it was his imagination or the chill in the air, but the old piece of wood seemed warm to the touch.

He'd discovered the staff decades ago in an archaeological dig on the island of Crete. He was rappelling down the wall of a subterranean cave when his rope snapped and he plummeted into the crystal waters of an underground lagoon.

When he surfaced, he saw a light dancing on a portion of the rock wall. He followed the ray into the water and saw a silver light emanating from the sand below. He dived down and pulled the long object from its resting place. He knew there was something unique about this old shaft of wood.

Years later he'd brought it to his friend Pope Augustine. One of the scholars at the Vatican who specialized in ancient artifacts concluded that it was partially petrified, and carbon dating estimated it to be thousands of years old. His research led him to believe it could be the same staff Moses held when he parted the Red Sea. O'Brian didn't know if that was true, but at the very least, he suspected the staff contained some hidden power. His recent dream seemed to confirm his suspicion.

For years it had been locked away in the pope's private library, and would-be thieves twice tried unsuccessfully to breach the Tower of the Winds looking for the staff.

Before he left the Vatican, the pope had returned the staff to O'Brian, hoping it would be safer with the priest. He was right. The most recent events at the Piazza San Pietro confirmed that whoever was hunting the staff was willing to commit mass murder to find it.

He shook his head. Supposedly, no one besides himself, a few at the Vatican, and the pope even knew the staff existed, let alone where it was hidden.

He thought about his dream. The man, whom he'd never seen before, had been holding this very same staff. There was no mistaking its markings.

His slid the staff back into the silk cloth and positioned it carefully in its new hiding place.

Father O'Brian was certain that whoever had ransacked his apartment was looking for the staff. But why?

He was also certain that whoever it had been would be back.

*"Dreams may contain ineluctable truths, philosophical pronouncements, illusions, wild fantasies, memories, plans, anticipations, irrational experiences, even telepathic visions, and heaven knows what besides."*
—Carl Gustav Jung

# CHAPTER 19

"Close your eyes, Detective," Dr. Jordan said. "Take deep breaths. Concentrate on my voice."

Santini repositioned his body as he lay outstretched on her sofa. Salvo sat quietly on the chair opposite, looking uncharacteristically nervous. The wind howled outside, but the doctor's voice had a soothing quality that seemed to overcome the battering of the rain. It seemed to Santini that her initial anger had subsided.

"Let all the tension in your mind release," she said. "Feel your body relax. Feel the tension drain from every muscle. Feel all the worry, fear, and anxiety melt away."

As Santini listened, he allowed himself to think he caught just a hint of affection in her voice. Was he imagining it? Probably.

He was tired, very tired. So he tried to concentrate on relaxing and followed the sound of her voice.

"Now it's time to sleep. A deep peaceful sleep."

Little by little, his body began to go limp and he felt as if he were drifting in space. Eventually, the doctor's voice faded, and despite the loud cracks of thunder and the incessant drumming of the rain, physical exhaustion finally took over, and when he could no longer hear the sound of Dr. Jordan's voice, he fell into a deep sleep.

Santini could see through the eyes of a man as he walked down a city street. The wind howled and whipped. The rain drenched his clothes, but he took no notice. He stopped at the corner of Madison Avenue and

Fifty-first Street and turned left. He stood in front of the church and looked around. A patrol car was parked out front. He walked up the steps to the entrance of the cathedral. Then he heard footsteps coming up from behind him. He pulled a knife from the inner pocket of his jacket. *No,* Santini screamed silently. With one swift movement, he turned and plunged the knife deep into the abdomen of the approaching police officer. The shocked officer crumpled onto the wet steps.

He continued up to the cathedral entrance and slowly opened the door. Except for the lightning that flashed through the stained glass windows, the inside of the church was completely dark. He turned on a flashlight and worked his way around the altar to a side door.

He swung his leg back and with one hard blow crashed through the door. The apartment was silent. He swung his flashlight from side to side, but there was no one. He approached another door and kicked it in. An old man stood in the corner of the bedroom, presumably a priest, staring defiantly at his intruder. He walked over and held the knife in front of the priest's face.

Santini could hear the man's menacing voice.

"Such a pure and virtuous mind. We'll have to do this the old-fashioned way." The man grinned.

"I have no money here," the priest said. "You're wasting your time."

He laughed, moving the knife closer to the priest's face. "The staff, old man. Where is it?"

The priest sighed. "I have lived a long life. I'm prepared to meet my God. Can you say the same, my son?"

"My son?" Santini listened as the man howled with laughter. "I've got about five thousand years on you, old man. And today your God is nowhere to be found. Today there's just me." He held the knife an inch from the priest's right eye, a flash of lightning illuminating the point of the blade. "I'll start with your right eye, then the left. You will be dismembered piece by piece until you tell me where it is."

The priest closed his eyes and began reciting a prayer.

"The Lord is my shepherd, I shall not want."

Simultaneously, out of the storm, there erupted a cacophony of screams.

Santini listened through the man's ears as the voices rose in a fury of anger, the screams echoing through the room.

"Yea, though I walk through the valley of the shadow of death, I will fear no evil. For thou art with me."

The entire room shook with the terrible screams.

Suddenly, there was silence and a deep voice emanated from the man who stood before the priest.

"Your faith is weak, old man," he hissed. "Your God has no power here."

He reared his arm back. Santini tried to stop it. *No!* The knife swung forward and plunged into the eye of the priest. The priest cried out.

Santini screamed. Then his eyes flew open and he bolted upright on the couch.

He sat on the edge of the couch and shook his head, trying to clear his mind.

"Salvo," Santini said. "What's the church at the corner of Madison and Fifty-first?"

Before Salvo could speak, Dr. Jordan answered. "That's St. Patrick's Cathedral. How could you not know that?"

"I'm not a churchgoer, Doc."

"Why?" Salvo asked.

"The priest. He's in danger. We need to get over there. Now!"

"Are you sure about taking the Doc with us?" Salvo said.

Santini stood up and faced Dr. Jordan. "Salvo's right. You don't have to do this. It could be dangerous."

"Or it could be nothing," she said. "Either way, I'm going. The pastor at St. Patrick's, Father O'Brian—he's a friend."

Santini raised an eyebrow. "I wouldn't have thought psychiatry and religion were a fit."

"That's a discussion for another day, Detective."

Salvo sighed. "All right, but she stays in the car."

Santini locked eyes with Jordan. "Understood?"

Jordan nodded. "Understood."

They quickly exited the doctor's house and piled into the Crown Victoria. Salvo slapped the siren onto the roof of the car and sped into the dark of the night

## CHAPTER 20

The Crown Victoria screeched to a halt behind the empty police car parked in front of the church. Santini jumped out of the car and leaped up the stone stairs. An officer was lying on the steps, rain washing away the blood from his wound. Salvo and Jordan trailed behind.

"I thought I told you to stay in the car," Santini said.

"I did a year in the ER before specializing. Now move over." She crouched beside the officer and felt for a pulse. "He's alive. But barely. I need to put pressure on the wound."

Salvo removed his jacket and placed it under the policeman's head. He pulled out his cell phone. "This is Detective John Salvo. Officer down. I repeat, officer down. In front of St. Patrick's Cathedral. Madison and Fifty-first. Abdominal wound. Send backup and an ambulance. Now!"

Jordan again felt for a pulse. "We're losing him. Apply pressure on the wound, Salvo." Santini glanced at the name on the officer's badge: Andrew Jenkins. He couldn't have been more than twenty-five. Jordan began compression on his chest.

After an agonizing minute she checked again for a pulse. Santini and Salvo looked at her. She shook her head. She continued working, unwilling to give up.

"Come on Jenkins," Santini said. "Come on."

She checked the pulse again and sighed. "He's back."

In the distance they could hear the sounds of approaching sirens.

Santini glanced up at the entrance to the cathedral. "We need to go inside, Salvo. The priest."

"Go ahead," Jordan said.

Santini hesitated.

"Go," she said. "I've got this."

Santini and Salvo ran up the stone steps to the large oak doors and entered the church. Except for the flickering flames from the prayer candles and the sudden flashes of lightning, the church was shrouded in dark shadows. No sounds emerged.

"Quick. This way, Salvo."

They used their flashlights to navigate down the center aisle of the church and worked their way around the altar to the side door.

Santini and Salvo stood on either side of the open door, and Salvo slipped a gun from his ankle holster and handed it to Santini.

"NYPD!" Salvo yelled.

No response.

Santini nodded to Salvo, and Salvo entered the room, gun drawn, flashlight searching in the darkness. The apartment had been trashed.

They crept toward another open door. Santini entered first with Salvo a step behind. A flash of lightning lit the room to reveal two men standing against the far wall, one with a knife pointed at the other's eye.

Santini felt like he was stepping into his own nightmare again.

"Put the knife down," he yelled.

The man with the knife, brandishing gang colors, his hair in tight braids, turned to look defiantly at Santini.

"Put the knife down or I'll put a bullet in your head."

With lightning speed the man spun the priest around to face the detectives and held the knife to the priest's throat. He smiled.

"Detective Santini. You're becoming a tiresome nuisance."

"Put the knife down," Salvo yelled.

"In a split second I can take his head off."

"Let him go," Santini said.

"I'm walking out of here with the priest." The man walked slowly toward the bedroom door, and the detectives let him pass. He backed his way through the apartment with Salvo and Santini following, guns drawn. The man edged his way into the church and passed the altar, the blade pressed firmly against O'Brian's throat. Outside they could hear sirens and cars screeching to a halt.

"There's no way out," Santini said. "Let him go."

The man seemed to consider for a moment, and then his face contorted, his eyes blazed red, and he let loose a deafening scream that echoed throughout the church. At the same moment, a tremendous bolt of lightning shattered a stained glass window into shards and splitting the altar in half. Smoke curled in all directions as fire spread rapidly from the altar toward the large wooden crucifix behind it.

The man screamed again, an unearthly howl that made Santini's hair stand on end, and another bolt shattered a second stained glass window and ignited the entire front of the church.

As the inside of the church burned, the man's eyes rolled up into his head and he fell to the floor. Salvo jumped on top of him, flipped him over and handcuffed him.

"Are you okay, Father?" Santini asked. "Father O'Brian, is it?"

The priest nodded and turned to look at the burning crucifix.

"We have to go, Father," Santini said.

Salvo hoisted the dazed gang banger to his feet, and Santini supported the priest. Santini looked all around, fearful that the thing from his dreams was still near. Then the front doors flew open and six police officers with guns drawn entered the church.

"Get him out of here," Salvo said. He pushed the gangbanger toward one of the officers and helped Santini lead Father O'Brian out of the building.

When they were outside, Dr. Jordan ran to them. "Father, are you injured?"

O'Brian placed his hand on his throat where the sharp blade had left its mark. "Kelly Jordan? What are you doing here?"

"It's a long story, Father."

"I'm fine, Kelly. Thanks to these two young men."

"What about Jenkins?" Salvo asked.

"He's lost a lot of blood," Jordan said. "But I think we got to him in time." She shook her head and gazed at Santini. "Thanks to you, Detective."

"No," Santini said, smiling. "Thanks to you."

"I have to go back inside." The priest said. "I must have my staff."

Salvo turned and watched the smoke curling through the front doors of the church. "How about we get you a brand-new cane just as soon as we can," he said.

"No. You don't understand. I have to go back." Father O'Brian headed up the stairs to the burning church.

Santini ran ahead and stood in front of him.

"Sorry, Father, we can't let you do that."

"Do you think I'd go in there if it wasn't important? I have no choice. That staff could mean all the difference." The priest glared at Santini.

"Where is it?" Santini said.

"You can't be serious," Salvo said.

They could hear the sounds of approaching fire trucks in the distance.

"I'll be fine, Salvo. Firemen are on the way. I'm soaked from the rain, which is a good thing. Where is it, Father?"

"As soon as you walk into the church, turn left past the pews. Take the side stairs to the upper level and you'll see a grand organ. As you face the organ, on the lower right-hand side is a small wooden panel, an access to the lower pipes. Slide it open. It's wrapped in a purple silk cloth."

"This is crazy," Salvo said.

"We're here for a reason," Santini said. "I don't know why, but this thing wants O'Brian's staff. So I'm not going to let him have it."

Santini dashed up the steps to the cathedral entrance.

Covering his mouth and nose with his wet cap, he entered the burning church. Holding his breath, he worked his way left toward the stairs, which were just barely visible. As he made his ascent, he could feel the heat from the flames now licking the bottom of each step.

When he made it to the top floor, he saw the organ and dashed over to where the priest had indicated. He pulled on the panel several times, but it wouldn't budge. He tapped it with his fist and tried again. This time it slid open. He rummaged through the space until his hands felt a soft silk cloth. He pulled it out and turned it over in his hands. He thought he felt a tingling warmth flow up into his arms. *Must be the heat from the fire.*

He ran back to the top of the stairs and stopped. Sporadic flames were now jumping up through the steps. Soon his only escape route would be destroyed. He tucked the staff under one arm, still holding the cap over his face, felt for the banister with his other hand, and leaped down the stairs.

When he made it to the bottom, the smoke had thickened and he could barely see. The intense heat was overwhelming, and his lungs burned with each breath. Slowly, he maneuvered in the direction he thought was the way out, but a piece of falling debris from the ceiling caught him on the side of the head and he went down with a thud. He tried to get up, but his legs wouldn't work. Santini closed his eyes, and as he was about to lose consciousness, he thought he heard someone calling his name.

Two firemen held Salvo back, as four others, with masks and oxygen tanks, charged into the burning church. They turned left, as Salvo had instructed, the lead fireman dousing the flames and creating a path before them as they edged closer to the fallen detective. When they finally reached him, they placed an oxygen mask over his face and hoisted him into a semi-upright position. As they raced toward the exit, hot embers fell from the ceiling, and they could hear the rafters groan and pop as large pieces snapped loose and fell to the floor. Just as they carried Santini out the front doors, the ceiling of St. Patrick's Cathedral came crashing down in a blaze of fire and smoke.

# CHAPTER 21

Santini was seated at the edge of the gurney just outside the back of the ambulance. He removed the oxygen mask from his face and inhaled deeply. He was a little dizzy but otherwise felt fine and so had refused the trip to the emergency room. A paramedic placed a small bandage over his right temple and removed the blood pressure cuff from Santini's arm.

"He'll be fine," he said to Salvo and Dr. Jordan, who were standing next to him wearing concerned expressions.

Jordan looked at Santini. "We need to talk, Detective."

At that moment, the once-ornate front doors of the old church fell forward with a crash. When they turned to look, the remaining stained glass windows exploded, sending hot shards of glass into the air.

The fire chief backed everyone away and walked over to Father O'Brian, who stood alone facing the cathedral. Even with the torrential rain, light from the soaring flames illuminated the dark night, and billows of black smoke commingled with the clouds from the storm.

"I'm sorry, Father," the chief said. "It's too late to save her." He shook his head. "I've never seen a fire burn so rapidly. The best we can do is control the burn and keep the fire from spreading."

The priest made the sign of the cross as tears filled his eyes.

"Your men saved the detective, Chief," O'Brian said. "For that I am grateful."

He walked over to where Santini and the others were. Santini could see that the water in the old priest's eyes was not from the rain.

Officer Sean Cassidy, who was a part of the team that entered the church, walked over to O'Brian.

"Are you okay, Father?"

"I'm fine, Sean," O'Brian said.

"We have your assailant in custody," Cassidy said. "Probably the same man who ransacked your apartment. When you feel up to it, I'm going to need a statement."

"We'll have our report filed tomorrow," Salvo said, "including Father O'Brian's. Right now he needs to rest."

Cassidy glanced at the burning church. "I'm sorry about the cathedral, Father." He shook his head. "I'll need to call Jenkins's family now."

"I'll pray for his recovery, Sean," O'Brian said. As Cassidy walked away, the priest turned to face Santini. "I should not have let you risk your life like that. I'm deeply sorry."

"What the—" Salvo caught himself. "What's so important about an old staff?"

"I can explain, Detective Salvo," the priest said. "But first it is vital I speak with your partner."

Salvo threw up his hands. "Doesn't anyone want to talk to me?"

Dr. Jordan smiled. "My place? It's closest."

They all agreed. Santini handed the staff to Father O'Brian, which the detective somehow managed to hold on to even as he was carried out of the burning church.

As Santini, Salvo, Jordan, and O'Brian piled into the Crown Victoria, a tall man with long hair and a beard, standing among the crowd of onlookers, watched as the staff was loaded into the car.

Drakin-Jackson smiled. He loved fire. The intense heat. The energy. Its uses were infinite. And on this occasion, it had flushed out a long-sought prize.

He hopped onto his motorcycle and slowly trailed his prey.

Santini stood near the gas fireplace rubbing his hands. They all seemed to be trying to escape the damp chill that had worked its way into their bodies. Wet jackets hung in the entryway to Jordan's home. The thunder and lightning continued unabated.

Father O'Brian sat on the couch next to Salvo with a blanket wrapped around him.

"I'm terribly sorry about your church, Father," Jordan said.

The priest seemed dazed. Then he looked up at Dr. Jordan, tears in his eyes.

"My home, my books, the organs . . . all gone." He shook his head. "Where will my parishioners go?"

Salvo placed his hand on O'Brian's shoulder.

"Is there something I can get for you, Father?" Jordan asked. "Something to drink, maybe?"

"A whiskey would be just what the doctor ordered," he said.

Santini quickly raised his arm. "A double, please."

"Since no one wants to talk to me," Salvo said, "I'll have a triple."

Jordan went into the kitchen and reappeared with a bottle of Jack Daniel's and four glasses. Santini glanced at the bottle and raised a brow at Jordan.

"It was a gift," she said. "I'm usually not a fan of hard liquor, but tonight . . ."

They sat quietly sipping bourbon, watching the flames in the fireplace, listening to the pounding rain and thunder, until Dr. Jordan broke the silence.

"I owe you an apology, Detective."

"Not necessary," Santini said. "I'd have done the same thing in your position."

Salvo punched a number into his cell phone and handed it to Dr. Jordan.

"This is Captain Johnson's cell," he said. "Time to clear this up."

Father O'Brian looked at Jordan and Salvo with a puzzled expression. Jordan took the phone.

"Captain Johnson? This is Dr. Kelly Jordan." She looked at Santini as she spoke. "I'm calling on behalf of Detective Santini . . . No, he's fine. I'm calling to give Detective Santini full medical clearance to return to work. I'll have the paperwork faxed to you first thing in the morning . . . Yes, yes I know. It was a big misunderstanding . . . Yes, I'm happy about it, too. All right. Good-bye." She handed the phone back to Salvo.

Santini nodded. "Thanks, Doc."

The priest sat forward on the couch. "And I want to thank you for coming to my aid."

"You said we needed to talk," Santini said. "I don't think it was to thank us."

"You're right." O'Brian locked eyes with Santini. "When I first saw you, I thought there was something familiar about you. But when we were standing outside and the flames from the church lit up you face, I was certain. You see, I had a dream about you."

"Great," Salvo said. "Another one. Doesn't anyone have normal dreams around here?"

This caught the priest's attention. "Have you been having unusual dreams also?"

Santini smiled. "I suppose you could say that."

"Tell me," O'Brian said. "I must know everything."

There was a sudden crash of thunder and flash of lightning, and the room was plunged into darkness except for the light from the fireplace.

Salvo peered out the window. "The entire block is out," he said.

Dr. Jordan maneuvered into the kitchen and returned with a flashlight and two candles, which she lit on either side of the room.

Between the candlelight and the flames from the fireplace, long dancing shadows were cast on the walls. Santini watched as the shadows seemed to shape themselves into ghoulish faces. He shook his head. This storm was starting to get to him.

He sat in a chair next to Dr. Jordan, with Salvo and O'Brian on the couch. He was relieved to be able to tell his story again to someone who wouldn't think he was crazy.

He began his narrative with the recurring apocalyptic nightmare and his harrowing experience with the voices on the observatory. He recounted the details of his precognitive dreams of the Gorman-family murders and saving the little girl in Jamaica Estates. He talked about the entity he seemed to be able to see in his dreams and the entity's attempt to kill him. Then he related his latest dream concerning the priest.

O'Brian stared intently at the detective. After several moments he spoke.

"This . . . entity, as you call it—it's been here for a very long time."

"How do you know?" Santini said.

"Throughout human history, the Church has recognized the existence of demonic forces," O'Brian said.

"To frighten people," Santini said. "So they turn to religion for protection."

The priest gazed into Santini's eyes and smiled. "I assure you, your contention couldn't be further from the truth."

"And people just have to take the Church's word on this?" Salvo said.

"Of course not," O'Brian said. "Let's just say I've been given access to some of the more secret archives of the Church, and the evidence for the existence of these forces is overwhelming."

"Suppose we believe you," Santini said. "What's this thing want?"

The priest closed his eyes and recited:

*When the Souls of Men have been Corrupted in Sufficient Numbers,*
*And Love Withers at its Roots,*
*When the Collective Mind of Man has turned away from the Light,*
*And in its Stead there Foments Hate, Fear, and Violence,*
*It is Then the Portal will Open,*
*And They will Ride Through,*
*Propelled by an epoch storm,*
*Thrusting Humankind into a Darkness so complete,*
*That there Shall be no Escape from Hell on Earth.*

There was a long silence.

O'Brian opened his eyes. "What it wants, Detective, is hell on Earth."

The priest looked old and tired. Santini could see the growing fear in his eyes.

O'Brian shook his head. "Man has turned his back on God. He's turned away from the light of His grace and love. If this portal opens, it will be the end of the human race as we know it."

"That's quite a claim," Salvo said.

O'Brian turned to look at all three of them. "Haven't you been wondering what this thing is and where it came from?"

"It's an evil force that can influence behavior," Santini said. "Beyond that, we don't have enough facts."

"Facts?" The priest shook his head. "The fact is, there is more going on than just random murders. Surely you have felt it. This storm, under its influence, is having a global effect. Spiritual leaders and people who devote their lives to prayer and contemplation have felt it. "

"Felt what?" Dr. Jordan asked.

"A growing spiritual darkness. A disturbance so strong it permeates the mind with negative energy and blocks our ability to communicate with God. And this entity is responsible. He's most likely a demon of the highest order. Some believe even the Anti-Christ himself."

Santini thought about how the storm was affecting him. Then he shook his head. "Those are some pretty wild conclusions, Father."

"I assure you, Detective, I'm not one given to exaggeration. Haven't you noticed anything unusual about this storm?"

"I've never seen so much lightning," Jordan said. "The bolts are lower and linger in the sky."

"And the thunder," Salvo added. "It never lets up."

"And I've noticed a rancid smell," Jordan said. "Not the usual fresh-air smell when it rains."

"This storm isn't natural," the priest said. "There are voices deeply embedded within it. The bolts of lightning that destroyed St. Patrick's Cathedral were no accident. This demon was responsible."

"Demon? Anti-Christ? It's just a damn storm," Santini said. "Some kind of global warming anomaly. Father, I concede that something out of the ordinary is going on here, but do you have any actual evidence?"

O'Brian glared at Santini. "Evidence? Facts? I assume that accepting your dreams as premonitions required a dramatic shift on your part, Detective. It required you to suspend your typical analytic, rational approach to reality."

"I think that can be said for all of us after tonight," Jordan said.

"It's still quite a leap to the Anti-Christ," Salvo said.

The priest stood up, seemingly energized by the course of the discussion.

"You must all listen very carefully. Anthony is not the only one having unusual dreams."

Everyone fell silent.

"Two nights ago, I also had a dream of a destroyed city. As I was standing in the midst of devastation, I was attacked by a creature who seemed to draw energy from its surroundings. A rescuer appeared wielding a staff." O'Brian focused his gaze on Santini as he picked up the staff wrapped in silk cloth. "The very same staff I asked you to risk your life to retrieve. And the rescuer in my dream, holding this staff, turned out to be none other than you, Anthony."

Santini stared straight ahead, unable to speak. The wind howled and the shadows from the candles danced on the walls. The priest pulled out the staff from its sheath.

"It wants this very badly," said O'Brian. "And this isn't the first time it's tried to obtain it."

"And you were willing to be tortured and to die before telling him where it was hidden," Salvo said. "Why?"

"Twice in the past five years, thieves have tried to breach the pope's private library, but none of them got very far. When the culprits were captured and interrogated, each stated they'd been commissioned to steal an antique staff. Millions of dollars in solid gold artifacts adorned the Vatican, yet the thieves were only interested in an old piece of wood."

"The recent bombing at St. Peter's square—was that an attempt to steal the staff?" Santini asked.

The priest shook his head. "It was a terrible tragedy. A diversion for breaching the Tower of the Winds. Luckily, it had been given to me for safekeeping. But apparently it has been discovered once again."

"Why? What does this thing want with it?" Jordan asked.

The priest turned to look intently at Santini. "My theory, and it's just a theory, is that it can somehow focus energy when wielded by the right person in the right state of mind. In my dream, you used it against him. This entity is trying to kill you for a reason. You can see him in your dreams. He knows you're a threat to his plans. So you must find it, Detective. And you must destroy him. Before he destroys us."

Santini stood up. "Why me? I'm no one special. Far from it. Why not someone like you whose faith is strong? Who at least might know what to do with this staff?"

"Don't underestimate your role in this, Anthony," O'Brian said. "When there are greater forces at work, it's not always possible to understand why things unfold the way they do. It's not just coincidence that you're dreaming of this entity. There must be a reason."

"Speaking of greater forces," Salvo said, "where is your God in all of this? If we're on the brink of annihilation, don't you think now would be a good time for the Almighty to show himself? Or is he too busy playing croquette in heaven with the apostles?"

"Because he doesn't exist, that's why!" Santini said. "And if he does exist, he doesn't give a damn!"

A heavy silence filled the room.

"So the wielder of the staff is an atheist?" O'Brian said. "How interesting."

"My mother prayed every day for my dad," Santini said. "And it didn't do a damn thing to prevent a good man from being gunned down. So if you were counting on faith, specifically mine, then we've got a big problem."

"I understand your anger," O'Brian said. "But since Eden, this has been the conundrum man has not been able to reconcile. It's not that God doesn't care. He's simply unwilling to take back His greatest gift. Free will."

Santini started pacing. "I'm sorry, but I don't buy it. You're saying my father's life was less important than the free will of a twisted murderer?"

"Of course not," O'Brian said. "It's difficult to witness the pain and suffering of the innocent, but that's where faith comes in. With faith we believe there's a greater plan. A plan beyond our understanding."

"If Humanity is in as much trouble as you say," Jordan said, "then how about a little help? Even at the expense of free will. Parents want their children to be independent, but that doesn't mean they shouldn't pull them away from an oncoming truck."

"We *are* being helped. Right now." He looked over at Santini.

"Are you trying to tell me these dreams are sent by God?" Santini said. "I don't believe that. So I ask again. Why me?"

"You and your partner have spent your lives chasing evil, Anthony. So why not you? I know you would do anything in your power to stop this thing. And I sense your friends would do anything to help you."

Salvo and Jordan nodded. Santini took a breath, knowing he was running out of ways to counter the priest's argument. He turned to face O'Brian. "I can agree with you on one thing. We need to find it and stop it. I have to dream about it again. I've no choice."

"I'm afraid it's the only course of action right now," O'Brian said.

"We'll be here with you," Jordan said.

"I just wish your dreams were a little more pleasant," Salvo said. "With each dream, we seem to find ourselves in deeper and deeper shit." He glanced sheepishly at O'Brian. "Sorry, Father."

"It's okay, Detective Salvo," the priest said with a smile.

The wind howled and shrieked as if attempting to worm its way through the walls of the house.

"Whenever you're ready, Detective Santini," Jordan said

# CHAPTER 22

President Tyler sat in the Oval Office listening to the torrential rain pound the windows. By nature he was a man of logic and reason, but even before his last meeting with Beaumont, his gut had told him there was something very wrong about this storm. *And now they've detected voices in the background noise? Unintelligible, but voices nonetheless. What the hell is that all about?*

Whitaker knocked on the door and entered.

Tyler's Chief of Staff was a short man, and when he stood next to the six-foot three President, they looked like something out of a Mutt and Jeff comic strip. His white hair was thinning and he carried about thirty extra pounds beneath an impeccably tailored collection of fine suits. In the world of politics it was easy to make enemies, but it was impossible to dislike Whitaker. He was good-natured to a fault, but at the same time he was fiercely loyal and devoted to his President.

"Anything new, Jim?"

"Actually, yes, Mr. President. Beaumont has something."

"Good. Let's hear what he has to say."

Back in the Situation Room, the director of NASA peered over his spectacles at the intense eyes staring in anticipation. Beaumont was excited but nervous.

"It seems," he began with a faltering voice. "It seems we've detected some unusual measurements over the New York City area."

"What could be more unusual than what you've already told us?" Tyler said.

"Well, Mr. President, in order for you to understand the extraordinary significance of these measurements, I should give you some background on what I'm about to tell you."

Tyler frowned. "Just keep it brief, Professor."

"For many years, scientists have postulated the existence of dark matter, a negative energy that binds the stars and galaxies together. All mathematical equations prove this postulation is true. But physicists have never been able to actually observe these dark energy particles. Even at the Soudan Iron Mine Laboratory, 2,431 feet below the surface of the Earth and completely shielded from interfering cosmic radiation, scientists have been unable to observe even one particle of this dark matter." Beaumont paused. "Until today. We're now registering a concentration of dark matter particles hovering over the island of Manhattan."

"And so what does that mean?" Tyler said. "Is this causing the storm?"

"We're not sure. This is something we've never come across before. But we do have a theory."

"I'm listening."

Beaumont took a deep breath and continued.

"Einstein's General Theory of Relativity allows for the existence of certain unique cosmic phenomena which you've probably heard about. Black holes and wormholes."

Tyler stared at Beaumont in astonishment. "Are you saying there's a black hole hovering over our city?"

"That would not be possible, sir," Beaumont said, "since the gravitational pull of a black hole would destroy our planet."

"Right. Of course. So what about these wormholes?"

"Wormholes are hypothetical, but it has been theorized they can connect two separate points in space/time. For the most part, current theories suggest these shortcuts through the universe are unstable and therefore non-traversable. They open up briefly, pinch off, and anything that tries to pass through them will be crushed."

"What does all of this have to do with this storm?" Tyler said.

Beaumont hesitated. All eyes in the room focused intently on him.

"It has been theorized that traversable wormholes would only be possible if what we call exotic matter with negative energy could be used to hold open the throat, or portal, of a wormhole."

Silence once again settled over the room.

"So let me get this straight," Tyler said. "You're saying the storm and this concentration of negative energy particles is the result of a traversable wormhole hovering over New York City?"

"Right now, Mr. President, that's our working theory, though at present, based on our calculations, there isn't enough dark matter to hold open the portal of a wormhole."

Tyler shook his head. Apparently his gut was right. There was something very wrong about this storm.

*"Come to the edge," He said.
They said, "We are afraid."
"Come to the edge," He said.
They came. He pushed them,
And they flew . . .*
—Guillaume Apollinaire

# CHAPTER 23

Santini fidgeted on Dr. Jordan's couch, trying to get comfortable as the wind howled and rain battered the windows and doors. His mind churned from the heated conversation with the priest, who now sat quietly in prayer across from him. Salvo finally stopped pacing and sat down.

It wasn't that Santini didn't want to believe. He envied those whose faith came so easily. He remembered praying with his mother when his father was late on patrol. He remembered sitting in church with his parents and feeling very comfortable with the whole religion thing. Until his father was shot.

"Are you ready, Detective?" Dr. Jordan asked.

"I'm ready."

"Let your entire body relax, starting with your feet and gradually working up to the top of your head. Take long, slow, deep breaths.

"Now imagine you're floating on a soft white cloud. It's so restful ... You can feel your body becoming more and more relaxed. Let all the tension go. Let the tension go so you can sleep. Sleep and dream."

Eventually, the soothing sound of Jordan's voice quelled the concerns and tension in his mind and he fell asleep.

He was standing on a beautiful green hilltop. On the hilltop was a lone tree, a magnificent old willow the likes of which Santini had never seen. There was a distinct sadness about the old tree, and he felt drawn to it. He walked over and sat on the stone bench beneath it and watched the long drooping branches sway and dance in the gentle breeze. He closed his eyes to relish the relaxation and felt the warm rays of sunlight spill onto his face.

He rested for what seemed like a very long time, and when he finally opened his eyes, a shimmering orb of light materialized out of nowhere directly in front of him.

He stood up and stepped back, shielding his eyes. The circle of white light was several feet in diameter and pulsated violet and purple from its center. A jasmine fragrance filled the air.

He began to speak, but just as he opened his mouth, the orb intensified in brightness and spoke to him.

"You have come for answers, Anthony Santini."

The voice seemed to emerge from inside his head rather than from the orb itself.

"Who are you?" he asked.

The colors of the orb shifted from blue to violet as the responses appeared in Santini's mind.

"I am what you and your race have the potential to become."

"What are you?"

"I am an Astrolite, a being of pure energy consciousness."

He lowered his arms as his eyes adapted to the light. There was something calming, something beautiful about it that he couldn't quite describe.

"Are you an angel?" he said.

"That is a difficult question to answer. We have had contact with your race before, and some have used that word to describe us."

"Were you sent by God?"

"Through the creator all things came to be. We recognize and honor the great creator and the underlying order of the universe. But we were not sent. We go where we will."

"How is it you don't have a body?"

"We have advanced beyond the limitations of a physical body. As your race is beginning to learn, matter and energy are much more interchangeable and fluid than humans can comprehend. Unfortunately, Drakin is a product of this evolution as well."

"Who is Drakin?"

"Your race calls beings like Drakin demons. They're the opposite of everything we are."

"Are you saying the entity I'm chasing is an alien?"

"Drakin was sent by his kind, to see if your species was vulnerable to thought manipulation. Unfortunately, he found humans to be very easy prey. Your race is aware of Drakin's existence, both consciously and subconsciously. Throughout human history, in books, art, sculpture and architecture, images of demons and devils were conjured up by the mind of man, and the name of Satan was given to express what they didn't really understand."

"So you're saying the Devil doesn't really exist?"

"Drakin is as good a devil as any Christian could have conjured."

"But if there's no Devil, then there's no God. He was supposed to have intervened to save the human race."

"It was the Astrolites who intervened, so in a way we are the emissaries of God and the underlying order of the universe. To counter Drakin's influence on your planet, we sent several of our own to Earth to teach and become examples of how to think and live. Buddha, Gandhi, Teresa, Krishna, and others. One of these emissaries became known in human history as 'The Christ,' teaching love, compassion, forgiveness, peace, and all of the positive attributes for humanity to emulate."

Santini was startled. "Are you saying Christ was an Astrolite?"

"There are many like him that have walked among you in human form. I know it may come as a shock, but it does not change the importance of the message he conveyed."

"You must know, since you've been watching us, that my attempts to stop Drakin have failed."

"Unfortunately, humanity has not yet learned from its own history and continues to make the same mistakes. Your negative and violent nature is your own undoing. We are saddened by this turn of events."

"Saddened? There must be something you can do to stop him."

"Your race has been given the gift of free will. We cannot help beyond what we have already done and are now doing. Humanity must take the next step together. Human destiny must find its own path, even if that path leads into darkness and destruction."

"Then at least tell me what I can do. There must be something."

"You must wield the staff, and you must wield it with faith and courage, with your heart and your mind."

"What exactly do I do with it?"

"You must discover that for yourself. But remember, you cannot do this alone. By yourself, you will not be able to invoke its full power."

The orb of light slowly began to fade. "It is now up to the human race to save itself from its own dark nature. It has always been that way."

"Wait," Santini said.

The orb of light flickered several times and disappeared.

Santini opened his eyes and sat up.

"How are you feeling, Detective?" Jordan said.

He looked at his three friends. "I'm not sure. Okay, I guess. His gaze fell on the priest.

"What is it?" O'Brian asked.

Santini's mind was reeling. He shook his head. "This dream was very different. It was more of a visitation."

"God sometimes communicates in that manner."

"I don't know," Santini said. "Maybe. You may not want to hear this, Father."

"Why? Tell us what you've learned."

"We'll drag it out of you eventually," Salvo said.

"Why don't I just start from the beginning." He looked at them with a worried expression. "I hope I'm doing the right thing."

"The truth is always the right thing," O'Brian said.

Santini closed his eyes. When he eventually spoke, he was surprised to hear himself relate his conversation with the Astrolite word for word. Apparently, the being had impressed their conversation perfectly into his mind. When he was finished, he opened his eyes.

No one spoke.

The priest looked troubled. "The truth is always the right thing," O'Brian said. "If it is indeed the truth."

"What are you saying?" Santini asked.

"It's lies," O'Brian said, "and the trickery of Satan. That Christ was not the son of God but an alien? An advanced being from another planet? I don't believe it."

"That's what it told me," Santini said. "The Astrolites came to save humanity from its destructive tendencies. We've just been looking at things through a different prism. The Astrolites acknowledge the existence of a God. He told me they're the emissaries of the creator."

"And what of this Drakin and his ilk?" O'Brian said. "Are they part of God's plan also?"

"Maybe there's good and evil on even the highest levels of existence," Santini said.

"No!" O'Brian's face turned red. "I will not toss everything I've lived for out the window based on a dream you had of an alien's explanation of history. No matter how advanced he may be. Don't you see? This dream was triggered by your own lack of faith. Your dream simply reflects your own beliefs, or lack of them."

Santini shook his head. "And what about the Astrolite's knowledge of the staff? He confirmed what you yourself stated: that I'm supposed to use it."

"So what?" O'Brian said. "This Drakin, disguised as a higher being, knows about the staff. That's why he wants it. Don't you see how perfectly all this would work to aid him by destroying humanity's faith? Without religion, the human mind would flounder. There would be hopelessness and despair."

"We can still have faith," Santini said. "God still exists. He's just not calling the shots in the ways we've imagined."

O'Brian jumped up and started pacing. "Faith? Faith in what? An alien race? Without faith, humanity is defenseless. You've been duped, Detective. My suggestion to you is to never utter another word of this blasphemy ever again, unless you want to be responsible for the destruction of the human race. I can't listen to this nonsense any longer." He stormed out of the room.

Santini looked at Salvo and Jordan. "Maybe that was a mistake."

"What if the priest is right?" Salvo said. "What if Drakin is masquerading as this Astrolite?"

"I didn't sense any evil intent from this being," Santini said. "On the contrary. And how could Drakin enter my dreams?"

They sat in silence as a blast of thunder crashed overhead and lightning lit the room.

Santini replayed his encounter with the Astrolite in his mind, wondering if there was any truth to the priest's argument. His cell phone broke his reverie.

"Yes, this is Santini . . . What? Who is this? . . . And how would you know that? . . . You were there?" Santini clenched his jaw. There was a long pause. "You saw who killed my father? Is this some kind of a sick joke, because if it is . . . And so now you just remembered after all these years . . . Pangs of conscience? So tell me then. Who was it? . . . Meet? Where? . . . Central Park. At the east entrance." There was a long silence. "All right. I'll be there."

Salvo stood up to face his partner. "Really? I thought you were smarter than that. What are the instincts you always rely on telling you? This is a setup."

"He said he was hiding in a food aisle," Santini said, "and caught a glimpse of an identifying mark on the killer. How else would he even know about the bakery shop?"

"Drakin was inside your head," Jordan said. "That's how it got your cell number and how it knows exactly where your father was shot."

"It might be a trap," Santini said, "but maybe not. I can't risk not going. This guy may have nothing to do with what's happening." He walked over to grab his coat. "I have to find out. What if this entity saw something in my mind that I have no memory of?"

"And why the hell would he share this information with you?" Salvo said. "I thought it was trying to kill you. Or did you forget that?"

"I'll be on high alert," Santini said.

"High alert? Is that something you just made up? . . . Great. I'm going with you. No argument."

"This doesn't feel right," Jordan said.

"He knows that," Salvo said. "He's too obsessed with his father's killer to think straight."

She turned to squarely face Santini. "Remember I said you always have a choice. You're choosing to place yourself in danger by following what could be a bogus lead and maybe even a trap."

Santini shook his head. "You're probably both right. But this could be an opportunity to catch this damn thing. It could also be a clue to my father's murderer."

He put on his coat. "Lock the doors until we get back."

Salvo trailed after him shaking his head.

# CHAPTER 24

The Crown Victoria stopped at the east entrance to Central Park, splashing water high into the air. There were just a few people walking with raincoats and umbrellas, but otherwise the park looked strangely deserted. Two large oak trees in the park had toppled sideways, partially uprooted by the storm. Santini and Salvo got out of the car and looked around. No one was there.

After about ten minutes of standing in the cold and wet, Salvo retreated to the inside of the car. Eventually, Santini followed.

"He'll show up," Santini said.

"Even if he does, how reliable do you think the information will be?"

"We'll find out," Santini said.

"And what use will the information be if you're dead?"

Santini didn't answer. Instead he just stared out of the water-strewn windshield.

Salvo pulled out his cell.

"Hey. How are you? . . . And the kids? . . . I'm fine. Yeah, they miss their soccer games. Every field is probably under water. Don't worry, and tell them I'll be home soon. Could be a late night . . . Give them a kiss for me . . . I will. Love you, too."

A dense mist slowly replaced the rain and floated over the street as the minutes ticked slowly by. In the distance, through the fog, Santini could make out a figure walking in their direction. He climbed out and Salvo followed. As the man approached, Santini pulled out his gun.

"Remember, high alert," he said.

They both stood with guns at their sides, watching as the man drew nearer. When he stopped before them, they could see he was just a kid. Maybe twelve or thirteen.

The kid looked from one man to the other. "Detective Santini?"

Santini nodded. "Who's asking?"

The kid reached into his coat pocket. Both detectives raised their guns.

"Don't move!" Salvo yelled. "Hands up, now!"

The young man's arms shot high into the air. "Whoa, hey, wait a minute. What's going on? I didn't do anything."

"What's in the coat?" Santini asked.

"It's a note! Some guy gave me a hundred bucks to give it to Detective Santini at the Central Park east entrance."

"What's your name?" Salvo asked.

"Ross . . . Ross Miller."

"What did this man look like?" Santini asked.

"He was a big dude. Had a beard . . . Oh, and long hair."

"What was he wearing?" Salvo asked.

"Uh, a black leather jacket. With, like, a snake on the back. He was riding a Harley." He swallowed. "Can you stop pointing those guns at me? Please?"

"How can we trust anything he says?" Salvo said. "This thing could be inside his head right now."

The kid looked quizzically at Salvo.

"Are you right-handed or left-handed?" Santini asked.

"What? Uh, right-handed."

"Okay Ross. With your left hand, I want you to very slowly pull that note out from inside your jacket. If anything other than a piece of paper comes out, you'll be facedown on the wet concrete with handcuffs on."

The kid nodded and slowly pulled out a small folded piece of paper and handed it to Santini.

"All right. Go on, get out of here," Santini said.

The kid bolted down the street and disappeared into the fog.

Santini unfolded the piece of paper. On it was a hand drawn swastika, with the letters *R* and *M* on either side of it. After staring at it for several moments, he handed it to Salvo. "A tattoo?"

Salvo looked at it. "Probably."

"It's something," Santini said.

"Or nothing. And why did it send a messenger boy? Why not come himself if he wants you dead so badly?"

"I don't know." Then Santini's jaw dropped. "Shit, the staff. We need to get back to Jordan's. Now."

They jumped into the car and peeled out into the flooded street.

## CHAPTER 25

Dr. Jordan turned up the gas fireplace, and as the flames danced higher, the warmth from the fire and the bourbon finally quelled the chill Father O'Brian had been feeling.

He took a gulp of his drink, his hands shaking.

If what Santini reported was true and this story became widespread, the effect on humanity and the Church could be devastating.

O'Brian knew he'd been hard on the detective, but his belief system was under assault and his conception of the world was unraveling. He tried to look at Santini's visitation from as many angles as possible. If what this Astrolite said was true, maybe there was something that could be salvaged from this new narrative. And yet there was still the possibility that this being's story was a lie, filled with half truths and deception.

"I have a spare bedroom, Father," Dr. Jordan said. "You should spend the night, at least until the archdiocese can find a place for you. The detectives can take you to the precinct in the morning for your statement. And a word of advice from someone who knows: you might want to leave out the part about demons in your statement."

O'Brian laughed. "That's very kind of you, Kelly. I accept your invitation."

"It's the least I can do after what has just happened. I haven't forgotten how you helped me. I'd never have thought religion would help me get through a divorce."

"We all need guidance in our lives at one time or another," O'Brian said. "Especially those of us who make a career out of guiding others. Unfortunately, because of our training, we have a tendency to think we can go it alone. But it's like trying to see into your own eyes without the aid of a mirror. My guess is your detective friend is similar to you in this regard."

"Your guess is right." She took a small sip of her drink. "If everything you're saying is true, this city is in danger."

"Unfortunately, it's not just this city."

O'Brian suddenly gasped. He closed his eyes, and what he saw made his body tremble.

"Father?" Jordan said. "Father O'Brian? Are you all right?"

He abruptly sat up on the edge of the couch and reached for Jordan's hand. "You must tell Detective Santini to ask for God's help. Tell him he must awaken the faith sleeping inside of him."

"You'll just have to tell him yourself, Father."

O'Brian quickly shook his head. "Please, Kelly. Promise me you will tell him. Otherwise the staff will be useless."

Jordan noted the sadness in the old priest's voice and squeezed his hand. "Okay, Father. I'll tell him."

O'Brian smiled. "I wonder if there is something simple in your kitchen to eat. This drink has gone straight to my head."

"Of course. I'll see what I can find."

As she surveyed the contents of the refrigerator, a loud crash caused her to jump. She turned toward the living room and heard the deafening sound of a gunshot. Her heart racing, she crept back toward the living room.

"Father?"

The only sound came from the rain pouring in through the smashed front door, and then there was the roar of a motorcycle being driven off. In the living room, Father O'Brian lay in a pool of blood, his right hand clutching a crucifix.

"No!" she screamed.

She knelt beside the priest and, for the second time tonight, frantically attempted to stem the flow of blood.

## CHAPTER 26

The Crown Victoria screeched to a halt just as the motorcycle took off. Santini and Salvo jumped out of the car and sprinted up the steps into Jordan's house, guns drawn. They found Jordan kneeling beside the priest applying pressure on his wound.

"Shit," Salvo said. He called for an ambulance.

"Forget that," Jordan said. "He needs to be transported. Now."

Santini and Salvo carefully carried the priest out the door, down the steps, and into the backseat of the Crown Victoria. Dr. Jordan sat in the back beside him, her hands firmly pressed on the wound. The car tore off into the storm, siren blaring.

"Stay with me, Father," Jordan said. "Do you hear? Stay with me."

Santini called the closest hospital, Mount Sinai.

"We're en route with a male, mid-seventies, gunshot wound to the chest. I want emergency personnel standing by . . . What?! What do you mean full? This is an emergency, damn it. I've got the pastor of St. Patrick's Cathedral bleeding out . . . New York-Presbyterian. Shit." He hung up. "Damn storm. Every hospital in Manhattan is overloaded. It's a mess out there. Closest trauma center is New York-Presbyterian in Queens. They can take us."

"How far?" Jordan said.

"Ten to fifteen minutes."

"I think I can do better than that," Salvo said. He slammed his foot on the gas pedal.

Santini turned to look at Jordan. She was covered in blood. "I'm sorry."

She didn't look up. "I hope it was worth it."

"You were both right. It was a setup."

"O'Brian knew," she said.

"What do you mean?" Santini said.

Tears filled her eyes. "Father O'Brian. He sent me into the kitchen. He knew what was going to happen."

Suddenly the car screeched to a stop in front of a kaleidoscope of emergency lights. A patrolman was turning traffic around. Salvo stuck his head out the window and flashed his badge.

"What's going on?" he asked.

"Downed power line, sir."

"He's fading," Jordan said. "No pulse. I need you to get back here and apply pressure on the wound while I start compression."

Santini climbed over the backseat.

Salvo looked around and found an opening. "Sorry, Officer."

He threw the car into reverse and then accelerated forward onto the far sidewalk, where he raced past a fire truck before sliding back onto the road.

"I've always wanted to do that," he said.

A few minutes later, they were barreling into the emergency-room entrance to New York-Presbyterian Hospital. A medical crew immediately sprang into action.

"I'm going in with him," Jordan said.

"He's going to make it, Kelly," Santini said. "He's tough."

Tears filled her eyes. "He made me promise to tell you something. He said you must ask for God's help. That you must find the faith sleeping inside of you." Then her face turned red. *"You find this thing, Detective. And you get that goddamn staff back."*

"I will."

Jordan turned and walked away.

Santini watched the gurney with Father O'Brian roll into the ER.

"I really screwed this up. And I'm afraid my faith isn't sleeping but dead."

"Pyth," Salvo said.

"Pyth? What are you talking about?"

"I caught part of the license plate as the motorcycle took off," Salvo said. *"P-Y-T-H."*

"Good eyes, Salvo. A custom plate. *Pyth . . . pyth*. Didn't that kid say something about snakes on the guy's jacket?"

"Yeah, he did," Salvo said.

"Python," Santini said. "Call Marissa at the precinct. Let's go."

## CHAPTER 27

Jackson Hollenbach, the longhaired bearded member of the Python motorcycle gang, ditched the Harley behind the building complex, ran over to his garage stall, unlocked the roll-up doors, and flicked on the light. He grabbed the chain saw in the corner, placed the staff in a large vise, and tightened the clamps securely in place. Then he cranked up the chain saw.

Sparks flew everywhere. Jackson pushed harder and harder, the sweat dripping from his forehead. Eventually, the saw just ground to a halt and the chain fell off, half-melted. Next, he grabbed his blowtorch, but the result wasn't any better.

Drakin-Jackson stared down at the unharmed shaft of wood. He wasn't too surprised—a talisman created by the Astrolites would not be so easily done away with.

Drakin had learned through centuries of manipulating people and events that fluidity was critical. Not everything could be controlled and predicted, especially when there were powerful counter-forces aimed at thwarting his moves, so he'd mastered the art of adapting to the current circumstances. Unforeseen variables, such as his pal Detective Santini, required a cool head, which was more apt to provide creative solutions.

So the next-best plan for the staff was to hide it and ensure that no one would get his or her hands on it.

Jackson leaped up the steps that led to his apartment door, ran into the bedroom, and stood staring into his gun safe, trying to decide which weapon to take with him. He decided on the Glock and replaced it with the old piece of antique wood he hoped would bring quite a ransom.

Back outside, he jumped into his Ford Explorer, slammed on the gas pedal and headed west on the Brooklyn-Queens Expressway.

From behind Jackson's eyes, Drakin glanced in the rearview mirror at the man's rugged face.

His present host, another victim of childhood abuse, had been wired for violence since he was a youth. So it was easy to steer Jackson in whatever direction Drakin chose, always letting the man believe he was about to exact revenge on the society that had kept him in a perpetual state of anger.

He had also planted the suggestion that the staff had been stolen from a research facility and that it was the one of the hardest materials known to man. All Jackson had to do was keep it safe until the highest bidder came calling. Greed was one of the easiest emotions for Drakin to tap into, and the man hadn't disappointed him.

Drakin had been surprised when the detectives interrupted him at the church. Santini's dream, no doubt. He'd have to continue to make adjustments for that as he moved through his plans, but having the staff in his possession after all these centuries was exhilarating. It would ensure that there would be no repeat of what happened at the Red Sea. Unfortunately, he could not take it with him as he moved from host to host, so he had Jackson lock it in the man's gun safe temporarily.

Maybe he was being overly cautious, but he didn't want anything to interfere with the wheels he'd set in motion. He'd waited too long, and it was time to claim his true place on this miserable planet.

Drakin knew that every mind had a key that would unlock it. And that key was a negative thought or emotion. If he was patient enough, a human would eventually radiate one of these negative vibrations, and it was this energy that allowed Drakin to ride into his host's mind.

He'd found a way into Santini's mind through his self-doubt, but once there he'd found the detective almost impossible to manipulate. And so he'd tried to kill him. But the detective was more resilient than he'd anticipated. Either that or he was very, very lucky.

But everyone had a dark side, and there was more than one way to kill a man. So the last time he entered Santini's mind, at the Nolan residence, Drakin had left a little present behind: a time bomb deep within Santini's subconscious mind. Given the right trigger, specifically anger, the next time the man entered the world of dreams and accessed his subconscious, things wouldn't be so pleasant.

Drakin-Jackson turned on the radio. There were reports of vast power outages, and the expression "storm of the century" was being bandied about. *Good. More fear and worry.*

First stop: the private Tri-Borough Heliport. He pulled alongside the office and walked in with a small satchel. There was only one man there.

"Captain Wagner?"

The man eyed Drakin-Jackson suspiciously. "Who's asking?"

"Hathaway. We spoke on the phone about commissioning a helicopter."

"Do you have the money?"

Drakin-Jackson turned over his bag. "As agreed, thirty-thousand up front and thirty-thousand upon completion of the flight."

Wagner shook his head. "Sorry, pal. Price has doubled. Look outside. I'll be taking a serious risk flying in this goddamn storm."

Drakin-Jackson stared at the man. Thanks to his manipulations of Josef Shahid, he had plenty of cash on hand. "Agreed."

Wagner extended his hand to seal the deal. "Top of the MetLife Building. Fifteen hundred hours."

Drakin-Jackson squeezed Wagner's hand with a strength that clearly took the pilot by surprise. "You must be fueled and ready," he said, glaring. "One minute late and the deal is off. And trust me, you don't want to be my enemy." Drakin-Jackson held the man's gaze.

"I'll be there, pal. Don't get in a tizzy."

"You'd better be." Drakin-Jackson turned and walked out.

It was unfortunate that he needed a helicopter to transport himself, but it was too difficult and spotty to hop from one mind to another as a means of leaving the city. It consumed too much energy. Besides, he needed a faster mode of transportation for the second part of his plan.

He pulled back onto the Brooklyn-Queens Expressway and eventually wormed his way onto the island of Manhattan.

He felt nostalgic being back in the heart of New York. He'd spent quite a bit of time here, sampling the diversity of the minds, sucking the abundant negative energy. It usually took more than inclement weather to rattle the average New Yorker, but Drakin could see the confusion and fear in their grim faces.

*They haven't seen anything yet.*

Drakin-Jackson turned left onto Forty-second Street and headed toward the Waldorf Astoria. It was time to dump Jackson and meet up with Josef Shahid once again.

Before he abandoned his current host, he placed a powerful suggestion deep into the man's subconscious mind: "Go home. Guard the safe and the staff with your life." He pursed the man's lips into a twisted smile.

# CHAPTER 28

Santini and Salvo sat parked outside a storefront in a remote back alley of east New York. The glass was painted black, and there were no signs or markings on the exterior. But Marissa at headquarters had discovered that the Pythons had had previous run-ins with the police, so their location was conveniently described in detail. Apparently, these were some very bad characters.

When Marissa ran the plates on the motorcycle, the registered name and address were bogus. So all they had to go on was the club location.

The rain pelted the windshield of the Crown Vic as the two detectives sat staring at the storefront.

"So, what's the plan?" Salvo said. "These Pythons deal in heavy drugs, firearms, prostitution, you name it. But somehow they've managed to escape prosecution. We could be walking into a snake pit, and without backup."

"I've been two steps behind this thing all along," Santini said. "That's not going to happen again. We don't have time."

"You're being reckless," Salvo said. "So what's the plan?"

"We politely ask where this guy is. He must be high up in the pecking order for him to be able to flaunt the plate with *Python* on it. These groups are pretty touchy about stuff like that."

Salvo shook his head. "Some plan. I'm calling for backup."

Santini climbed out of the car and walked toward the front door. It was also painted black. He could hear the sound of loud music coming from inside. He knocked on the door.

There was no response.

He knocked again, but this time with more enthusiasm. Salvo came up beside him.

The door eased open and a bald, bulging man in a black tank top with two earrings in each ear, two more through each eyebrow, and shoulders wide enough to block the entire doorway stood glaring at them. He grinned and jiggled his enormous chest muscles a few times.

"This is a private club," he growled. "Get the hell out of here before I break your fucking necks."

Santini assessed the situation and quickly determined that there was only one possible course of action: surprise.

His fist shot out with lightning speed and crashed into the bridge of the man's nose. The man toppled backward and landed with a thud on the wooden floor, blood pouring from his nose.

"What the hell are you doing?" Salvo said. "What happened to asking politely? Are you trying to get us killed?"

"You know what's at stake here," Santini said. "These guys respect only one thing: brute force." He stepped over the man.

The inside of the place was dimly lit and smelled of a noxious blend of stale beer, cigarettes, pot, and vomit. Everyone had gone silent—the only sound was the music on the jukebox. Four bikers were seated at the bar, two were standing at a pool table with two women, and three were sitting at a table in the corner. Each was holding a bottle of beer, and each looked almost as big as the greeter at the front door. Most had long hair and beards, tattoos, and piercings in every conceivable location, and all had python tattoos on the bulging muscles of their right arms. It looked to Santini like they'd stepped into a pirates' den.

He knew they could get in trouble for this—private property, no warrant—but he was not about to let the man who shot O'Brian get away. "NYPD," he announced.

No one spoke.

"We're looking for one of your boys with Python plates on his Harley in connection with the attempted murder of a priest," Salvo said.

Silence.

Santini looked around at the smug expressions.

"There's two ways this can go down," he said. "You tell us where we can find this asshole and we walk away, or I call the precinct, we close this place down indefinitely, and we haul your asses in for obstructing justice and accessory to murder." Santini turned to Salvo. "I'm sure this little group of Boy Scouts has squeaky clean records. They don't have to worry about the three-strikes law. What do you think, Salvo?"

"I think there's probably an outstanding warrant on each one of these scouts."

Silence.

Santini walked over to the man behind the bar. "Give me his name."

One of the men at the pool table charged forward with a pool stick held high in the air. Santini hadn't been sure which one would make the first move, but by the way this guy had been slapping the pool stick into his open palm, he'd known not to take his eyes off him.

As the man barreled toward him, Santini pivoted, sidestepped, and used the man's momentum to smash his face into the bar counter. He fell limp to the floor.

At the same moment, the man behind the bar reached below and pulled out a shotgun, but Salvo had been watching his every move and put a bullet in the man's shoulder before he could fire off a round. Santini grabbed the bartender by the hair and pushed his face and wounded shoulder onto the counter. While the man howled in pain, Salvo kept his gun pointed at the remaining bikers.

"My partner is an excellent shot," Santini said. "He could have put that bullet right between your eyes. So it's like you've been given a second chance here. Don't squander it. Give me a name."

"He'll kill me if I do," the bartender whined.

"Not if we find him first." Santini pushed the man's shoulder harder into the counter.

"Jackson," he yelled.

By this point, the rest of the bikers had had enough. Several stood up in unison, brandishing weapons pointed at Santini and Salvo. But that was also the moment when the police SWAT team charged through the front door shouting for the bikers to drop their weapons.

One of the women raised her hand. "Stand down, Pythons!"

There was hesitation, but the bikers finally lowered their weapons.

Santini turned to the bartender again. "Where can I find this Jackson?"

"I don't know. I swear."

The woman, who seemed to be the leader, walked slowly over to Santini. A cigarette hung from her lower lip. "It's not cool to kill a priest. Jackson's a piece of shit. Four seventy-seven East 147th Street."

Santini nodded. "You'd better get these guys to a hospital."

The commander of the SWAT team looked questioningly at Santini. "What are your orders, sir?"

Santini looked around the room. "Stand down, Commander."

Then he and Salvo walked slowly out the front door and into the street.

# CHAPTER 29

Santini and Salvo pulled up to a dilapidated apartment building on East 147th street, and with the key they'd obtained from the on-site manager, they ran up the stairs looking for apartment 2G, the residence of Jackson Hollenbach.

The detectives stood on either side of the door. Salvo knocked several times. "Jackson Hollenbach. This is the NYPD," he announced. "Open the door."

When there was no response, Santini used the key. They both entered with guns drawn. After a preliminary sweep, they could see Jackson wasn't there.

"Any sign of the staff?" Santini said.

"No, but look at this." In the bedroom closet was a stand-up gun safe. Salvo inspected it. "It might be in here."

Santini heard the front door ease open, and they stood silently in the hallway, guns drawn. The shadowy figure, holding a Glock, crept into the kitchen. Salvo walked around and came up behind him. "Don't move."

Jackson Hollenbach hesitated until Santini appeared in front of him.

"Drop the gun," Santini said. "Down on your knees. Hands behind your head. Now."

The man let the gun fall from his hand and dropped to his knees. In a flash, Salvo was on top of him.

"Jackson Hollenbach, you're under arrest for the attempted murder of Father Timothy O'Brian." He turned to Santini. "Do you think it's still here? Inside his head?"

"Don't know."

"I didn't mean to shoot him," Jackson said.

"Then why did you?" Santini said.

The man seemed to think about it. "I don't know. I had to have the stick."

Santini and Salvo glanced at each other.

"Why?" Salvo said.

Jackson hesitated. "To sell it. Why else?"

"How did you know about the staff?" Santini asked.

The man looked puzzled for a moment. "I don't know. I was just standing there watching the flames from the burning church when I saw you hand it to the priest. That's when I knew I had to have it."

"Tell me where it is," Santini said.

"Fuck off," Jackson said.

"If you cooperate, I'll tell the prosecutor there were extenuating circumstances."

The man started shaking.

"Possibly even a temporary insanity plea," Salvo said.

Then Jackson started babbling as if he were having a heated argument with himself. "I can't, I cant, I can't," he whined.

"Is it in the safe?" Salvo said.

Jackson started moaning as if he were in pain, but eventually his head moved up and down.

"What's the combination?" Santini demanded.

"No. Can't tell. Can't tell."

"Shooting a priest," Salvo said. "I'm guessing the jury will deliberate for five minutes. Then it'll be the injection for you."

Jackson's whole body trembled.

"It's the only way to save yourself," Santini said. "Otherwise we can't help you."

His bodied jerked from side to side and he started moaning again.

"Forty-seven, thirty-four," he blurted, and his head snapped backward. "Sixty-eight, twenty-four." As he voiced the final number, he let out a scream and blood started dripping from Jackson's nose. Then he fell over onto his side.

Salvo checked his pulse. "Shit. I'll call an ambulance."

Santini went to the safe and started spinning the combination lock with the numbers Jackson had given them. When the lock disengaged, he pulled on the handle and the steel door swung open.

A plethora of firearms, drugs and cash filled the space. Leaning in the back of the safe was an object wrapped in a purple silk cloth. Santini reached in for the staff and pulled it from its sheath.

He turned it in his hands. It was old and weathered and unusually light and smooth to the touch. The fine grains of the wood created interesting patterns throughout its length. The small curves at the top end of the staff seemed to fit his hand perfectly. For a brief moment, he thought he felt a tingling sensation through his right arm.

"Great," he said. "Now what am I supposed to do with this damn thing?"

Salvo walked into the room. "Ambulance and police are on the way. What the hell happened to Jackson?"

"Damned if I know."

"Great. Now what?"

Santini shook his head. "Since we can't question Jackson about his recent movements, I'm afraid we've lost the trail on this thing."

"At least you have the staff. It doesn't want you to have it."

"For now all we can do is go back to the hospital once we're finished here," Santini said. "Check on O'Brian and Jordan. Last I spoke to her, it was touch-and-go. But he should be out of surgery by now."

"Where the hell is this thing now? And what's it up to?"

Santini shook his head. "Nothing good, I'm afraid."

*Satan's successes are the greatest when he appears with the name of God on his lips."*
*Mahatma Gandhi*

# CHAPTER 30

When Drakin-Shahid finished shaving off his beard and mustache, he gazed into the mirror and ran the palm of his hand over his face. He couldn't remember the last time he'd felt his smooth cheeks. The sensation intrigued him.

He threw off his long robe and white undercoat and traded them for a gray pinstripe suit, a charcoal shirt, and a silver tie. A man of many appearances, it was time for a more western look.

He rode the elevator down to the lobby of the Waldorf Astoria and saw his driver parked outside waiting.

Drakin was in cruise control mode with his host. Josef Shahid had proved an excellent accomplice over the last several months and, as such, required very little nudging. Nevertheless, Drakin would be along for the ride to make sure things went according to plan. The helicopter was commissioned, the devices were in transit, and now he was going to see to yet another important piece of the puzzle.

The storm had gotten worse, but cars could still navigate the streets that were not completely flooded.

They slowly wormed their way across Forty-second Street to an apartment building called The Terrace. Drakin-Shahid slipped the doorman a Ben Franklin, and the man's face lit up, clearly happy that his generous benefactor had returned.

Drakin-Shahid rode the elevator to the twelfth floor and proceeded to apartment 22. He knocked on the door.

"What time is it?" a voice from inside asked.

"It is the end of time," Drakin-Shahid responded

"And what day is it?"

"It is the day of retribution."

The door was unlocked and a young man, maybe twenty-five or twenty-six, cracked open the door, holding a gun in his hand.

"Put that down, you idiot," Drakin-Shahid said.

"I didn't recognize you," the young man stammered. "You look different, and I didn't know when to expect you."

"There will be no further cell phone communications," Drakin-Shahid said.

When the young man lowered his weapon, Drakin quickly unraveled his invisible tentacles from the brain of Josef Shahid and coiled them about the head of an unsuspecting Allam Bashir. At this stage, there was no need to take any chances. He had to be sure that everything was prepared and that there would be no qualms of conscience on the part of his accomplice.

There was a slight shudder of the nervous system, but it was otherwise uneventful.

Allam's hatred for America gave Drakin easy access. The episode with his older brother and younger sister was the clincher—five and eight years old, both killed in a U.S. drone strike in 1995.

When Drakin had first encountered Allam, the young man had just graduated from Syracuse University with a degree in electrical engineering. His main ambition then was to create a uniquely powerful body-vest bomb and blow himself up in a crowded shopping mall. Drakin had convinced him that with Shahid's help he could accomplish much more.

The portal required a major shock of energy to open. The storm was evidence that there was a drastic thinning of the veil that protected the planet. Electromagnetic disturbances were already widespread. The focal point for that thinning was over the island of Manhattan. One more push and a tear in the space-time fabric would occur.

That push would consist of the dark energy created by the cumulative negative emotions and thoughts generated by humans, especially fear. But he needed more of it. Much more. And so his plan was to create a catastrophic event that would provide the necessary catalyst for intense emotional discharge.

As Drakin settled into his new host, his tentacles tingled with excitement.

Fifth Avenue was deserted as the truck pulled into the service delivery entrance of the Empire State Building. The high-altitude lightning and wind was so intense that the old edifice rocked and swayed in a way the engineers hadn't designed for. So for the first time in history, the entire building, including security personnel, had been evacuated. And that was exactly what Drakin-Shahid and Allam Bashir had hoped for.

They jumped out of the truck and quickly opened the back of the vehicle. They rolled out the first device and loaded it onto the service elevator. With Allam's technical skills, they were able to temporarily disable the surveillance cameras.

The ride up to the observatory was bumpy, and the elevator clanged precariously from side to side.

"Why do we have to plant it so high?" Bashir said as another jolt knocked him against the wall of the car.

"The higher the explosion into the atmosphere, the greater the effect will be," Drakin-Shahid said. "Also, this building has symbolic significance. It will amplify the devastating emotional impact. And the emotional impact is crucial. Isn't that what terrorism means, to strike terror into the hearts and minds of your enemy?"

Bashir nodded. "You must fulfill your promise to help my parents in Kabul," he shouted over the clanging of the elevator. "You must see to it they get the money."

"Don't worry. They'll get their money, and your sacrifice will make history."

The video, to be orchestrated by Bashir and delivered live, was also part of Drakin's plan and would hit as many Internet and television air waves as possible. He'd given Bashir some leeway in the production, and it would be the usual crap. He'd rant on about how naughty America had been. He'd present a litany of crimes the Americans had perpetrated against Islam and the rest of the world as justification for today's act of terrorism. The name of Allah would be invoked as the true God and ultimate slayer of the "Great Satan." But Bashir didn't know his people would wind up in the same prison camps, torture chambers, whipping posts, and "food banks" as the rest of these miserable humans. Religious fanaticism had always worked well for Drakin.

The most important part of the message was to announce to the world, and to the residents of New York, that Manhattan Island and its occupants were about to be obliterated. This part was critical. It was the vital ingredient of his recipe. There must be enough time for intense emotional discharge: fear, panic, anxiety, and the like. Just enough time to let the negative emotions rise like a tsunami and commingle with the nuclear blast.

When they reached the 102nd floor, the double doors slid open with a grinding sound and a final jolt.

The observatory was deserted. The winds howled frantically and whipped into the deck with a relentless pounding force. A few windows shattered, sending lethal shards of glass the size of swords raining down on the streets below. Slowly they rolled the device onto the windy platform and against the far wall.

Drakin-Shahid placed his hand on Bashir's shoulder. "Now I want you to gaze out over the infidels' greatest city. Look down upon your enemy. Pray for strength. Let the courage for what you are about to do fill your heart."

Drakin thought about Santini and exited the mind of Josef Shahid. He then coiled his tentacles of awareness around Bashir's mind as he gazed out from the platform of the observatory.

Drakin filled Bashir's mind with thoughts of hatred and vengeance. He turned to look at the device and smiled.

As instructed, Josef Shahid then took the elevator back down to ground level, where another accomplice waited. They rolled the second device out of the truck into the elevator and up to the seventy-fifth floor.

# CHAPTER 31

Santini and Dr. Jordan stood in the hallway just outside the door to Father O'Brian's hospital room. Salvo volunteered to find coffee.

"How is he?" Santini asked.

"They just placed him in the intensive care unit," Jordan said. "The surgeon was encouraged because the bullet missed the heart and major blood vessels. But he's lost a lot of blood. Fortunately, the transfusions are working. The surgeon said he has a strong constitution, so he's cautiously optimistic."

Santini closed his eyes and shook his head. "This is all my fault. If I hadn't been so damn blinded he wouldn't be in here right now."

"Who's at fault doesn't matter," Jordan said. "What matters is what you do now. This thing was inside your head, so it knows you, maybe better than you know yourself."

"You're right. It's difficult to know yourself, let alone someone else." He placed his hand on her shoulder. "I owe you an apology, Kelly. For throwing Reilly's suicide in your face. That wasn't fair. I'm sorry." He could see the sadness in her eyes.

"The golden rule in psychiatry, 'Don't get attached.' Keep a professional distance." She looked down. When she looked up again, there were tears in her eyes. "I can't help think about what I might have done differently. He had a wife and three kids."

"No one, not even a trained professional, knows what's really going on inside a person's head. You should know that. You can't blame yourself."

She remained quiet and then extended her hand. "Apology accepted."

Santini glanced at the blood on her sweater. "I thought all psychiatrists did was talk. You're amazing in a crisis. But you must be exhausted."

She looked down at her sweater. "I'm fine."

Salvo returned with three large coffees. "Who's that?"

There was an older woman sitting at O'Brian's bedside.

"His younger sister drove through the storm by herself to be here," Jordan said. "All the way from Jersey."

"I'll bet there are a lot of people praying for him right now," Salvo said. "I hope his God is listening. The priest deserves his attention."

"If he doesn't, then nobody does," Jordan said.

"Why don't you go home and get some rest?" Santini said. "There's nothing else you can do here."

Jordan locked eyes with Santini. The intensity caught him by surprise.

"Did you find it?"

"We found the man who pulled the trigger," Santini said. "And the staff."

"That's good. Very good. But what about it?"

Santini averted his eyes. "We've lost the trail. We can tell you all about it when we get you home, rested and cleaned up."

"Rest? There's no time for rest," she yelled. "If you've lost its trail, there's only one thing we can do. You need to be on my couch again, Detective."

Salvo crouched outside at the bottom of Jordan's front door with a screwdriver and a hammer, trying to repair some of the damage.

There was still no power in the area, so Dr. Jordan relit the gas fireplace. In a few minutes, the flames began to warm the room. Shadows from the flames danced on the far wall.

Santini glanced at the photographs on the mantelpiece. "I assume that's Dayna. She's a very beautiful young lady. Can't imagine why."

Jordan nodded. "She's very special. I tried to steer her into medical school, but she always wanted to be a teacher. She loves her third-graders and doesn't give a damn about the pay."

"Sounds like she's very dedicated," Santini said. "Like her mother."

"I hope not as dedicated."

"Is that what happened?"

"What do you mean?"

"Your divorce."

Jordan crossed her arms. Santini could tell she was taken aback.

"Wouldn't it be helpful to talk to someone about you for a change," he said.

She stared at Santini and sighed. "We were both to blame. We didn't make enough time for each other. For years we stayed together, going through the motions for Dayna's sake. Eventually it just fell apart."

Santini nodded. "Sounds familiar. Although it was me who was to blame. Casey tried, but I'd become too distant. I would come home and just . . . couldn't seem to shift gears the way Salvo is able to do. Maybe if there had been kids in the house. I don't know."

"What you do, and what you see, would take its toll on anyone."

He shook his head. "It's no excuse."

Salvo walked into the house. "Should keep out the rain and wind for now. But you'll need to replace the door frame, and you'll need a new lock."

Jordan didn't respond. She was watching Santini roll up the blood-soaked carpet.

"Just get rid of it," she said.

Santini and Salvo carried the carpet out the front door. When they returned, Salvo stood by the fire to warm his hands.

"So it was this biker who shot O'Brian?" she asked.

"Jackson Hollenbach. Bad character," Salvo said. "This thing convinced him the staff was priceless."

"His behavior was strange," Santini said. "When we asked him about the staff, he began arguing with himself and his body started jerking. We finally pried the combination to the safe out of him. Then he screamed and fell over, blood dripping from his nose." Santini paused and shook his head. "Hollenbach died on the way to the hospital."

Jordan's eyes widened. "And the entity wasn't manipulating him at that moment?"

"Who the hell knows?" Salvo said. "We didn't think so. But his mind was really screwed up."

"This thing wanted to make sure he wouldn't open the safe," Santini said.

Dr. Jordan looked pensive for a moment. "It must have planted a suggestion deep in his subconscious. Like a hypnotist would do, only much stronger for that kind of reaction. Probably a suggestion triggered by a certain thought, idea, or emotion."

"What are you saying?" Santini said.

Jordan looked concerned. "Apparently, it can influence behavior even after it leaves its host."

"That's not good," Salvo said. He looked at Santini and frowned. "We could be walking around with a time bomb in our heads, just waiting for the fuse to be lit."

"This guy was weak," Santini said. "Easily manipulated. You and I are different."

Salvo and Jordan didn't seem convinced.

"Let's hope so," Jordan said.

Santini stretched out on the couch. He couldn't help think about what happened to Hollenbach. Salvo sat in a chair opposite. Dr. Jordan pulled up a chair next to Santini. The wind rattled the broken door, but Salvo's tinkering seemed to hold firm and denied the rain entry. The incessant thunder and lightning continued.

It didn't take long for Dr. Jordan to get Santini into a relaxed state, and in just a few minutes, he fell into a deep sleep.

The elevator doors slid open with a grinding sound and a final jolt.

Santini placed both hands—not his hands, on the cold metal of a large rectangular object and pushed. He could hear the strained breathing of the man beside him as they rolled the object out onto the north side of the observatory platform. The normally bustling deck was deserted. Powerful gusts of wind ripped across the platform, shaking the old building and shattering windows.

When the device was positioned, he turned and placed his hand on the shoulder of the young man next to him. "I want you to gaze out over the infidel's greatest city. Look down upon your enemy, and let the courage for what you are about to do fill your heart."

Then Santini felt a snapping sensation and his awareness shifted.

He felt hands, not his hands, gripping the cold railing tightly as he looked out over the skyline. Intense thoughts of hatred and vengeance filled the man's mind.

He looked over at the device in the north corner of the platform and his mouth curled into a smile.

Then he glanced at the elevators. The lit arrow indicated it had stopped on the seventy-fifth floor. *The other man must have gone down,* Santini thought.

Then a blast of wind and rain forced him to close his eyes, but when he opened them again, the scene had completely changed.

Santini found himself in a charred, barren landscape that stretched as far as the eye could see. Blazing fires were everywhere and erupted like volcanic explosions, sending forth a turbulent tower of dust and debris. Burned rubble from collapsed buildings spewed pungent smoke into the air, and huge pieces of twisted metal and glass stood like giant skeletons plastered against the bleak horizon.

He was right in the middle of his recurring apocalyptic nightmare.

He looked up but saw no sun, no clouds, and no sky. Instead, there hung a dark layer of black soot and ash that bellowed and rumbled and rained down hot embers that burned his skin.

Then, as he began to walk through the wreckage, he heard moaning. Men, women, and children, crying out in agony and pleading for help, their bodies severely burned and broken. Most could barely see and were in shock, their charred and shredded remnants of clothing clinging to wounds open to the bone.

He went over to a little girl lying facedown in the debris, crying for her mother, and turned her over. Part of her arm had been blown off, and half her body was burned so badly that the skin still sizzled and smoked.

Santini knew she was only seconds away from dying. She looked pleadingly into his eyes as he cradled her in his arms and gently stroked what was left of her hair.

"It's okay," he said. "What's your name, sweetie?" The little girl struggled to form the words with the half of her mouth that was still left. Finally it came out.

"Emily."

"Emily," Santini repeated. "Soon you'll be with your parents in a very beautiful place, where there are flowers and trees and sunny skies."

The little girl stared at Santini with a blank expression. Thankfully, seconds later, she closed her eyes and died. He continued to hold the little body as the tears rolled down his cheeks. And then in a fit of rage, he screamed defiantly at the sky.

"What kind of a God are you? Is pointless suffering how you teach your lessons?"

As if in reply, a familiar deep voice filled his mind.

"What's the matter? Lost what little faith you have? Poor Detective. Unable to find Daddy's killer. Unable to save Stephanie Winchester and little Emily. Unable to save the old priest. You're worthless and incompetent."

Santini looked all around, his anger growing. Then he remembered. Drakin had tinkered with his subconscious mind. The thought made his skin crawl.

Drakin's voice howled with laughter. Santini tried not to listen, but the voice in his head continued.

"You are worthless and incompetent. No wonder Casey left you."

Santini's body trembled as his anger swelled.

"That's right, Detective. Let all of your dark emotions out. I will savor them. You're no different from the rest of your pathetic race. I will use humanity's negative thoughts and emotions to destroy you all."

Santini's rage boiled to the surface and a white flame exploded in his mind. At the same moment, the ground beneath him quaked and split open. He teetered at the edge and then fell like a rock, tumbling through a dark abyss.

As he plummeted, he heard Drakin's laughter, along with screams and strange voices that pressed deep into his mind. Black shadows chased him, and beasts with razor-sharp teeth danced in his head.

As he fell, he felt an acute pressure in his chest and breathing became difficult.

He'd fallen into a trap, triggered by his own anger.

He tried to breathe, but the pressure and the constriction in his throat wouldn't allow it. *I must wake u*p, he thought, but try as he might, his eyes wouldn't open.

Though he strained to hear the sound of Dr. Jordan's voice, all he could hear were the creatures that howled and chanted vile obscenities. He tried to calm his mind, but his rage was out of control, and the creatures, apparently fueled by his anger, squeezed his mind harder and harder. The onslaught continued, and he knew that if he didn't awaken soon, he'd die.

Dr. Jordan's living room rattled and shook with each explosion of thunder, each episode more violent than the last. Salvo and Jordan sat next to the sleeping detective with anxious expressions. Then Santini's body began to tremble.

Salvo jumped to his feet. "What's happening? Why is he shaking?"

"Is there any history of seizures?" Jordan asked.

"I don't know!"

Jordan quickly went for her first-aid kit. As Santini's chest heaved, she pulled out a syringe, filled a vial, and injected the contents into Santini's arm. For a moment, it seemed as if the drug had worked, but abruptly he began shaking again, only more violently. Salvo looked anxiously at Dr. Jordan and grabbed Santini's shaking hand.

"Get him back," he said. "Wake him up! What's wrong?"

"I've no idea," Jordan said. She placed her hand on the detective's perspiring forehead. Then she knelt beside Santini and began whispering in his ear.

Santini tried to take a breath, but the pressure in his chest wouldn't allow it. He felt a wave of dizziness as the shadows and creatures from his subconscious mind closed in.

But he couldn't give up. He thought about the metal object on the observatory.

With all his might he summoned his will, and deep within the recesses of his mind, beyond the vile shadows and creatures seeking to devour him, a tiny crack opened and a bright sliver of light poured through.

A wave of hope surged within him as he focused all his strength and will on that small ray of light, pushing his mind ever and ever closer. But still he couldn't breathe. Still he was falling and spinning. He felt as if his lungs were filling with water and his chest were about to burst.

Then, from the crack of light in the darkness, he heard a voice, muffled at first but then slowly recognizable as Dr. Jordan's.

"Wake up, Anthony. Wake up. It's just a dream. Come back to your friends. Salvo and I are right here waiting. Just follow the sound of my voice. It's time to wake up now. Time to wake up."

He listened intently as she guided him back, back out of the nightmare that had ensnared him, back from the clutches of the dark creatures that chased him.

Slowly, the ray of light brightened, and Jordan's voice became louder and clearer.

"Fight, Anthony. Fight to come back to us. Wake up. Wake up now."

Finally, the pressure in his chest eased, and he heard the angry howls of the frustrated creatures. Then, like a drowning person who bursts through the surface of the water, the pressure on his chest released and he opened his eyes.

Santini heard a collective sigh of relief as he woke up, but his breathing was still labored. Somebody quickly sat him up, and cold water was splashed onto his face. Although his eyes were open, they weren't focusing. Somebody slapped his face.

Santini gasped and inhaled. Slowly his vision cleared, and he looked around the room. His gaze fell on the doctor.

"Thank you," he said.

"Please tell me all of this drama was worth it and you have something of value to tell us," Salvo said.

Images of the dream cascaded into Santini's consciousness and his face turned pale. "Drakin. He has a bomb! We need to contact Homeland."

"That's definitely not what I wanted to hear," Salvo said.

"It's a nuclear device. I'm sure of it. On the Empire State Building. That's why I've been dreaming about it. We have to stop him."

"And what proof will you give to Homeland?" Salvo said. "That you had a dream?"

"Can we take the chance a bomb threat is imminent and do nothing?" Santini said.

There was silence.

Dr. Jordan pulled out her cell phone. "My daughter. She was taking her third-graders on a field trip to the Guggenheim. Damn it. Answer the phone, Dayna."

Santini placed his hand on Jordan's shoulder. "I'm sure the trip was canceled because of the storm."

"You don't know my daughter, Detective. The rain won't stop her. Even so, her school is near Fifth Avenue."

"Keep trying," he said.

Salvo pulled out his cell, too. "Mari. Listen very carefully. Take the kids, get in the car, and drive out to my mom's house . . . I can't explain right now. Just do it . . . I'll be fine . . . Yes, drive carefully and stay there until you here from me . . . I love you, too."

"I don't want them anywhere near this blast if it does go off," Salvo said.

"Let's hope it doesn't come to that," Santini said. "There's a friend of mine at the FBI. Agent Beckman. He knows me, he trusts me. I can call him and he can mobilize Homeland."

"That's if they believe it's a credible threat," Salvo said.

Santini pulled out his cell. Reception was poor, but the call finally went through.

"Beckman, this is Detective Anthony Santini. I have intel of an imminent attack in New York City involving a nuclear weapon."

"What! Where?"

"Manhattan. The device is on the observatory platform of the Empire State Building."

"And how reliable is this intel?"

Santini glanced at his friends. "One hundred percent."

"And what is the source?"

"Me. Look, Beckman, we don't have time to waste. How long will it take to get your people up there?"

Beckman hesitated. "In this storm, twenty, maybe twenty-five minutes."

"Then don't waste time talking to me."

"All right, Santini. But this better be real. My neck will be on the chopping block if this turns out to be bogus."

Santini hung up. "I'm going up there. We're closer, and our pilots are just as competent as theirs. We need to defuse this damn thing. Call Captain Johnson, Salvo. He owes me. We're going to need a chopper."

Salvo stared at his partner. "Did I just hear you say you're going up there? On top of the Empire State Building? In this storm? Flying a helicopter? To defuse a nuclear bomb? Don't they have specialists for this, Santini? Are you crazy?"

"I have no choice." Santini's body shuddered. "I've seen what could happen. I have to try. Once we get to the heliport, you and Jordan get out of the city."

"Not a chance. We're partners, remember?" Salvo got on the phone and called Captain Johnson. He was the only one with authority to okay a helicopter deployment. It took some convincing, and embellishment of the facts, but eventually he relented.

"We have to go," Santini said. He closed his eyes. "I can still hear the screams."

"But it could be just a dream," Jordan said.

"I think we all know by now my dreams shouldn't be ignored. I hope I go up there and find nothing. Either way, this city needs to be evacuated."

She helped Santini to his feet. "You're not leaving me here alone again," she said. "I'm coming. At least to the heliport."

Santini knew better than to argue with her.

Salvo got off the phone. "There's a chopper on standby. Remember, I'm going up with you. No discussion."

They filed out the door and into the Crown Vic. Salvo stepped on the gas and sped toward the heliport.

Pilot Ethan Roberts completed his preflight check of the police copter just as Santini, Salvo, and Jordan walked in. The heliport looked deserted.

"You're lucky I'm still here," Roberts said. "Everyone else is helping with the evacuations of the flooded areas. And things are getting worse with this bizarre storm. Are you sure about this?"

"Electric company confirms intermittent power to the skyscraper," Santini said. "So use of the elevators is out of the question. There's no other way. I have confidence in your skill, Ethan. I know we're asking a lot, but if this thing detonates, we'll all be in big trouble."

"Since you put it that way, I guess I'm left without a choice. Still, it's crazy to go up there, Santini."

"Right, crazy," Salvo said. "That's why he won't go anywhere now without a psychiatrist."

"Except now." He walked over to Dr. Jordan and took her hand.

"Here's the keys to our car. You get out of here. Find your daughter. Head east on the expressway."

Jordan shook her head. "Outrun a nuclear blast? I don't think so, Detective."

"The further away from the epicenter, the better your chances," Santini said.

Dr. Jordan looked into Santini's eyes. "I can't bear the thought of losing my daughter. Please. Stop this."

"We will. I promise." Then he turned and walked toward the helicopter.

# CHAPTER 32

President Tyler's pen tapped the large mahogany conference table.

"Any theories as to why this mysterious dark matter is forming over New York City, Beaumont, and nowhere else?"

The director of NASA shook his head. "It's the focal point, but we're not sure why, Mr. President."

The Situation Room door flew open and Deborah Wright interrupted. "Mr. President, there's an urgent call from Director Carter."

"Put him through on speaker." A short crackle of static filled the silence.

"Carter! What's going on?"

"Mr. President, moments ago one of my agents received a call from a Detective Anthony Santini of the NYPD claiming he has evidence of a nuclear bomb on the observatory platform of the Empire State Building."

"What?!" Everyone in the room fell silent.

"Because of the storm, surveillance cameras on the observatory are intermittent, but our satellite imaging has detected a large metal object in the north corner of the platform. Our experts feel it could very well be a nuclear device."

"How certain are they?"

"Until we get there and open the damn thing up, there's no way to know. But if it is a bomb, we've no idea when it's set to detonate."

The blood drained from Tyler's face. "I want a complete and immediate evacuation of New York City."

FEMA Director Jack Reynolds and Serena Morales of Homeland Security immediately sprang into action.

"I want all appropriate agencies alerted and all first responders mobilized, General."

"Yes, Mr. President."

"I've passed on the coordinates," said Carter. "You should have a visual in just a moment."

The large screen in the Situation Room blinked twice before coming to life. Despite the static and jiggling of the image, they could still make out the observatory platform and a rectangular metal box sitting in the corner.

"Experts here say if it is a nuclear device, it's an exceptionally large one. Large enough to do a significant amount of damage," Carter said.

"How much damage are we talking about?" Tyler asked.

"There have been various case scenario estimates, Mr. President, based upon the time of day. With a daytime detonation that high above the ground and the population of Manhattan ballooning to three million, six hundred thousand would die. However, because we've already evacuated portions of the island, that figure would be reduced significantly. We're looking at one hundred to two hundred thousand casualties."

President Tyler felt the blood drain from his face. "What's being done to stop this?"

"We've mobilized the Counter-terrorism Unit and Bomb Squad and they're on their way. Two stealth Black Hawks with two of the best pilots we have to navigate through this storm, and two bomb experts."

"If it can't be defused, can it be destroyed?" Tyler asked.

"Negative, sir. A missile will only trigger the plutonium. But we're confident our people can disarm this thing, if there's time."

"How far out are they, Carter?"

"I'm switching over to Commander Larson right now, sir."

A static blip filled the silence of the Situation Room.

"This is squadron commander Richard Larson, Mr. Pres—" A blast of static interrupted the communication. "We're making visual . . . act with the skyscrap— . . . and estimate a two-minute contact, sir. It's a bumpy . . . up here, sir. We're flying into . . . powerful headwinds and crosswinds."

"We're getting a visual now, Mr. President," Carter said.

Tyler felt the tension in the air as the men and women in the Situation Room watched the two helicopters approach the spire of the Empire State Building. Surrounding the helicopters were angry black thunderclouds that raced across the sky, pushed by winds that hammered the two aircraft.

The conference room was silent except for the sound of the helicopter engines. Each second passed like an eternity.

"Let's pray they're not too late," Tyler said.

As they watched the approach of the squadron, it struck—a bolt of lightning of such power and intensity that the lead helicopter exploded in a burst of light and sound that caused everyone in the room to jump. Time shifted into a surreal slow-motion nightmare. The big screen flickered several times, and observers watched plumes of black smoke and blazing debris fly through the air. One of the flying pieces hit the rotor blade of the remaining copter and sent it spiraling into a tailspin.

"Mayday, Mayday. This is Lieutenant Commander Richard Larson. We're going down."

The pilot of the spinning copter tried desperately to regain control. Had it not been for the relentless wind and rain, his skills might have prevailed, but instead, the assembled men and women watched in horror as the second helicopter crashed into the north side of the Empire State Building. Another stupendous explosion filled the dark sky.

Smoke billowed from the side of the wounded building as a stunned silence filled the room. No one had ejected. The old building rocked and swayed but managed to stay erect.

President Tyler removed his glasses and rubbed his eyes. "My God! What now?"

Everyone looked back to the screen when the sound of chopper blades once again filled the room. Rising from behind the south side of the observatory was an NYPD helicopter. It hovered there for a few seconds before passing directly over the platform. The aircraft bobbed and weaved and bucked as the rain and wind came from all directions.

The president and those assembled watched as a ladder descended from the aircraft. The ladder swayed in the storm as the pilot struggled to keep the copter still.

"Are you sure about this?" Salvo shouted.

They saw the smoke spiraling upward from the side of the building where the helicopter had crashed.

"Not much of a choice, is there?" Santini shouted back.

"Wear the gloves," Salvo yelled. "The rope ladder will be wet and slick. I'll hold it steady." He put his hand on Santini's shoulder. "We'll be waiting right here. Get it done."

Santini nodded, slung a small tool bag over his shoulder, put the gloves on, and stepped out the door of the helicopter.

It was like stepping into a hurricane. Wind and cold rain pelted his body, and the ladder swayed and snapped as he made a slow, careful descent.

"Who the hell is that?" President Tyler said.

"Not sure," Carter said.

They watched as Santini dropped onto the platform and walked to the metal box. All that could be heard was a round of intermittent static. Finally a voice prevailed.

". . . is Detective Santini. I hope someone up there that can talk me through this."

# CHAPTER 33

Santini heard a jumbled confusion of voices on the other end. Finally one voice emerged.

"This is Special Agent David Earnest, Detective. Describe to me what you're looking at."

"A six foot-by-four foot rectangular metal box, about four foot high. Set on wheels. Screws on the top and sides. Looks like stainless steel."

"Unscrew the top panel, Detective, and lift it off. Carefully."

Santini opened the tool satchel and chose a flat-head screwdriver. He had to lean his upper body into it, and several times the tool slipped off the slick screw heads. Finally he succeeded.

"Shit!" Santini could see the digital timer. "Two minutes and counting."

"Now look for the four wires that lead from the timer to a battery, and from the battery to the detonator."

"I see them. But they're covered in a plastic compartment."

"Pry it off."

He worked at it with the screwdriver, but it wouldn't budge.

"One minute fifteen seconds," Carter said.

Santini grabbed a hammer out of the satchel and raised it.

The casing shattered.

Agent Earnest shook his head. "Okay, that worked. Now look for the red wire that goes to the battery and cut it."

"Got it."

"Thirty-five seconds," Carter said.

"Can you see the wire that goes from the battery to the detonator?" Earnest asked.

"Yeah, it's green."

"Green? Are you sure?"

"I know my primary colors, Agent Earnest."

"Fifteen seconds," said Carter.

"Cut it."

Santini cut the green wire. The timer stopped at five seconds.

Cheers rose from the men and women in the Situation Room.

Chief of Staff James Whitaker walked over to President Tyler. "It's time to evacuate you and your family and the cabinet to a secure location, Mr. President. We don't know the full extent of this attack."

Tyler frowned and stood up. "How the hell did this happen? I want a full report. This was a major intelligence failure. We were lucky, and we're in indebted to this detective. So who is this man and how did he know about the bomb?"

"Apparently, he's an old friend of Agent Beckman, Detective Anthony Santini of the NYPD. You may have heard of him."

"I vaguely remember his name mentioned in the news a few years back," the president said. "But how did he have foreknowledge of this attack?"

"That's precisely what we'd like to know," Whitaker said.

"Keep me informed, Jim. We need to speak with this detective."

Santini looked up at the dangling ladder swaying in the wind and rain. With shouts of encouragement from Salvo, he leaped and caught the bottom rung. Grasping the ladder firmly, he slowly pulled himself upward. As he climbed, a powerful gust of wind forced the copter sideways and away from the platform, and he found himself flying through the air, hanging precipitously a hundred stories above Fifth Avenue.

Salvo reappeared in the entrance to the copter after having been thrown down.

"You hold on, Santini," he yelled. "Don't you let go. Do you hear me? Don't you dare let go."

His muscles stretched and strained as he tried to hold on, but eventually one hand slipped off. He thought about his nightmare and felt himself falling, but Salvo's screams snapped him back and he found the strength to grasp the rung tighter. Then the helicopter lurched in the opposite direction, and this time the wind pried him loose and he fell with a smack onto the observatory platform.

Santini lay very still. He tried to move his legs but couldn't. Then he heard someone call his name.

"Santini!" He heard someone drop down from the ladder onto the platform as the wind howled. "Santini."

His eyes fluttered open, and for a moment, he thought he saw the bald man standing over him. He lurched at him.

"Whoa. Take it easy partner. It's me, Salvo. We have to go, Santini. The copter can't hang here forever."

Then Santini's vision cleared and he saw Salvo.

"You did it. The bomb is defused. Now let's go."

Salvo lifted Santini to his feet, then caught the ladder, gripped it firmly, and helped Santini onto the first rung. They climbed slowly upward, the wind and rain pounding them. With Salvo's encouragement, they managed to make it to the top as the copter once again swayed precariously.

When they flopped into the copter, Salvo shouted to the pilot, "Let's get the hell out of here!"

# CHAPTER 34

The helicopter carrying Drakin-Shahid lifted off the rooftop of the MetLife Building as powerful winds threatened to send it plummeting to the ground. The pilot fought for control of the aircraft, which jerked and swayed in the torrential rain.

Drakin sensed Wagner was suspicious of his passenger, but he'd researched the man thoroughly, which was his custom when requiring an important accomplice, and knew the man had serious financial problems. Drakin had appeared out of nowhere and made him an offer he couldn't refuse.

The helicopter swung sideways. It was a roller coaster ride, with sudden jerks and dips, but the pilot was in control. Drakin's research had revealed Wagner was one of the best helicopter pilots out there.

Finally, after righting the helicopter and gathering enough speed to clear the Manhattan skyline, the pilot lowered the altitude to reduce the intensity of the wind shear.

As the winds diminished, the pilot found the optimum cruising speed. They hugged the Atlantic coastline, headed due south. Drakin-Shahid heard Wagner breathe a sigh of relief.

"Now maybe you can tell me what our destination is," the pilot grumbled. "I need to make calculations so I can navigate."

Drakin-Shahid didn't respond. He stared at the Manhattan skyline, which grew smaller as they flew. He curled Shahid's lips into a twisted smile.

"I need to know where I'm going," Wagner persisted.

Drakin-Shahid pulled out a piece of paper and handed it to the pilot. "These are the coordinates. It is an open field suitable for landing near the D.C. area."

Drakin-Shahid saw the frown on Wagner's face. The man hadn't anticipated a mysterious landing site. But he made the necessary calculations, punched in the coordinates, and settled back in his seat.

Adaptation was everything. It was how his kind had evolved beyond the needs of a physical body, how they'd learned to utilize negative energy for sustenance. And now, partly due to Santini's interference, it had prompted him to devise a contingency plan.

"We're about ten miles from the landing area," Captain Wagner announced. "I'll expect payment in full as soon as we land."

Drakin-Shahid looked out the window, blurred and rippled from the driving rain. "You'll have your payment."

As they approached, Drakin-Shahid saw the vehicle he'd commissioned parked along the small road that led to the landing site.

It was difficult at first, but after a few circles around the area, Captain Wagner maneuvered the aircraft safely onto the designated spot.

As soon as Wagner turned off the engine, Drakin-Shahid plunged the long knife deep into the base of the pilot's skull just above the first cervical vertebra. There were three or four body twitches before Wagner's head fell limp.

Drakin-Shahid grinned. "Payment in full, *mon capitaine*." As Drakin-Shahid exited the helicopter, he tossed a grenade into the cockpit.

Drakin loved grenades. He found the damage inflicted upon the human body to be quite satisfying. He jumped into the black Cadillac, slapped it into gear, and peeled through mud and water, fishtailing about until he finally found traction and headed down the dirt road.

The helicopter exploded behind him as Drakin thought about the next part of his plan. About thirty minutes from now, he would intercept the man as he waited for transport to his next assignment. Manipulating the disciplined mind of an FBI agent would be a challenge, but as usual, he'd discovered one who would suit his needs very nicely. An agent Robert Brooks.

His research had shown that the advancement of the man's career had always been his first priority, even at the expense of his wife and family. Agent Brooks had stepped on a few toes, and even on a few necks, to get to where he was today and so had made more than a few enemies. That made him the perfect candidate for the next phase of Drakin's plan.

Drakin-Shahid parked the car just outside the perimeter of the Secret Service heliport, clipped the wire fencing, and strolled toward the tarmac. He could see a man standing under an overhang impatiently pacing back and forth. Drakin-Shahid approached.

"Agent Brooks?" he said with a grin.

Brooks was clearly puzzled. "Who the hell are you?"

There was some resistance, but ultimately Drakin accessed the deep layers of the agent's subconscious mind that despised the pompous fools he risked his life to protect. He fanned the flames of this hostility and anger and entered through these doorways.

As Drakin settled into his new host, Josef Shahid turned and disappeared into the night.

Drakin-Brooks checked his watch. In five minutes, a helicopter would take him to the secret bunker that housed the president of the United States.

## CHAPTER 35

When Roberts landed the aircraft at the NYPD heliport, two wet and haggard-looking detectives emerged. Salvo gave a thumb's-up sign. Dr. Jordan walked up to Santini and put her arms around him. He couldn't hide the surprised look on his face.

"You were supposed to have left the city," Santini said.

"We always have choices, Detective. Remember that. As it turns out, Dayna's school was closed and she went to White Plains to visit a friend. So I chose to wait here."

"You shouldn't have done that," Santini said. "Things may not have worked out so well."

"But they did work out, thanks to you and Salvo. And right now we need to get both of you into some dry clothes. My place is closest. I have a few things my ex left behind that are at least dry."

"So you're going to dress us in your ex-husband's clothes," Santini said. "What if I don't like his style?"

"Come to think of it, you just might be a little bigger than my ex," Jordan said.

Santini grinned. "I bet I'm a lot bigger."

She laughed. "Maybe you should stay in your wet clothes, Detective."

They all got into the Crown Victoria and headed for the Long Island Expressway. After a few minutes of driving through the continuous downpour, Salvo spoke.

"That was just a little bit too close."

Santini had his eyes closed.

"Is he asleep, Salvo?" Jordan asked.

Santini opened his eyes. "Something isn't right. That was too easy."

"Easy?" Salvo said. "Two helicopters destroyed. Two special ops teams dead. We almost crashed our helicopter and you defused the bomb with five seconds to spare. If that's easy, I'm curious to know what you would consider hard."

"I don't know," he said. "It's just a feeling I'm missing something."

"Well, Drakin is still out there, and I'm sure he's not finished," Jordan said.

"And that's what I'm worried about," Santini said.

They sat quietly as Salvo steered the vehicle through a storm that grew more intense by the minute. Visibility was difficult, and Salvo squinted as the wipers banged noisily back and forth.

"Tell us about your last dream?" Jordan said. "Maybe by talking about it, you'll remember something important."

Santini sighed. At least she didn't think he was crazy anymore.

"My recurring nightmare was nothing compared to this." He closed his eyes. "I walked among the dead and the dying. It was horrible . . . the screams." He hesitated. "A little girl died in my arms. After that my anger grew and things spiraled out of control." He frowned as he opened his eyes. "He left his calling card in my head. He knew I'd try to track him and sabotaged my subconscious."

Dr. Jordan placed her hand on Santini's shoulder. "But you overcame it and survived."

"Without you to guide me back, there might have been a different outcome." He turned toward Salvo. "We have to let the government know this wasn't simply a terrorist attack."

"And just who do we tell our story of mind-manipulating entities to?" Salvo said.

"That's what I've been trying to figure out," Santini said.

Salvo shook his head. "So, do we just march into FBI headquarters without a shred of hard evidence and tell them you dreamed about the bomb?"

"The evidence is, and the truth is, I knew beforehand about the device."

They sat in silence as the rain drummed the windshield. Dr. Jordan's cell phone rang. Santini listened anxiously to the conversation. She hung up and closed her eyes. "Thank you," she whispered. She turned toward Santini. "You were right, Detective. He's tough. O'Brian is in and out of consciousness and insists he speak with you."

Santini breathed a sigh of relief. "I owe him that much. Step on the gas, Salvo."

*"I tell you the truth. If you have faith as small as a mustard seed, you can say to this mountain, 'Move from here to there,' and it will move."*
—Matthew 17:20

# CHAPTER 36

"He needs to rest," Dr. Markson said. "Now's not the time for a police interrogation. He's lucky to be alive."

"We're thankful for all you've done," Dr. Jordan said, "but we're his friends."

"Father O'Brian asked to speak to us," Salvo said.

"Look, Doc," Santini said. "This is police business and a matter of life and death."

The surgeon sighed. "Keep it brief."

Father O'Brian was asleep when they entered the room. Dr. Jordan tapped his shoulder lightly and the priest slowly came awake.

He looked around blearily, and his eyes found Santini. After several moments he spoke.

"You have an intensity in your eyes. There is strength and determination within them." Then he looked at Salvo and Dr. Jordan. "And your friends, they have these same qualities. You're very lucky to have them with you."

Santini nodded. "I'm sorry I left you and the doctor alone. I shouldn't have done that."

The priest shook his head. "It would have come for the staff sooner or later, Detective. Do not blame yourself."

"We got it back," Santini said. "I'll keep it safe for you."

He shook his head again. "It's yours, Anthony. It belongs to you now." Then the priest beckoned for them to come closer. "There's something I must tell you." He took a deep breath. "All of you."

They came nearer to his bedside.

"A long time ago, in another life, I had a beautiful wife and daughter. But then . . . a drunk driver, on the wrong side of the road. Both killed." O'Brian closed his eyes. When he opened them they were filled with water. "For years, anger consumed me. Every waking moment was misery. So I drank and lost myself . . . Eventually, suicide seemed a welcome relief . . . But thankfully, I was saved. God spoke to me. Not in words, but with a blanket of hope that warmed my soul and lifted my spirit with his grace. Since then Christ has been my savior."

He paused as if gathering strength.

"You must forgive me, Anthony, for what I said earlier. I don't know if what this Astrolite said is true. I only know what is true for me. Faith in God has saved my life, and it has saved millions throughout human history. But faith is difficult. It is elusive and fragile. It ebbs and flows like ocean waves. Even I have struggled with it."

He reached out for Santini's hand.

"You have seen horrible crimes committed against innocent people. You've seen much suffering. And because you're compassionate, you've felt their pain, and over time it is understandable your faith has been shattered. Whether this thing is a demon, or an alien, or both, I don't know, but what I do know is you must not rob humanity of hope. If you want to defeat it, you must arm yourself with faith, and you must ask for God's help. Now listen very carefully to what I'm about to say, Anthony. I had a vision. While under surgery."

Santini edged closer.

"You were standing on a pile of broken rubble with thunder and lightning crashing all around you. There were fires everywhere. In your outstretched hand you held the staff, and you were pointing it upward. But there were thousands of people, maybe more, who had their eyes closed and were concentrating intently. They weren't there with you, but I could sense them."

They sat in silence for a very long time, Santini at a loss for words.

"Anthony, please unfasten the chain from around my neck."

Santini unclasped the chain and placed it in the priest's hand. Then Father O' Brian held it out to him.

"My mother gave me this cross. She said one day I would pass it on to someone who would need it more than me."

Santini took the gold crucifix and placed it around his neck.

The priest squeezed his hand. "God has not abandoned us," he said. "You need only ask for his help."

"I'll try," Santini said

"And remember what the Astrolite said. You cannot do this alone."

The doctor poked his head into the room. "Please. I must insist. He needs to rest now."

Santini, Jordan, and Salvo said their good-byes and left the hospital. They climbed back into the car and headed down the Brooklyn-Queens Expressway toward Dr. Jordan's home. Santini felt the gold medal that now hung around his neck along with his father's badge.

"Arm myself with faith," Santini said. "How am I supposed to do that?" He shook his head. "What about you Salvo? You go to church."

"I'm not as consistent as Mari," Salvo said, "but I go. It helps me get through some of the crap we see. So I try to have faith." He looked pensive for a moment. "I have to think, since I personally am not responsible for showing up on this planet, that there's someone or something out there a lot smarter than me."

Santini smiled. "That's not saying much, Salvo." He turned around to look at Jordan in the backseat. "Were you a parishioner at St. Patrick's?"

"Now and then. The priest helped me out of a rough time after my divorce. I used to think psychiatry was the only answer to our emotional problems, but I've come to believe that at times, turning them over to God can be useful, too."

Santini closed his eyes and thought about what the priest had said.

Suddenly they could hear a deafening roar coming from directly overhead.

"What the hell is that?" Salvo yelled. He rolled down the window and poked his head out into the pouring rain. A searchlight in the sky focused on their moving vehicle and lit the interior, prompting Salvo to shield his eyes. An amplified voice emerged from beyond the light.

"Detective Anthony Santini, please pull your vehicle to the side of the road. I repeat, pull your vehicle to the side of the road."

"I think we should do what the man in the helicopter says," Jordan yelled.

"You'd better pull over," Santini said.

Salvo turned off the engine. They watched nervously as an Army helicopter landed directly in front of their car and four armed soldiers emerged from the aircraft. They quickly surrounded the vehicle.

"They look like Navy SEAL uniforms," Salvo said. "We must have been driving with a broken taillight."

"I think we all know why they're here," Santini said.

"Detective Anthony Santini?" The man looked from the photo in his hand to Santini. "My name is Lieutenant Giffords of Navy SEAL Special Operations. I have orders to take you and your friends here for a little ride. I hope you all have strong stomachs, because things will be getting a little bumpy."

"I'll pass," Salvo said. "I've had enough of helicopters for one day."

"Do we have a choice?" Santini asked.

"I'm afraid not, sir."

"Where are you taking us?" Salvo demanded.

"I'm sorry, sir, but that information is classified."

"Something to do with my call to Beckman," Santini said, "right?"

"I'm sorry, sir, but there isn't anything further I can tell you," Lieutenant Giffords said, his uniform soaked through. "Except you'll need to turn over your firearms."

Salvo didn't look happy. "What about the car?"

"I'm sorry, Detective, but it must be left behind. We might be able to find someone to pick it up, but as you can imagine, since this storm and terrorist attack, all personnel are currently being deployed."

"There's a priceless museum artifact in our trunk," Santini said. "We can't just leave it."

"We can store it in the cargo bay of the helicopter." Giffords was starting to lose patience as the water streamed over his face. "Now if you'll all please follow me, we really must be going."

The three were loaded onto the helicopter and securely fastened in. The pilot then lifted off and headed straight into the rain and wind.

## CHAPTER 37

An elite helicopter squadron had whisked President Tyler, his family, and the cabinet to a bunker, code name "Lifesaver," constructed out of a mountain in Raven Rock, Pennsylvania. And it was here that the helicopter containing Santini, Salvo, and Jordan was headed.

Lieutenant Giffords cautiously initiated their descent, and the three passengers watched nervously through water-strewn glass as the side of the mountain grew larger.

"I've heard about these bunkers," Salvo said.

"In the early 1950s, the Washington establishment was convinced World War III could break out at any moment," Lieutenant Giffords said. "So they built over fifty of these radiation-proof babies in strategic secret locations. This one is carved out of greenstone granite, some of the hardest rock on the East Coast. Tunneling into this mountain was no easy task, but Eisenhower insisted it be done. Beneath is a vast underground complex meant to shelter the Pentagon and the president."

Santini turned to Salvo and Jordan, and then he reached over and took Jordan's hand. "Whatever happens, just tell them the truth."

Salvo chuckled. "We tell the truth and we'll be waterboarded. How long can you hold your breath?"

After the helicopter finally landed, they were escorted into separate interview rooms. Salvo and Santini were given a change of dry clothing.

Jason Carter, director of the FBI, and James Whitaker, Tyler's chief of staff, walked into the room where Santini was being held. It was a bland, white, sterile-looking room lined in concrete, with fluorescent lighting and exposed pipes that ran along the length of the ceiling. There were a few metal bunk beds on the far side and a few chairs scattered about. They introduced themselves, although Santini had seen both of them several times on the news.

"Sorry about your accommodations," Whitaker said, "but we are, unfortunately, in a bunker."

Santini couldn't help noticing the way Carter glared at him.

"I want to thank you for what you did out there today, Detective," Whitaker said.

"Why the armed escort?" Santini said. "You scared the hell out of us."

"Sorry about that," Whitaker said, "but we needed to speak to you. And this was the quickest way to get you here."

Santini couldn't hide his annoyance.

"So how did you know?" Carter asked.

Santini had known this was coming and had thought hard about how he would handle it. "I saw it in a dream."

Silence.

"So your statement is, you had a dream about the bomb?" Carter said.

"My friends will confirm this. Dr. Jordan used her suggestive skills to put me to sleep." Santini hesitated but decided to take his own advice and go forward. "I'd had previous dreams about the event, but this time I actually saw the bomb."

Carter stood and walked to the side of the room. "So who did you actually see plant the bomb in your dream?"

"There were two men. One was young, maybe late twenties, probably Middle Eastern."

"And the other man?"

Santini hesitated. "Didn't see him."

"You said there were two men," Carter said.

Santini shifted in his chair. "I didn't see him because in my dream I was seeing through the eyes of the other man."

"So it was you who planted the device," Carter said.

"No. It was him."

"And who is him?" Whitaker asked.

Santini knew this was going to be the hardest part of the conversation.

"When I dream, I'm able to perceive the actions of an entity that has the ability to enter the human mind and influence behavior. It was this entity, using accomplices, that almost destroyed the city."

"Bullshit," Carter said.

"It's the truth."

"What do you mean by 'an entity'?" Whitaker asked. "What kind of entity?"

"It's an alien intelligence," Santini said, "invisible, some form of energy consciousness."

"And this so-called entity can manipulate people?"

"Yes."

"And just how does it do that?" Carter asked.

"It plants suggestions by using an inner voice masquerading as the person's own thoughts."

"Forgive me," Carter said, "but how does an invisible nothing secure and plant a nuclear device on top of the Empire State Building?"

"Like I said, it had accomplices."

"Could this entity be manipulating you?" Carter asked.

Santini held the director's gaze. "It tried, but it was not successful."

"This is all horseshit," Carter said. "And there's something that has me a bit concerned."

"What?"

"It is my understanding you're traveling with your psychiatrist and were under her treatment. Is that correct?"

"Yes, but—"

"And you were suspended because of mental instability and potentially suicidal thoughts."

"Yes, but that was before I was able to convince the doctor that my dreams had become precognitive."

Carter moved toward Santini and stood over him. "Isn't it possible, Detective, you yourself planted that bomb so you could play the hero and save the day?"

"That's not how it went down, Director. I've been with Detective Salvo and Dr. Jordan for most of the last forty-eight hours. So that would be impossible."

"Not unless you, too, had accomplices, Detective," Carter said.

"Now *that's* horseshit," Santini said.

There was a long silence as Santini and Carter locked eyes.

"I think we should have a conversation with your friends and continue this interview later," Whitaker said.

Carter and Whitaker walked out of the room.

*That went well*, Santini thought.

# CHAPTER 38

Santini sat in an uncomfortable metal chair in what they'd called the "guest quarters." Having the president's chief of staff as well as the director of the FBI interrogate him was nerve-racking. Usually he was the one doing the questioning. He wondered how his friends were holding up.

The cave-like silence was oppressive. For days he'd heard crashing thunder, howling wind, and pounding rain. Now . . . nothing. But at times he thought he could still hear the storm, though he knew that was impossible.

He rubbed his temples and closed his eyes. Images of his recent nightmare surfaced. The little girl, the screams . . .

But the bomb had been defused, so why was he so apprehensive?

The door opened and Carter and Whitaker walked in.

"Am I a prisoner?" Santini asked.

"Should you be?" Carter said.

He glared at Carter. "You insinuated it was me who planted the bomb Salvo and I risked our lives to disarm."

"We had to corroborate your story, Detective," Whitaker said. "Put yourself in our position. We have two renowned detectives and a psychiatrist describing supernatural forces and precognitive dreams. Not something we hear every day. Both Dr. Jordan's and Detective Salvo's account of the last forty-eight hours supports your story. And her testimony convinced me, at least for now, to entertain the possibility that what you've told us is true." Whitaker glanced at Carter. "Although Director Carter thinks you're all crazy."

Carter remained expressionless.

"There's someone else who would like to interview you," Whitaker said. "He's head of one of our more, shall we say, obscure agencies. And we'd like to monitor your blood pressure and heart rate during the interview."

"So now you're going to hook up the person who saved your asses due to your intelligence failures to a lie detector?" Santini felt his face flush.

"Similar, but much more sophisticated," Whitaker said.

Carter gave Santini a cold stare. "And extremely accurate."

"Do I have a choice?"

"You must realize the profundity of your assertions," Whitaker said. "It's now a matter of national security."

"What do you mean by 'obscure agency'?" Santini said.

"During the Cold War," Whitaker said, "American and Soviet researchers were interested in the possibility of using psychic abilities for military applications. They even set up several agencies to research such possibilities. The U.S. Defense Advanced Research Projects Agency, or DARPA, was one of these agencies."

"A bunch of bullshit and a waste of taxpayer money," Carter said.

"Nevertheless," Whitaker continued, "the U.S government has spent decades searching for individuals with abilities such as ESP, telepathy, clairvoyance, precognition, and psychokinesis. Unfortunately, most of the scientific evidence remains inconclusive."

Carter huffed. "Like I said, a bunch of bullshit."

Whitaker glanced at Carter and frowned. Santini got the impression they were not the best of friends. He turned toward Santini. "Bottom line, Detective, if there's even a remote possibility you have the ability to foresee events potentially damaging to the United States of America, we'd like to know about it."

"It's just in the last few months I've been having these dreams," Santini said. "And you should know, my . . . ability . . . only seems to connect to this entity."

A short thin man with gray hair, a goatee, piercing black eyes, and wire-rim spectacles walked in. He was carrying a large suitcase and sat at the metal desk in the corner of the room.

"This is Dr. Richard Cleveland," Whitaker said. "Head psychologist and research director of DARPA, Paranormal Division."

"Please have a seat, Detective." Dr. Cleveland said. "And if you will please remove your shirt."

He opened the suitcase and proceeded to tape electrical wires to Santini's temples, neck, and chest.

"I hope you're not going to ask me to bend a spoon," Santini said.

"That isn't a test we find very helpful, Detective," Dr. Cleveland said. "I suggest you just relax."

As Carter and Whitaker observed, Dr. Cleveland began with some basic preliminary questions to establish a baseline pattern. Then the course of questioning changed.

"You say you had a dream about the device you and your partner defused on top of the Empire State Building earlier today?" Cleveland said

"That's right."

Cleveland stared intently at the monitor in front of him. "When did you have this dream?"

"Maybe ten-twelve hours ago."

"Tell me the details of this dream."

Santini narrated the dream but left out the sabotage of his subconscious mind and his near-death experience.

"Was this the only time you dreamed about the device and the destruction of New York City?"

"No. For several months I've had a recurring dream of a destroyed city, but this last dream was the first time I'd actually seen the device on the observatory."

"Have you had any other similar-type dreams?"

"Yes." Santini talked about his dreams of the Gorman murders, the Nolan child, and Father O'Brian.

"Is it only in the dream state that you have precognitive ability?" Cleveland asked.

"Yes."

"And because of your dreams, you were able to prevent two violent crimes?"

"Detective Salvo and I were able to get to the Nolan kid and O'Brian in time."

"And this has been documented in the police records?"

"It was documented I prevented the crimes, but not because of my dreams."

"And was this . . . alien intelligence responsible for these crimes?"

"Yes."

"According to Dr. Jordan and Detective Salvo, this entity is trying to kill you?"

Santini nodded. "It sees me as a threat."

"Why?"

"Because I have dreams about it."

"And this entity tried to manipulate you into jumping off the observatory?"

"It tried, but obviously failed."

"And you were seeing Dr. Jordan for insomnia because of your recurring dreams at the time?"

"Yes. I didn't yet understand what was happening to me."

"And when you told her about this episode, she suspended you because she was concerned you were suicidal?"

"Yes, but afterwards when I dreamed about Father O'Brian being assaulted and we rescued him, she had me reinstated."

Cleveland checked his readings before continuing.

"Is it your belief this entity used terrorists to plant the bomb on the observatory?"

"That would seem a logical conclusion."

Deputy Director Vance Lundy walked into the room. "I need to speak to both of you," he said, looking at Whitaker and Carter.

The three stepped out of the room, and when Whitaker and Carter returned, they both wore grim expressions.

"Another one of our copters has made it to the top of the Empire State Building," Carter said. "Their evaluation of the bomb you disarmed confirms that it was a very sophisticated hoax. Extremely high tech. Made to look like a nuclear bomb but without radioactive material."

"What!" Santini said. "Are they sure?"

"When they finally opened the damn thing, there was a load of C4 that would have killed anyone standing nearby, but no plutonium." Carter glared at Santini. "Any idea as to why someone would go through all of that trouble to make it look like a nuclear device, Detective?"

Santini was stunned, his mind spinning. Could it have been that Drakin's plan all along was to kill Santini with C4 explosives but not to destroy the city? He flashed back to his dream on the observatory. He'd seen the elevator moving and assumed it was Drakin's accomplice leaving after he had helped position the bomb.

Then it came to him. Drakin knew Santini would dream about his plan and see the bomb, so he devised a contingency plan. One in which he was not directly involved. They had planted a decoy, knowing Santini would see it in a dream. It was possible Drakin's conspirators then rode the elevator up to the seventy-fifth floor to plant the real device.

Santini jumped up. "Because it's a decoy," he blurted. "There's another device inside that building! You have to find it."

A heavy silence filled the room. Carter and Whitaker looked at each other as if trying to assess what the other was thinking. Finally, Cleveland broke the silence.

"Based on my preliminary evaluation, gentlemen, I suggest you take what Detective Santini says very seriously."

"Are you sure about this, Cleveland?" Whitaker said.

"As sure as I can be."

"Can you be more precise, Detective?" Carter said.

"No. Somewhere on the seventy-fifth floor."

Whitaker turned to Deputy Director Lundy. "Find the president and assemble the security council immediately."

"I hope you're right about the seventy-fifth floor, Detective," Whitaker said.

"So do I," Santini said.

# CHAPTER 39

Santini looked nervously around the room, which resembled a small airplane hangar. The powerful men and women seated at the long conference table seemed just as anxious as he was. Several large monitors lined the concrete walls conveying live satellite feeds.

Drakin had outsmarted him. He prayed he had discovered his error in time.

Whitaker walked Santini over to the president, who had just finished a discussion with the head of homeland security. Santini had seen the man on television, but in real life he had a much more commanding presence.

"This is Detective Anthony Santini, Mr. President."

Tyler looked him over carefully as if trying to assess him. Santini held Tyler's gaze. Then the president extended his hand.

"Thank you for defusing that bomb, Detective, but it seems according to your, shall we say, intuition, we've been duped and are now searching for the actual nuclear device. Carter and Cleveland have briefed me."

"I pray we still have time, sir," Santini said.

"Dr. Cleveland suggested he be here, Mr. President," Whitaker said, "in case the live feed from the team triggers any dream memories of the location of the second device."

"That's if it even exists," Tyler said. He glanced at Santini with a serious expression. Then he beckoned Santini and Whitaker aside out of earshot of the rest of the cabinet.

"The blueprints of the seventy-fifth floor reveal hundreds of potential hiding places for a device that size, Detective," Tyler said. "We're sending another team to assist, but it could take hours to check every nook and cranny. There's twenty-five thousand square feet of office space. Is there anything else you can give us to help narrow down the search?"

"I'm afraid my dream was only of the observatory device, Mr. President."

"And nothing else?"

Santini hesitated. "I did dream of the city's destruction, Mr. President."

Tyler glared at Santini. "That's not acceptable. What if you were to dream again, now, and find the location of this second device?"

"That wouldn't work, Mr. President." Santini said. "I can't control what I dream."

The large monitor on the center wall blinked to life. Navy Seal Commander George Hastings's voice and image came through on the live feed. "We're beginning our sweep of the seventy-fifth floor, Mr. President," he said. "We've divided the team in half, one approaching from the east and one from the west. We're working on restoring power to the building, but for now we're searching with flashlights."

"The second team is on the way," Tyler said. "If ever there was a time for speed, Commander, it's now."

"Yes, Mr. President." Hastings said.

As Santini listened, he observed that the man he recognized as Secretary Hessling, seated at the conference table, was not focused on the live feed from the Navy SEAL operation but was staring directly at him. Santini held his gaze until Tyler walked in front of him

"To be honest, I don't know what to think of all this dreaming bullshit," Tyler said. "But stay here. Maybe you'll remember something."


Drakin was surprised to see the detective here at the bunker, and surprise was not an emotion he was accustomed to. It was always Drakin who was the orchestrator of events.

A human's senses were much more acute when Drakin rode its host, so he was able to easily overhear their conversation. It was obvious the detective was here because of his foreknowledge of the decoy device on the observatory. And now it was obvious they were aware of the device on the seventy-fifth floor. No matter.

He looked at Hessling's watch. He'd used Jerry Slater, the maintenance man at the Empire State Building, to case the skyscraper several times in search of a proper location for the video camera and for concealment of the device. There was no way the humans would find it in time.

Drakin's energy tentacles of awareness wound tighter around the secretary of state's brain. He'd gained access to the man's mind through his jealousy and hatred of the president. They were both from opposing parties, and Tyler had appointed Hessling as a gesture of reconciliation. Politically, they had nothing in common, so Hessling, a vain and ambitious man who had made a run in the primaries, had to dance to Tyler's tune. All Drakin had to do was feed these negative emotions long enough that he'd be able to access the man's memory.

Drakin-Hessling glanced at the man in uniform standing at attention in the corner of the room. He wore no identification badge, but from the recesses of Hessling's memory, the name Major Steven Custer surfaced.

Major Custer was a shadow—the president's shadow. Wherever the president went, there he was. Always in the background. Not too close but never very far away. And with the recent turn of events, he was staying even closer. His sole purpose was to carry the atomic "football," or "black box."

Custer stood at perfect attention. Drakin could sense the tension focused in the man's right arm where he held the briefcase cuffed to his wrist and secured by manacles constructed of a specially designed steel alloy that made it virtually impossible to cut.

The contents of the briefcase were to be used by the president to authorize a nuclear attack while away from fixed command centers such as the White House Situation Room. It contained a secure sat-com radio, a handset, a nuclear playbook, and the nuclear launch codes.

Based on his exploration of Hessling's mind, Drakin knew of the "two-man rule." The president had the unilateral authority as commander in chief to order a nuclear strike, but it required a secondary confirmation from the secretary of state. And it was his personal authentication codes that Drakin now hunted for in Hessling's memory banks. It was an art Drakin had mastered, similar to scrolling through a computer's files.

Eventually, Drakin was able to illuminate the part of Hessling's brain that stored the code. Now he need only acquire the second set of authorization codes.

Drakin prided himself on his ability to foresee potential disruptions to his plans. And one of these potential disruptions was the use of nuclear missiles. Control and diversion of America's nuclear arsenal would provide a nice safeguard for the next phase of his plan.

He watched through Hessling's eyes as the president took the seat beside him. The secretary of state smiled at him, awaiting the opportunity he knew would come.

"Status report, Commander," Tyler said.

"We're about halfway through our sweep, Mr. President. Nothing yet."

As everyone anxiously watched the live feed of the bomb squad's progress, Deborah Wright rushed into the room, brushing past Santini.

"I think you should see this, Mr. President," she said.

All eyes turned toward her as she walked to another monitor in the room and switched to a live Internet broadcast. There on the large screen, standing motionless in front of a white backdrop, was a young man in Muslim garb.

Santini's eyes opened wide. It was the young man from his dream.

"Who is this?" Tyler said.

"He's yet to identify himself, but his signal is originating from the Empire State Building. And it's all over the Internet."

As soon as she'd said those words, the man began speaking.

*"Infidels! The day of retribution has arrived, and I, Allam Bashir, shall be the instrument of your demise. I've prayed for this day, the day I will strike a blow deep into the heart of the Great Satan."*

Drakin pursed Hesslings's mouth into a smile. His boy was right on time.

*"You, America, are the pinnacle of evil. Your collective sins are beyond atonement. You flaunt your vices for all the world to see. Your obsession with freedom to do whatever you please gives license to all manner of vile activity."*

"Can we isolate the exact location of the signal?" Tyler asked.

Deborah Wright shook her head. "We're trying, sir."

*"You mock God by peddling sex and pornography. You promote a life of indulgence and promiscuity. You know nothing of sacrifice, sacrifice for a greater cause."*

As Santini listened, his heart began to race. Drakin's accomplice no doubt, bent on destroying western civilization, convinced his God condones mass murder. He glanced over at the monitor showing the progress of the search team. This rant could mean only one thing. They were running out of time.

*"Well, I'm here today for a greater cause. To bring justice to all those you've murdered in the name of your imperialist democracy."*

Santini closed his eyes and frantically searched his memory, his dream images, his intuition for anything that might hint at where the bomb was hidden.

Bashir's eyes blazed. *"To my brother, Hamed, slaughtered by your government, today I bring you justice."*

Tyler stood up. "Status report, Commander."

"Still searching, sir. About ten offices left."

*"To my sister, Basma, murdered when just a baby, today I bring you justice."*

"Comander Hastings!" Tyler yelled at the monitor. "Find that goddamn bomb!"

*"Soon, I will join you both in paradise."*

"Hastings!" Tyler yelled again.

Allam Bashir closed his eyes. *"Allahu Akbar."*

Drakin-Hessling fought to keep from laughing as he watched Santini's face.

Tyler turned to Santini. "Anything?"

Santini's heart pounded as he opened his eyes. He shook his head. He had come up with nothing.

All those assembled then watched in horror as a remote camera zoomed in on a large device with a digital clock that was, at this moment, counting down from three seconds.

"My God!" Tyler said.

Two seconds.

One second—

A shrill screech filled the room and the screen went static. Everyone around the long conference table sat motionless for a moment before turning toward the second monitor, showing satellite feed of the city.

A black mushroom cloud was rising into the sky.

*"There are more things in Heaven and Earth,
Than are dreamed of in your philosophy."*
—William Shakespeare

# CHAPTER 40

Santini, Salvo, and Jordan sat in the room where Santini had initially been questioned. They were all in shock. Santini's whole body was numb, and a heavy silence filled the air.

He couldn't get the image of the mushroom cloud out of his head. So many dead, and he'd been powerless to prevent it. How many had perished because of him?

"I should have warned the precinct," Santini said.

Salvo looked up. "None of this is your fault. We did our best to stop it. How the hell could we have known there was another bomb?"

Santini stared straight ahead, dazed. "I've spent my life trying to protect people. Thousands dead. Drakin has made my life's work seem an insignificant joke."

"Santini!" Salvo said.

"I can hear him, his taunts, saying I'd always be one step behind him. He was right. I've been outsmarted. I should have caught my mistake sooner."

Santini felt a hand on his shoulder and looked up to see Jordan standing over him. Her eyes were still red from crying.

Whitaker walked into the room, a somber expression on his face.

"Is there somewhere I can get a drink around here?" Santini asked.

Whitaker began to speak, but Salvo interjected. "Any update on the extent of the casualties?"

"With all the chaos, an accurate assessment is not yet available," Whitaker said.

"Weren't there some evacuations due to the flooding?" Jordan said.

"That's the only saving grace in this whole disaster," Whitaker said. He looked at Santini. "We intercept all cell phone communications in the bunker for security purposes. You have a call. A Father Timothy O'Brian. Says it's urgent he speak with you. Punch in 7183 on your cell to take the call."

After Whitaker left, Santini pulled out his cell phone and sat staring at it.

"Take the call," Salvo said.

"Why? So he can tell me to rally my faith?"

He sighed and punched in the numbers. "This is Santini."

The voice on the other end was weak and raspy. "Hello, Anthony."

"Father."

"This isn't over yet, Anthony. The explosion." The priest struggled to get out the words. "The fear. The panic. The raw emotions . . . They've destroyed the barrier. I can feel it."

Santini shook his head. "I don't know anything about a barrier. What I do know is that Manhattan is gone. Where's the help your God was supposed to have given?"

"It's devastating. I know. But there's more at stake . . . 'When the Souls of Men have been Corrupted in Sufficient Numbers, It is then the Portal will Open' " The priest paused to take a breath. "And do you remember the vision I had?"

"You were under anesthesia," Santini said. "I don't know what to make of your hallucinations while under surgery."

"Hallucinations? Is that what you think they were? You mean like your dreams?"

"What is it you want me to do, Father?"

"Stop him. It's not too late. He wants you dead for a reason. Use the staff."

"And just how do I do that?"

"I can't answer that. But I pray it will become clear to you in time."

"In time? Well then, I'd better let you get to your praying. You have a lot of it to do." Santini put his phone down and shook his head. "Faith? After what just happened?"

"What did he say?" Salvo said.

"Does it matter?"

"Father O'Brian is a wise man," Jordan said. "I'd listen to his advice."

Santini shook his head and recounted his conversation.

"Stop blaming yourself," Jordan said. "Clear your head. We need you."

"If what the priest says is true," Salvo said, "now is not the time to fold."

"There's still more you must do," Jordan said. "Both the Astrolite and the priest have said so."

Santini gazed at his two friends. He thought about what Drakin had said of the darkness growing in his mind: "Like a cancer." His head ached. Maybe Drakin was right.

Then he abruptly stood and walked out of the room.

# CHAPTER 41

The somber faces of the men and women surrounding the president reflected their pain. Many had lost family or dear friends.

Homeland Security Director Morales began her briefing.

"Presently, we estimate the death toll at fifty thousand and counting, Mr. President. The wounded, burned, and maimed, twice as many."

President Tyler seemed to be staring off into space.

Morales looked around the room unsure of whether to continue. "Mr. President?"

After a long uncomfortable silence, Tyler responded. "Survivors?"

"The National Guard and first responders are doing what they can outside of the radiation zone," she said, "but their movements are impeded by the storm. Explosions from broken gas lines compound the problem. So even with helicopters and hazmat, it's difficult at this time to approach ground zero. We have aerial footage." She hesitated. "But be warned, sir, it's not a pretty sight."

Morales turned on the central monitor.

The president's face turned gray. It was a mass grave. Charred bodies were scattered everywhere. Fires burned out of control. What was once the most beautiful skyline in the world had collapsed into rubble.

"All of Manhattan destroyed?" Tyler said.

"I'm afraid so, sir. And all bridges into Manhattan, except for possibly the Williamsburg Bridge."

Deborah Wright walked into the room. "Director Beaumont is very anxious to update you on the storm," she said. "He says the blast has done something unusual to the edge of space above ground zero."

Tyler seemed annoyed. "He'll have to wait."

"People everywhere are in a state of panic," Whitaker said. "Social media is overloaded. It's an outpouring of emotion the likes of which the world has never seen."

"Americans are terrified, Mr. President." Morales said. "There's fear, confusion, anger. They're worried about another attack."

Tyler looked around the room and sighed deeply. "It's time the American people heard from their president."

President Tyler stood before the cameras in the communications studio of the Lifesaver Bunker as they prepared him, but despite their efforts, they couldn't hide the anguish emanating from the deep furrows of his brow or the redness and swelling that plagued his eyes. The advancing gray that seemed to afflict every man who held this most arduous position seemed to have gained more ground in the past few hours.

He took a deep breath and stepped closer to the podium.

"My fellow Americans, I come to you today with a heavy heart. An atrocity has been committed on our soil. Hundreds of thousands of our fellow Americans have been killed in a most horrific act of terrorism. This day will forever be etched in the minds of all Americans as a day of great sorrow.

"Our first priority is the survivors of the blast. Emergency response plans have been implemented, and as is the American way, offers of help have been pouring in from across the nation. And I want to thank all of the world leaders that have offered their country's resources to help us in this time of great tragedy.

"Tonight I ask for your prayers. Prayers for the dead, prayers for the wounded, and prayers for the families of the loved ones who have perished.

"For the cowards complicit in this heinous act, I have this to say. From this day forth, you will live every second of your miserable lives knowing the power and wrath of America is breathing down your neck. Never again will you place your head comfortably on a pillow and sleep. Never again will you know peace. No matter where you hide, no matter what dark hole you crawl into, we will dig you out and make you face the light of justice.

"Though we have been wounded, we will never be defeated. Though we have suffered, we will never give in to fear. Our beloved city has fallen, but from the rubble and ashes, like a great phoenix rising from the fires, the American spirit will rise once again. Stronger and more determined.

"We will rebuild our city and it will stand as a shining testament to who we are as a people.

"So tonight let us cry and grieve together. Let us stand united, and let us pray for God's strength.

"Good night, and may God bless the United States of America."

When it was over and the cameras were turned off, President Tyler cradled his face with his hands and inhaled deeply. As skillful as his presentation was, in the end, it was just another speech, and it wasn't enough to lessen the mounting fear, sorrow, and anger sweeping the country and the world.

James Whitaker, Tyler's lifelong friend, placed his hand on the president's shoulder. Tyler looked at him with an intensity Whitaker had never seen before.

"So many dead," Tyler said. "As commander in chief, I swore an oath." His voice began to tremble. "To protect the country . . . from all enemies, both foreign and domestic. I've failed the American people."

"You did everything you could, Mr. President. The circumstances surrounding this attack were not normal."

Tyler shook his head. "Circumstances? History will only remember I was at the helm when the worst terrorist attack occurred on American soil."

"Sir, the country needs you now. The cabinet is assembled and waiting."

"There's going to be payback for this Whitaker. Big time. I swear my life on it."

*"When a distinguished but elderly scientist states that something is possible, he is almost certainly right. When he states that something is impossible, he is very probably wrong."*
–Arthur C. Clarke

# CHAPTER 42

"What do we have on this Allam Bashir?" President Tyler asked.

"All agencies are collaborating and gathering intelligence as we speak," Whitaker said.

"What we know," Serena Morales said, "is that he's originally from Afghanistan, came here on a student visa, received a degree in electrical engineering from Syracuse University, and was residing in a small apartment on the Upper East Side of Manhattan. It's safe to assume Al-Qaeda or ISIS was behind the procurement of the device."

NASA Director Beaumont quietly entered the conference room. His eyes were bloodshot and he was as pale as a ghost. All eyes turned in his direction when Tyler addressed him.

"What is it, Beaumont? Your unusual storm isn't the biggest problem we have at the moment."

"Well, Mr. President," he said nervously, "that may not be entirely true."

"What are you talking about?"

"We've been taking continuous readings since the blast. The findings could be very significant."

"Don't make me drag it out of you."

"If you remember, Mr. President, before the nuclear explosion we were discussing the detection of dark matter particles and the theory of a wormhole portal in the area."

"Yes, and I distinctly remember you stated there was not enough dark energy, or whatever you call it, for the wormhole to be viable."

"That *was* correct, Mr. President."

"Was?"

"If I can call your attention to the big screen over here." Beaumont fiddled with some controls and, with the assistance of Deborah Wright, turned on the monitor.

"This is a live feed, Mr. President, taken by telescopes from around the country, of the area one mile above the blast."

All mouths dropped open. Before the assembled group was what looked to be a shimmering circular orb, the boundaries of which were an iridescent blue and green. In the center of the orb was a cluster of stars that shone brightly but were intermittently obscured by flashes of white light resembling lightning. There was a slow, mesmerizing whirlpool-like clockwise turning of the stars within the orb.

"What are we looking at Beaumont?"

"This, Mr. President, is a portal into another universe."

More stunned silence permeated the room as all eyes focused on the swirling stars and flashing lights.

"Our measurements calculate the portal to be one half mile in diameter, Mr. President."

"It doesn't seem possible," Whitaker said.

"So you're telling me what we're looking at is the result of the nuclear explosion?" Tyler said.

"It would seem so, Mr. President. Somehow the blast was a catalyst for the production of enough negative energy to stabilize the wormhole."

"Could the people responsible for the explosion have known this would be the result?" Tyler asked.

"I suppose it's possible," Beaumont said. "Although I can't imagine how."

Tyler drummed his fingers on the table and then turned to his chief of staff. "I want to know what the hell is going on here. Bring this Dr. Cleveland from DHARPA. And also Santini and his crew. Beaumont, you stay here, too. Everyone else take a break."

Dr. Jordan found Santini wandering down the hallway that led to the elevator that would eventually lead to the exit from the bunker. She grabbed his arm.

"They won't let you just stroll on out of here. You know that."

"Why not? There's nothing left for me to do here."

"You're wrong, Detective."

Santini turned and looked her in the eye. "If these dreams were God-inspired as O'Brian seems to think, why give me these visions if I can't change the course of events? Nothing I've done has made a difference."

"You tried. The president tried. The bomb squad tried. We all did. But just maybe O'Brian is right and you're not finished with Drakin. We can't just give up. Besides, I have faith in you."

Santini shook his head. "There's that tricky word again. But you've come a long way since thinking I was crazy."

She smiled. "Actually, my initial instincts were right. But not about that. I knew there was something special about you. But the clinical side of me pushed those feelings away. I guess I've been overly cautious of getting involved with a patient."

"Well you're involved now," he said. "I know you were just doing your job, but you know more about me than anyone."

"And what I know is that you're a good man. She placed her hand on Santini's face. "You've sacrificed a lot to help people. Remember that. You've risked your life more than once. You have courage and compassion. Like I said, I knew there was something special about you."

Santini was embarrassed and at a loss for words. Finally he spoke.

"How about I fire you? No more doctor-patient etiquette to worry about." He stared into Jordan's eyes. "When I first met you, I knew also."

"Knew what?"

"That you would get me on the couch."

She laughed. Santini edged closer to her lips. She closed her eyes.

"So there you are." Salvo's voice echoed loudly in the hallway as he approached. He looked at both of them with a puzzled expression. "Am I interrupting something?"

Santini sighed. "Not at all, Salvo." He smiled at Jordan.

"We can't keep the president waiting," Salvo said.

"What are you talking about?" Santini said.

"That's why I came for you," Salvo said. "The president has called a meeting and wants our input. There's something he wants us to see."

"Well then, we'd better get going," Santini said.

Santini, Jordan and Salvo sat at the conference table with Dr. Cleveland, John Beaumont, James Whitaker, Director Carter, and, at the head of the table, President Tyler. They all stared at the swirling orb of stars on the central monitor.

"This must be the portal Father O'Brian referred to," Jordan said. "The one mentioned in his book."

"Yeah, but he said it was the portal to hell," Salvo said.

"I assume this portal–to-hell business is a metaphor," Tyler said.

"Not to hell but to another universe," Beaumont said. "That's somewhat different."

President Tyler turned toward Dr. Cleveland. "Let's start with you, Cleveland, since you deal with, shall we say, the unusual all the time. What is your take on all of this?"

Cleveland stood up, stroking his goatee, his wire-rim spectacles hanging low on his nose.

"In my twenty years of experience with the Paranormal Division of DHARPA, I've witnessed much that's unexplainable. That being said, with what I've witnessed recently, I believe what is happening now is the result of supernatural forces."

"Based on?" Tyler said.

Cleveland turned toward Beaumont. "Is there anything normal about this storm? Does it follow any of the laws of meteorological science?"

"No. But that doesn't mean it's the result of supernatural forces. When our ancestors witnessed an eclipse, they assumed supernatural forces, angry Gods, and the like because they didn't understand what they were seeing."

Dr. Cleveland nodded. "I think we're somewhat on the same page, Beaumont. Unfortunately, the word *supernatural* is tainted and misunderstood. My definition of *supernatural* is events attributed to some force beyond scientific understanding or the laws of nature."

"I can agree with that," Beaumont said.

"Prior to the nuclear blast, your team of scientists postulated the existence of a wormhole."

"That's correct," Beaumont said.

"And your team also concluded the astrophysical conditions were not conducive to opening the throat of the wormhole."

"Not enough dark matter or negative energy," said Tyler, who was concentrating intently on the exchange.

"Also correct, Mr. President," Beaumont said.

"So what has changed?" Cleveland asked.

"The blast has somehow produced enough negative energy to create what we're looking at right now."

Cleveland turned toward Santini. "Your dreams are precognitive. One day there may be a scientific explanation as to how that's possible, but at this point I think we can all concede the precognitive nature of your dreams. And you've been dreaming of an entity that has succeeded in destroying Manhattan. But it seems to me this was a steppingstone to a grander design, which was the creation of the wormhole portal we now see on the screen."

Santini stood up. "You're correct except for one important fact. The entity said it was humanity's negative thoughts and emotions that would destroy us. Although a necessary trigger, I believe it wasn't the explosion that directly created the portal."

"Then what did?" Tyler asked.

"It was the surge of negative emotions, sir," Santini said. "That's what created the dark energy needed to open the wormhole." He paused and took a deep breath. "I speak now on behalf of Father Timothy O'Brian, who is presently in the hospital as a result of this entity's attempt to kill him."

"So now we're bringing religion into the discussion?" Carter said.

Santini ignored him. "According to O'Brian, this entity has been on this planet for centuries and has manipulated the minds and hearts of men, pushing them to commit violence and wage wars. This thing feeds off the negative energy produced by these acts, and it is this negative energy that has escalated, created this storm, and, with this explosion, created enough negative emotion to open the wormhole."

Everyone looked surprised. Cleveland stroked his goatee. "That's a very interesting assertion, Detective."

"This is all mumbo jumbo," Carter said. "We have terrorists that need to be caught and brought to justice. This is a waste of time."

Cleveland spoke up. "Our research has shown thoughts and emotions do have energy, Mr. President. The frequency of the vibrations varies with the quality of the thoughts. The more explosive emotions such as anger, hatred, and fear seem to have a higher energy associated with them."

"Which is why this entity nurtures and feeds off these emotions," Santini said.

"So what the hell is this thing," Tyler said. "And what does it want? Why did it go through all this trouble to create a wormhole?"

Deborah Wright walked into the room. "I have an urgent call for Beaumont from his team at NASA, sir."

Beaumont walked to the side of the room to take the call. When he returned, his face had turned another shade of gray.

"I know that look," Tyler said. "What now?"

Beaumont began fidgeting and clearing his throat. "I believe we have an answer to your question, sir."

"And what is that?"

"The team has detected several objects moving at considerable speed within the portal of the wormhole, Mr. President."

The room became very quiet.

"Any indication as to what these objects might be?"

"Our instruments and telescopes indicate they're not asteroids or satellites or any other kind of space debris." Beaumont hesitated. "Our analysts have also determined the objects have their own propulsion system. And, Mr. President, they're headed toward the Earth."

# CHAPTER 43

President Tyler addressed the group. "We're all in agreement. We should treat these alien vessels as hostile."

"After what happened to New York, and what it did to you, we have no choice," Whitaker said.

"We need to know what this damn thing is planning next," Tyler said.

After a pause, Santini spoke up. "I might be able to help with that, sir."

Salvo and Jordan gave each other a concerned look.

"I can dream again," Santini said. "Try to find out what its next move is."

"With all due respect, Mr. President," Carter said, "I can't agree to this nonsense." He glared at Santini. "His dreams sure didn't help the people of New York."

Santini stood up. Both fists clenched, he looked like he was ready to lurch at Carter.

"Take a breath," Tyler said. "Both of you."

Dr. Cleveland stood up. "If there's anything we can learn from the detective's dream, it would be helpful. I don't see a downside."

Tyler nodded.

"I insist the detective's vitals be monitored," Dr. Jordan said.

"The rooms in the bunker hospital are high-tech," Whitaker said. "Everything you need will be made available to you."

"Make it happen, Whitaker," Tyler said.

Santini stopped pacing the hospital room and rubbed his eyes. "I know we're deep underground, but I can still hear the storm."

"I don't like this," Jordan said. "Even with the monitors, things could turn bad in a hurry." She grabbed Santini's hand. "He knows you'll try to dream about him."

"I'll be fine," Santini said. "Doing nothing isn't an option. Any information I can get about Drakin's plans is worth the risk."

"All right then," Jordan said. "But the second your vitals show any signs of distress, I'm going to awaken you. And this time, I'll be doing the slapping as opposed to your timid friend over here. Understood?"

"Understood." Santini grinned and glanced sheepishly at Salvo. His partner didn't look happy.

"So I just sit here while you dream and hope you don't stop breathing again," snapped Salvo, who now took Santini's place pacing the floor. "This is bullshit. There's nothing I can contribute. Maybe I should just leave."

"Leave?" Santini said. "I already tried that. We're a thousand feet under a mountain in a fortified bunker in the middle of who knows where." He walked over and placed his hand on Salvo's shoulder. "I understand your frustration. But you've been in this every step of the way and you've risked your life more than once. This is different from anything we're used to. We have different parts to play. And I need you here. I need your support. I need to know you have my back. That's what partners are for. Now sit down and shut up."

Salvo stared at his partner. "All right. But like the doc said, you find this fucking thing. This is personal now. He can't blow up our city, kill our people, and get away with it."

Santini could see the intensity in his partner's eyes. He looked at Jordan.

"Remember," she said. "The subconscious suggestions Drakin left deep in your mind will use your weaknesses and fears against you."

"I know." He lay on the bed. "Let's do this."

He couldn't tell if he was angry, nervous, depressed, or hopeful. His last dream was so intense it had nearly cost him his life. But it didn't matter. There was no other choice. He closed his eyes.

Either Santini's mind had become conditioned to the sound of Dr. Jordan's voice or he was emotionally exhausted or both, for just as she started the relaxation suggestions, he fell sleep.

He was sitting at a long conference table. Large monitor screens lined the concrete walls. People he recognized were staring at him. Then he abruptly slammed his fist, no not *his* fist – on the table. "Once again, General, I'm ordering an immediate DEFCON 1." He then stood up, and walked away.

He walked down a long corridor. A young man in uniform, who seemed to look familiar, trailed behind him carrying a suitcase. He came to an office and walked in. The young man stood outside the door with an anxious expression on his face, a bead of sweat sliding down his forehead.

He sat at a desk and rubbed his temples. Then he stood and began pacing around the room. He sat again and called to the young man standing outside the door.

"Bring me the suitcase, Major Custer."

The soldier complied and placed the briefcase on the desk.

"Open it."

The young man looked questioningly at him. "Of course you know, sir, you'll need the secretary's authorization codes for any actions."

"I'm aware of that, Major. Now, if you'll please open the briefcase and close the door behind you."

"Yes, Mr. President."

After punching in a set of numbers, he stood and paced the room again. Then he sat down again, covered his face with his hands, and finally punched in a second set of numbers. A button began flashing on the keyboard. Santini felt his right hand hovering over the blinking red button. He struggled to pull the hand away, but it remained there, hovering. Slowly his hand descended.

Something began to stir in Santini's mind, and abruptly the scene shifted.

He found himself in a courtroom. There were shackles on his hands and feet. He looked up at the judge and saw the blazing red eyes of the tattooed man who had tried to choke him staring back at him. The man smiled.

Then he glanced at the jury and felt a jolt in the pit of his stomach. They were the lifeless faces of all the victims he'd investigated—the pain, anguish, and horror of their moment of death as captured in Santini's memory. Their hollow eyes stared at him.

The tattooed man stood and slammed his gavel on the bench. "You've been found guilty, Detective Santini. Guilty of failure. Failure to protect all these innocent souls." The man gestured toward the jurors. "You've been found guilty of a wasted and barren existence, devoid of joy, devoid of hope, and devoid of love. No wonder your wife left you. And your crowning achievement: failure to protect the people of New York City."

Whispering at first and then rising slowly raising their voices to a crescendo, the dead jurors chanted. "Guilty, guilty, guilty."

"And your sentence," the tattooed man yelled over the escalating chant, "is to join those you've hunted. And to join all those you've allowed to die. To join them in the dragon fires of hell."

His gavel crashed down on the wooden bench, splitting it in two and releasing a blinding bolt of light. At that moment, Santini's subconscious mind unlocked and a cascade of memories came spilling out. All the sinister faces of the men he'd hunted danced in his head, beckoning to him. All their crimes—the rapes, the murders, the tortures—filled his mind in a kaleidoscope of ghoulish images.

Then everything turned black and he was inside a giant mushroom cloud that billowed and heaved with smoke and fire. Parts of the black fiery cloud coalesced and formed fierce dragons that flew directly toward him.

As they approached, he heard the horrific screams of thousands of dying souls. He closed his eyes and covered his ears to stifle the screams, but it was to no avail. The screams grew louder as the dragons drew closer, until they finally overcame him and enveloped him in a shroud of fire and darkness. He tried to breathe, but the heat was too intense. Then his heart rate skyrocketed and his chest pounded to the point where he was certain it would explode at any moment.

Dr. Jordan acted quickly. As soon as she noticed the spike in vitals, she splashed cold water onto his face. There was no response. Salvo jumped up. She then smacked his cheek and he shot upright, his eyes flying open.

"Drakin!" Santini yelled.

Jordan and Salvo breathed a sigh of relief.

"What about him?" Salvo said.

Santini stood up. "Drakin . . . He's here!"

# CHAPTER 44

President Tyler sat at the head of the long mahogany conference table. General McGuire was seated to his left, along with the joint chiefs of staff. Secretary of Defense Hessling sat at the opposite end along with the rest of the cabinet. Whitaker sat to the president's right.

"I've thought long and hard about what I'm about to say," Tyler said "and the conclusions reached haven't come easily. Our nation, our freedom, our way of life have been savagely attacked. The explosion in New York City, perpetrated by Islamic radicals, is an outrage. Thousands are dead, thousands are suffering, and our financial system has collapsed. For hundreds of years, since this great country's inception, generations of Americans have had the freedom few peoples on Earth have had the opportunity to realize. The freedom to pursue their dreams. But now fear has taken the place of dreams. During World War II, Truman made a tough decision. One that required strength and courage. A decision for which he did not require approval from the Congress."

Tyler paused as he locked eyes with each individual.

"His oath, as president, was to protect the United States of America at all costs. When he ordered the dropping of nuclear bombs on Hiroshima and Nagasaki, the Japanese surrendered immediately. Thousands of people were killed. But in the long run, had the war continued, thousands of American lives would have been lost. It was a simple decision really. Japanese bodies or American bodies. And since it was the Japanese who drew first blood, Truman felt he had the moral high ground."

Tyler once again looked around the room, locking eyes with each person, before continuing.

"I also feel I have the moral high ground. Therefore, as commander and chief, I'm ordering an immediate DEFCON 1. I want nuclear missiles cocked and pointed at all major populated cities throughout the Middle East. Tehran, Baghdad, Beirut, Cairo, Shiraz, Damascus, Istanbul, and Riyadh. The immediate threat, ladies and gentleman, is not the unknown ships traveling though the wormhole in outer space. The immediate threat is right in our own backyard, and it is Islamic jihad."

A heavy silence filled the room. Finally Whitaker spoke up.

"Mr. President, we can't blame the entire Middle East for the actions of a few crazed individuals. In World War II there were clear dividing lines. Not today. The world is a different place."

There was an intensity in Tyler's eyes Whitaker had never seen before.

"As usual, you miss my point entirely, Whitaker. Since the attack on New York, the dividing lines have become all too clear for me." A smile seemed to glide across his face. "I want to blast them and their violent religion back to the Stone Age, where they belong."

"Mr. President, with all due respect, you're ignoring the facts."

"Facts? That's all bullshit. Nobody who is sane believes in supernatural forces. The enemy I see is tangible and real, not some nebulous ghost floating in space. You cannot deny that Islamic terrorists were involved."

Tyler slammed his fist on the table. "Once again, General, I'm ordering an immediate DEFCON 1." Then he stood and walked away, leaving a stunned cabinet in his wake.

Several moments later, after General McGuire reluctantly gave the order for a DEFCON 1 alert, Whitaker finally spoke again.

"He won't launch those missiles. I know the man. It's impossible." He looked around at the grave expressions of the men and women at the conference table.

"Are you certain?" Secretary Hessling said. "Our damn missiles are awaiting a launch command."

"He would need your authentication codes," Whitaker said. "And that's not going to happen."

"But you heard him," Hessling said. "He wants to blast them back to the Stone Age."

"He's blowing off steam. We've all been rattled by what happened."

"Blowing off steam?" Hessling shook his head. "There's millions of lives at stake. His judgment is impaired, and I think he should be made to step down."

"In the middle of one of the worst crises this country has ever faced?"

"All the more reason."

Whitaker stood and locked eyes with Hessling. "What you're suggesting is drastic. There's not enough evidence to indicate the president is unfit, either physically or psychologically, to carry out his duties as commander in chief."

"We're on the brink of a possible alien invasion," Director Morales said. "Now is not the time for a constitutional crisis. You talk to him, James. He trusts you. Find out what he's really thinking."

"He must be made to step down," Hessling demanded.

Whitaker glared at him. "And I still think there's not enough evidence for that action. Let me talk to him. That's where we should start."

Deborah Wright walked into the room and asked to speak to Whitaker in private. He met her at the side of the room.

"It's the detective," she whispered in his ear. "He says he needs to speak with you right away. That it's a matter of national security. And it has to do with the psychological health of the president."

> *"Evil is a fact not to be explained away, but to be accepted;
> And accepted not to be endured, but to be conquered.
> It is a challenge neither to our reason nor to our patience,
> But to our courage."*
> *–John Andrew Holmes*

# CHAPTER 45

Drakin-Tyler sat at his desk gazing down at the keyboard that controlled the atomic launch codes.

He'd gained access to Tyler's mind through the man's anger, guilt, and desire for revenge. All he had to do now was fan the flames.

Drakin's relationship with Josef Shahid was unique in that his host was fully aware of Drakin, accepting his influence and guidance as a steppingstone to power. Tyler, of course, was not aware of his presence. The man was, unfortunately, far less corruptible than most politicians Drakin had occupied over the years. His current emotional state was all that allowed Drakin entry, and that would eventually pass. Which meant Drakin needed to act quickly.

He cared little about the fate of the Middle East. It was a mere diversion. Although the ensuing bloodshed would help in conquering the planet, the main objective was to prevent America's nuclear arsenal from being pointed at the vessels that were, at this moment, traveling through the mouth of the wormhole.

It wasn't a large fleet, six ships with about eighteen hundred beings similar to Drakin. They rode human-like bodies acquired from a planet in the Tetron Galaxy. The bodies were necessary to commandeer the ships—otherwise, they couldn't pass through the erratic electromagnetic fluctuations of the wormhole.

This would not be a war fought in the traditional sense with soldiers, bullets, bombs, and missiles, though some of that was inevitable. It would be a war fought within the mind of man. Having amassed a wealth of experience in manipulating the human mind, Drakin had narrowed down the emotions his allies would do best to focus on. Nurturing fear, greed, and hatred were at the top of the list.

His strategy was simple. Disrupt energy grids, food and water supplies. Destroy communications networks. Infiltrate government agencies, law enforcement, and military installations. And most important, manipulate world leaders. Then, like dominoes, the planet would collapse and Drakin would rule the Earth. To say, after so many centuries, that he would enjoy the enslavement of the human race and the ensuing blood bath would be an understatement.

But suddenly Drakin felt a wave of resistance from Tyler.

President Tyler couldn't comprehend what was happening to him, but he knew something was terribly wrong. He was seething at the terrorists for what they'd done to his city. And he wanted more than anything to make them pay. His anger grew like a volcano about to blow. Images of the city up in flames, and of the men, women, and children who had been mercilessly incinerated, danced before his eyes. They deserved justice. They demanded retribution.

But not this.

His mind was filled with voices as the pressure in his head escalated. "Push the button, protect America, push the button, you must avenge their deaths." His hand trembled as it hovered over the red button. "You cannot let this atrocity go unpunished."

Then something stirred from deep within. He closed his eyes and filled his mind with thoughts of his wife and child and the love he had for them. He pictured their faces, and he heard his daughter's laughter. A warm glow filled his mind and replaced the burning anger.

Suddenly, Tyler felt the pressure release from his skull. The snakes that coiled around his brain abruptly unraveled, and his mind snapped back into awareness.

He was seated at his desk with an open briefcase he recognized all too well, and his right index finger was poised directly over the ominous red button. He pulled his hand away. Then the room began to spin and he could hear banging and yelling coming from the other side of his office door. An explosion caused him to jump and the door came crashing inward.

Four armed secret service agents entered, unsure of what to do next. Whitaker followed behind and Carter was last to enter. Several Navy SEALs stood peering in from the hallway at the ready.

Whitaker looked stunned. "The missiles . . . were they launched?" he asked.

Tyler stood up. His eyes glazed over. "No, Jim. They were not."

Whitaker let out a deep exhalation. "Thank God."

"Yes, thank God." Then Tyler spoke slowly and with great effort.

"Effective immediately, under Section 3 of the Twenty-Fifth Amendment to the Constitution, I am temporarily transferring the powers and duties of my office to the vice president until such time as I can be cleared by a thorough medical examination."

"What the hell is going on here, Mr. President?" Whitaker said.

Tyler began to sway and Whitaker quickly caught his shoulder. He gave his chief of staff a puzzled look just before his eyes fluttered and he passed out.

## CHAPTER 46

Santini, Salvo, and Jordan were back in the guest quarters after Jordan had found the detective's heart rate and blood pressure to have stabilized.

"At first Whitaker didn't believe me," Santini said. "But then his expression changed and I could tell he'd noticed something strange about Tyler. He's known the president for years, and I think he knew at that moment something was very wrong about him."

"Thankfully, Tyler didn't follow through on his threat," Salvo said.

"Despite his anger and Drakin's influence, he still couldn't do it," Jordan said. "Score one for humanity."

"We were lucky," Santini said.

Salvo nodded. "Your dream was right on the mark."

"Yeah, in more ways than one."

Salvo and Jordan had insisted Santini relate every detail of his dream. At first he was reluctant to mention the courtroom scene, but he relented.

"Do you think you're the only one with crap in your subconscious mind?" Jordan said. "Unfortunately, you've seen so much of the dark side of humanity you believe that's all there is."

"I thought our patient-doctor relationship was over," Santini said.

"Apparently not. Drakin amplified your issues all out of proportion and twisted them to suit his needs. He stirred the pot of your fears. He left the seeds of guilt and doubt, and from that your subconscious created the courtroom scene. Don't you see? He knows you're a threat. He wants to make sure your mind is so screwed up you can't act against him."

"She's right," Salvo said. "You're a good detective. Maybe too good. Your ability to get inside a killer's head is uncanny. But it comes with a price. You used to have a sense of humor. You were like a second father to my kids. Now they never see you."

Santini stared at Salvo for a very long time. "Great," he said. "Now I have two psychiatrists."

"The majority of people are good and decent," Jordan said. "You seem to have lost sight of that."

Santini chuckled, then grimaced. "You haven't seen what I have. What do you think is driving this storm? Why do you think Drakin has become so powerful?" Santini felt heat rush to his face. "If I'm down in a pit, you both have your heads in the clouds. And at least I wasn't disappointed. God wouldn't intervene to save New York. Even the Astrolites, the so-called emissaries of God, sat idly by. Score one for free will."

"The negative effects of the dream are lingering," Jordan said, "Like a bad hangover. Try to calm down."

"Calm down? How can I calm down when everyone around me is blind to the truth of what humanity has become?"

"He's still influencing you," Salvo said. "He has your head tangled up in a knot."

Jordan walked up to Santini and got right in his face. Then she spoke with an intensity that took him by surprise.

"There's something going on here, and it's something that's been puzzling me. What's your connection to Drakin? Why can you dream about him and see through his host's eyes? It has to be something more than your intuition in tracking down criminals. And I have an idea I'd like to test."

For a moment, Santini's anger subsided. "And what idea is that, Doctor?"

"I can't tell you, because it would effect the outcome. But it involves hypnosis."

Salvo frowned. "Hasn't he been through enough with these nightmares?"

"Hypnosis is very different from dreaming," Jordan said. "In hypnosis, you are in a very deep level of relaxation, but your mind is in a state of hyper-awareness and you are conscious of everything that's happening."

"What's the purpose of this?" Salvo said.

"In general terms, hypnosis allows the subject to access memories that are buried deep in the subconscious." She looked at Santini. "And it requires a high level of trust on your part."

Santini was still agitated, but also intrigued.

"It won't be easy," she said. "And I wouldn't put you through this if I didn't think it was important."

Santini stared at her. "Sure. Fine. Why not?" He looked around. "There's no place to lie down."

"Actually, I'd prefer you sit in a chair."

"Let's do it then."

Santini sat straight up in the chair with Jordan directly across. Salvo sat off to the side with an apprehensive expression.

"Take slow, deep breaths, Detective. Follow the sound of my voice. Let your body completely relax. Feel the tension drain from each muscle. Your body is asleep, but your mind is keenly aware of everything."

After a few minutes, she took a different tack.

"I want you to go back to another time in your life, when you were a young boy. It's your twelfth birthday. Can you see yourself at that age, Detective?"

Santini nodded.

"Your father has tickets to the baseball game at Yankee Stadium. Are you excited, Anthony?"

He smiled. "It's my first major league game—the Yankees and the Dodgers."

"What's the weather like?"

"The sun is warm. There's blue skies."

"You and your father stop at the neighborhood bake shop to buy doughnuts."

Santini licked his lips. "Mr. Nunziato has the best doughnuts in town."

"Can you smell the doughnuts, Anthony?"

Santini sniffed the air and nodded. "The warm jelly doughnuts are my favorite."

"Then what happens?"

"Mr. Nunziato goes to the back of the shop to get a fresh batch of doughnuts. My father puts his hand on my shoulder and says, 'Guess who's pitching today . . . Tommy Rose.' Wow, I say. He's my favorite pitcher." Then the expression on Santini's face changed and his body clenched.

"Then what happens, Anthony?"

"I see an arm, outstretched. Off to the side. There's a gun." Santini began breathing deeply.

"What happens next, Anthony?"

"Then . . . pop, pop, pop . . . I jump." Tears filled his eyes. "Blood everywhere." Tears rolled down his face. "Please, don't die. Don't leave me."

"What are you feeling, Anthony?"

"I'm so afraid. Please don't die."

"What else do you feel, Detective?"

Santini began to tremble. "There's something else there."

"Where?"

"All around me."

"What is it?"

"I don't know. I can feel it. It's cold, black." Santini put his hands over his head. "A shadow . . . covering me!" He grimaced. "A sucking sensation . . . inside my head. I try to fight it. Get away from me! Get away!" He screamed.

"It's all right, Anthony," she said. "Take deep breaths. Listen to the sound of my voice. You're safe now. It can't hurt you. The black shadow is gone. Just breathe."

Santini's body continued shaking.

"Just keep breathing slowly. Long deep breaths. Listen to my voice."

Gradually he stopped trembling.

"You're going to awaken now, Detective. Whenever you're ready, you can open your eyes."

Santini's eyes fluttered open, and he abruptly stood up and walked toward the door.

"Where are you going?" Jordan said. "We have to talk about this."

"I'm done talking. I need a drink, and I'm going to find one in this damn hole in the ground."

He slammed the door behind him.

He walked aimlessly through the dimly lit maze-like tunnels of the underground bunker, feeling as if he were wandering through the deep passages of his own subconscious mind. Even though he was a mile underground, the clamoring voices in the storm had found him, gnawing and badgering, trying to weaken whatever resolve he'd mustered.

He'd never been claustrophobic, but now he could feel the oppressive weight of millions of tons of granite pressing down. And the pressure squeezed unsettling pictures from the inner recesses of his mind.

The images of his father being shot surfaced again, along with a new memory. His anger boiled.

It was Drakin. All along. Orchestrating a random murder to quell his appetite. Killing his father so he could feed off the young boy's fear and sorrow. He had left his mark. Left his footprint in Santini's mind.

He had been chasing Drakin his whole life.

And Jordan was right. Drakin knew him better than he knew himself. What he'd said was true—the changes had been slow and gradual but relentless.

He had no faith. His life was devoid of love and joy. The victims of his cases haunted him. His clash with Drakin as a child had caused his obsession with chasing evil and eventually led to his ability to see Drakin in his dreams.

Santini wandered down another long corridor and came to a large metal door. The sign above read "Radiation Decontamination Area."

In a way, his mind had become contaminated by Drakin. Poisoned with negative thoughts and negative energy. As a child and now as well. He wished there were a decontamination room for that. And his friends were right. Drakin was still influencing him. Right here and right now. And Santini had allowed it.

He closed his eyes and recalled what the Astrolite had said. "I am what you and your race have the potential to become." He thought about the beautiful shimmering orb.

Then Father O'Brian's words came to him. "In your outstretched hand you held the staff, and you were pointing it upward. But what was most interesting to me were the thousands of people who seemed to have their eyes closed, concentrating intently."

*Concentrating on what?*

Santini abruptly turned about and, with a quickened pace, retraced his steps to the room where he'd left Salvo and Jordan.

"Did you find your scotch?" Salvo said.

"Something better. I need to speak with President Tyler. Now."

## CHAPTER 47

An emergency cabinet meeting had been convened and the men and women at the conference table waited anxiously for the vice president to appear.

Director Morales leaned next to Whitaker, who was seated beside her. "Do you think he's up to the task?" she asked.

"Vice President Sanchez is highly intelligent. IQ off the charts. And he's a shrewd politician." He hesitated. "But he's not a leader. Overthinks everything."

Finally, the vice president's image was projected onto the screen from another secure location. "How is the president?" he asked.

"President Tyler is undergoing just about every conceivable test there is," Whitaker said. "Other than fatigue and a headache, there seems to have been no permanent effects as a result of the alien intervention."

"That's a blessing," Sanchez said. "What security measures are being taken?"

"Security?" Whitaker shrugged. "There's no security against alien psychological attacks on the government. That being said, all personnel have been instructed to report any and all unusual behaviors immediately."

"So we don't know exactly where this thing is," Sanchez said.

"I'm afraid not."

There was a long pause. "That's not very comforting. I've instructed my closest aides to observe my behavior very closely. What happened to the president could have happened to any one of us."

"Thankfully, he didn't succumb to this alien's pressures," Whitaker said.

Sanchez glanced at the tracking monitors. "How much longer?"

"The alien vessels are estimated to be within ninety-five minutes of the mouth of the wormhole," General McGuire said, "at which time they'll enter the sovereign airspace of the United States of America."

"What is the present consensus regarding a missile strike?"

"Beaumont's team postulates that the physics within the wormhole would make an accurate missile launch difficult," Whitaker said.

Sanchez looked thoughtful. "What do you think we should do, Whitaker?"

The chief of staff looked around the room. "Everyone agrees it's worth a try, sir. At least detonations within the wormhole shouldn't affect our atmosphere."

Sanchez nodded. "I concur."

"Of course, you'll need to contact world leaders," Whitaker said. "Especially the nuclear powers. Give them our appraisal of the situation and our intention to utilize our nuclear warheads."

Sanchez nodded. "Yes, of course."

"You should be able to assure them, based on this alien's attempt to subvert our nuclear arsenal and the prior destruction of New York, that our visitors are hostile."

Sanchez seemed lost in thought. "I don't think this is the way mankind wanted its first alien encounter to turn out."

"We have no choice," Whitaker said.

President Sanchez sighed. "All right, General. Send them a welcoming committee."

*"He who does not believe in miracles is not a realist."*
*—Anton Rupert*

# CHAPTER 48

The headache had dissipated, and President Tyler felt better. All tests having come back negative, he was deemed to be in excellent health. Whitaker had spoken with him that morning and explained what had happened. He was thankful to know he wasn't losing his mind. But he couldn't emerge from the residual fog.

The experience had shaken him to the core. What was to prevent the same thing from happening to Vice President Sanchez, now president? And who knew how many beings like the one he'd battled were coming though the wormhole? He shuddered to think of the consequences.

There was a knock on the door and Whitaker popped his head in. "How are you feeling, Mr. President?"

"I'm fine, Whitaker, but I believe I would be even better sipping a glass of scotch. There must be a stash somewhere in this gopher hole."

Whitaker smiled. "I'll be right back, Mr. President."

Ten minutes later, Whitaker walked back in. "I just happened upon a bottle of GlenDronach 1996, a gift from the British prime minister."

"That will do very nicely, and please join me. God knows you deserve it."

Tyler poured two glasses and handed one to Whitaker.

"Thank you, Mr. President."

"Can you give me an update?"

"We've decided to launch an attack while the alien vessels are within the wormhole."

"And what do the scientists think our chances are?"

Whitaker frowned. "Fifty-fifty. We fear the missiles will penetrate the wormhole but their trajectory will be altered upon entering it."

"And if that happens?"

"Once the alien ships come through and enter the airspace over New York, we've no idea what their defensive or offensive capabilities are."

"And what about launching additional warheads at that time?"

"We're debating this, Mr. President. The fallout from exploding nuclear missiles in the upper atmosphere may spread to other parts of the city or even beyond, and the winds from this storm will make matters worse. The environmentalist contingent is going nuts."

Tyler shook his head. "Nobody wants further radiation contamination, but the fate of the entire world is at stake. Let's hope our missiles do the job before we're faced with that decision."

There was a knock on the door. "You have guests, Mr. President," Whitaker said as he went to the door. "I met them on their way here as I was procuring the GlenDronach. I thought you wouldn't mind hearing what they have to say."

Santini walked into the room, followed by Dr. Cleveland and Beaumont.

Tyler smiled. "You made a valiant effort to save the city, Detective. But I'm afraid we all fell short."

"I wish there had been a different outcome, sir," Santini said.

"How are you feeling, Mr. President?" Beaumont asked.

"I've been better."

"You're not responsible for what happened," Santini said. "My guess is the entity used tremendous pressure on you."

The president shifted uncomfortably and took a long pull on his scotch glass. "Please, Whitaker. Find these gentlemen some glasses. They all look like they could use a drink."

"Is it that obvious?" Santini said.

Tyler smiled but, then his expression changed. "If I hadn't experienced firsthand this alien's influence, I would otherwise have to conclude you belong back at Blackthorne, Detective."

Whitaker handed each of the men a glass of scotch, and they sat in a semicircle facing Tyler. "Drakin," Santini said.

"What?" Tyler said.

"Drakin. That's its name."

"And how do you know this? From your dreams?"

"Yes."

Tyler looked perplexed. "I still find it hard to understand how thoughts and emotions are responsible for opening this wormhole. And what is this barrier, anyway?"

"The barrier is the nature of space/time itself," Beaumont said. "Unless the curvature of space/time is acted upon by an intense application of energy, there can be no opening of a wormhole that might exist in the area. But my team doesn't believe it was solely the nuclear explosion that changed the nature of space/time above New York."

"Then what was it?" Tyler asked.

Dr. Cleveland cleared his throat, shifting attention to him. "I've thought a lot about that, Mr. President. Imagine thoughts and emotions not as just neuronal firings within the brain but as real energy wavelengths. And the frequency of that energy is determined by the quality of the thoughts. Take carbon monoxide gas. It's invisible, colorless, odorless, and yet it's partially responsible for destroying the ozone layer. In the same way carbon monoxide has created a hole in our atmosphere, negative thought energy has created the portal."

Santini put down his glass. "Thoughts are more powerful than we've ever imagined, Mr. President."

Cleveland nodded in agreement, his black eyes shining. "Especially the totality of thoughts generated on the planet."

"The collective mind of man is the key," Santini said. "It is the battleground for fighting these aliens."

"What do you mean?" Tyler said.

Santini stood up. "To fight them, we must all be brought together, Mr. President. If only for a brief moment. As many minds as possible, concentrating and focusing our energy, thinking of only the positive attributes of life and of humankind. Thinking about all the things we hold dear as part of the human family."

"There must be a tsunami of positive thought energy," Cleveland said, "focused at a single point and at a single moment in time."

Tyler seemed lost in thought. After a long pause he looked up. "Why are you telling me this? I'm not the president. You should be telling Sanchez your theories." He shook his head. "Just why are you three here?"

"If we are to avoid an invasion of Earth," Santini said, "you must reinstate yourself as president of the United States."

Tyler leaned back in his chair and gazed intently at Santini. "You have my attention, Detective."

Santini locked eyes with the president. "With all due respect to the vice president, he is not the orator you are. Your ability to stir emotions and minds and connect on a deep level is remarkable."

"It's true," Whitaker said. "You're loved and admired not only in this country but around the world."

"You can convince the people of the Earth to align together," Santini said. "For their own survival." He paused. "It is your destiny to deliver your greatest speech, Mr. President. A speech that can save our planet."

Silence hung in the room. Tyler took another long pull from his glass, and Santini could hear the clinking of the ice cubes. Tyler looked intently at Santini.

"And how do you know this coming together of minds will have an effect on the wormhole?"

Santini hesitated. "Well, we don't know for sure."

"I think it would be prudent to have a backup plan, sir," Cleveland said. "Just in case the warheads are ineffectual."

"I would concur," Beaumont said. "I've seen too much recently that questions my notion of what is possible and what is real. The storm, the wormhole, a mind-manipulating alien, and now this damn staff."

"What staff?" Tyler asked.

Beaumont glanced at Santini. "I think I'll defer to the detective, sir."

Santini sat back down. "It's an ancient artifact discovered in an archaeological dig by Father O'Brian and kept secret by the Vatican. Until recently. This entity wants it. And will kill to get it."

"We've had our team analyze the thing, Mr. President," Beaumont said. "Using every method of physical analysis we know of, from X-ray to MRI to spectral analysis. It looks like an old piece of wood on the surface, but it's virtually indestructible. It's made from a material we've never seen before."

"Apparently, Drakin is afraid of the staff," Santini said.

"Why?" Tyler asked.

"Father O'Brian's thinks it can focus positive energy. And if this is true, I can use it against Drakin." Santini took a deep breath. "I must return to ground zero. It's where this all started for me."

Tyler and Whitaker exchanged glances.

"And what about the radiation exposure at ground zero?" Whitaker asked.

"I'm willing to take my chances," Santini said.

Tyler put down his glass and looked intently at Santini.

"When this entity, or Drakin, as you call it, was pressuring me, the suggestions were so strong I almost pushed that button. But suddenly, my thoughts shifted and focused on the love I have for my wife and child. It was then the pressure released."

"And that's how Drakin and his allies can be defeated, sir," Santini said.

Tyler became quiet.

"So do you feel up to it, Mr. President?" Santini asked.

Tyler looked at Whitaker. "Do I have the Constitution behind me on this?"

"You voluntarily stepped down from office, and since you've been cleared by your physicians, there's nothing in the Constitution to prevent you from reinstating yourself as commander in chief of the United States."

Tyler folded his hands in front of him. "I'm willing to try what you're suggesting, Detective."

"There is one other important detail, sir," Santini said. "When I do use the staff, it must be synchronized with your speech."

"How do you know this?"

"Just my intuition, sir."

Tyler nodded. "We will provide transportation for you as near to ground zero as possible, and I'll make arrangements for an address to the nation."

Santini, Cleveland, and Beaumont rose to leave.

"You must address everyone, sir," Santini said. "Not just Americans."

Tyler nodded. "What you are asking will not be so easy, Detective, but I will do what I can." He walked over and shook Santini's hand. "Good luck, Detective."

"Thank you, Mr. President."

## CHAPTER 49

Drakin's energy consciousness skittered through the heavy lead bunker doors the moment they were opened. Lead always posed a problem for him, and in his weakened condition he didn't even attempt to pass through.

His battle with Tyler had left him drained. He'd attempted to exert too much influence on him, and he could feel the vibrations of his ethereal body pulsating at an erratic level.

Drakin knew they might attempt a strike on the ships, so he'd attempted to distract them by forcing a nuclear launch into the Middle East. He wasn't sure if the humans could score a direct hit within the wormhole. And he didn't like not being sure.

Fortunately, as soon as the vessels passed though the wormhole, hyper-drive would be initiated and it would be impossible for the humans to target the ships. This quelled his anger. Although he still had a loose end to tie up: his pal Santini.

But right now his main priority was his own well-being. He needed to be re-energized.

Drakin floated across an open field and through a short stretch of forest and emerged onto a little-used dirt road. He perceived the black Hummer and swirled in its direction. When he was near the vehicle, the door swung open and it was then that he could see the wide grin of Josef Shahid.

Due to Drakin's weakened electromagnetic state, the joining was a little more difficult than in the past. Shahid's body trembled, but eventually the shaking subsided, and with his energy tentacles securely in place, he accelerated the Hummer down the road.

Drakin-Shahid pushed the Hummer to the limit, racing at eighty mph, slicing through the wind and rain, skidding here and sliding there, the vehicle straining to clutch the road.

The storm had intensified since the creation of the wormhole. The rain continued nonstop, and lightning bolts incinerated trees, leaving gaping holes in the earth.

They were fifty miles outside New York City. Except for an occasional fire truck, ambulance, police car or National Guard vehicle, the highways were empty. People were hunkered in their homes, afraid, trying to figure out how to survive the storm.

Drakin was not overly concerned about the radiation fallout at ground zero. His energy consciousness would not be adversely affected in the short term. Josef Shahid's body might get a little toasty, but a slow death gave him plenty of time to evacuate his host. It was the sudden death of a host that could cause him to be trapped inside, which would not be good. Not good at all.

Drakin had been thinking a lot about the staff. One of the few mistakes he'd ever made was letting Moses escape with it centuries ago. But that was just another Chapter in a long saga of battles for the mind of man. Drakin had always relied on hatred and the mob mentality to create wars and chaos. Little by little, he'd created divisions and suspicions among the nations and races of the world. Thanks to him, throughout history human blood had flowed like water.

But it had taken longer than expected to destroy the barrier, due to the interventions of the Astrolites with Buddha, Christ, and Gandhi, just a few in a long list of annoyances. Still, they slowed his project down only temporarily, and he was very patient. In the end, the human mind always faltered, lost traction, and skidded back into the negative emotions.

Drakin didn't want any more surprises, so he was determined to stop the troublesome detective. He didn't know if Santini had discovered the key that would unlock the power of the staff. And even if he did, Drakin was convinced the humans couldn't muster it up. They were too steeped in negative energy.

His allies would come through the portal shortly, and Drakin wanted to be ready. He thought about the last conversation he'd overheard between Tyler and Whitaker concerning the transport of Santini to ground zero. He sensed the detective would go back there. And Drakin was sure he'd have the staff with him.

The Hummer crossed into the City of New York and eventually onto the island of Manhattan, where it came to a sudden stop. Drakin could wait no longer. He quickly got out of the vehicle and climbed atop a pile of rubble. He grinned as he gazed at the apocalyptic scene, proud of his handiwork. Fires had erupted everywhere, and thunder and lightning crashed all around him. Drakin-Shahid squinted, his face pelted by the black ashen rain.

He inhaled deeply and filled his lungs. The smell of death was exhilarating, and Drakin's tendrils of awareness tingled with excitement. Thousands were dead, but many still survived, barely alive, trapped beneath the rubble of what were once skyscrapers.

It would not even be necessary for him to absorb the energy of any particular individual. The energy of fear, pain, and suffering was so thick in the air that all Drakin had to do was allow it to wash over him. The last time he could remember feasting in this fashion was in the gas chambers of Auschwitz.

He unraveled himself from the brain of Josef Shahid and let his energy consciousness float just above the man's head. Then he extended his tentacles of awareness outward and immediately felt an intense wave of negative energy surge through his tendrils.

He stayed like this for several minutes, savoring the fear and horror that permeated the air until he was certain his ethereal essence could take no more.

No one could stop him now.

Drakin slid smoothly back into the brain of Josef Shahid. It was time to bring all his hard work to fruition. His newly invigorated tentacles tingled with power as he waited for Anthony Santini.

## CHAPTER 50

When President Tyler walked into the conference room, all eyes turned toward him.

"Esteemed colleagues," he said, "unless there's an objection, I've been examined thoroughly and have been cleared to resume my duties as president and commander in chief of the United States of America."

The video feed of acting President Tom Sanchez couldn't mask the look of surprise on his face. After a long silence, he spoke.

"You have my complete support, Mr. President." Actually, Sanchez looked relieved.

Tyler nodded. "I know this has been difficult, Tom, but I want you to know I, and your country, appreciate everything you've done in this time of crisis." He turned to face his cabinet and joint chiefs. "Update."

"We're ready at this moment to launch fifty warheads into the wormhole at the five moving targets," General McGuire said. "Awaiting your command, sir."

Tyler looked around the room at the serious faces.

"I know this is difficult. And there is no one here who would have preferred a peaceful welcoming of our visitors more than I would have. It is sad that our first contact with life from outside our galaxy is an act of war. But we've debated this at length. Manhattan has been destroyed. Given the nature of this alien, its power, and intentions, we really don't have a choice. We must act on behalf of our own survival." Tyler shook his head. "May God forgive us."

General McGuire handed the phone to the president.

"This is President Reginald Tyler, code Sirius 7472. Initiate launch, Colonel."

After he spoke those words, a heavy silence filled the room. Everyone was aware of what was at stake. Grim faces watched as the first set of missiles appeared as little green triangles on the radar tracking monitors. President Tyler thought about the nature of the aliens riding inside those starships, his mind still keenly aware of what had been done to him.

The triangles continued inching slowly across the screen until the warheads entered the portal. All present held their breath.

Then . . . nothing. The missiles disappeared from the radar. No explosions were detected. Within a few seconds, it was obvious to everyone that the initial attack had failed. The missiles had fizzled out. The alien vessels continued their approach.

"Initiating second wave of missiles," McGuire said. "We've altered the trajectory pattern."

They all watched the monitor as the little green triangles once again inched toward the wormhole. And once again they disappeared from sight.

A long silence permeated the room. President Tyler finally broke it.

"When our visitors pass through the mouth of that wormhole, I want every available missile pointed at them."

"We've discussed the danger of using our nuclear arsenal in the atmosphere above the city," Whitaker said.

"I realize that," Tyler said, "but if they cross that threshold with whatever weapons they have blazing, we will have no choice." He stood up. "And now, ladies and gentleman, it's time to return to the White House. If need be, the bunker below the White House is safe enough. The American people, and the world, need to see that the American government is no longer in hiding. I'll be contacting all foreign leaders asking them to prepare for war. I'll also be making a live address to all people on Earth capable of receiving our feeds, the exact time of which will be announced in advance. Everyone needs to know the truth about what is happening."

One by one, Tyler locked eyes with everyone present.

"We will not go down without a fight."

# CHAPTER 51

"And so you're just going to march onto ground zero, with no plan, where the earth is still simmering, holding nothing but your stick in your hand?" Salvo said.

"Very funny, Salvo, but I told you I had a gut feeling about this. Ground zero, and specifically the Empire State Building, has been a consistent focal point in my dreams. Now isn't the time to ignore my instincts."

"We're coming," Jordan insisted.

"Unfortunately, arrangements have been made for only me to be transported to ground zero."

She placed her hands on her hips and glared at him. "Is that so?"

Lieutenant James Giffords walked into the room. "Copter is ready. Are you three ready to take another ride?"

Santini gazed at his friends. "Apparently, you two have made other arrangements."

Jordan's eyes twinkled. "A psychiatrist can be very persuasive when her mind is set on something."

Santini knew when to throw in the towel. At least for now. "Give us five minutes, Lieutenant. There's someone I need to speak with first."

He called the hospital, and after a few moments he heard the sound of the old priest's voice.

"You sound much better than the last time we spoke," Santini said.

"My sister used to be a nurse. She won't leave me alone for a second. If she doesn't stop hounding me, I'm going to wind up on Dr. Jordan's couch."

Santini smiled. "I wanted to apologize for what I said during our last conversation. I know you were only trying to help."

"There's nothing to apologize for, Detective."

"I think I know who the people you sensed in your vision were," Santini said. He told O'Brian about the president's upcoming speech.

O'Brian thought for a moment. "I'll call the pope and ask him to rally spiritual leaders from around the world in leading a mass prayer at the time of the president's speech. And I'll pray for you, Anthony."

"Thank you, Father." He ended the call and turned to Jordan. "How did you know?"

"Know what?"

"That Drakin manipulated some lowlife to kill my father so he could feed off of my emotions. That he'd left his imprint in my subconscious. And that was how we were connected."

She tapped her temple and smiled. "You're not the only with intuitive abilities, Detective."

The helicopter carrying Santini, Salvo, and Jordan approached what was left of Manhattan Island from the southeast. They sat in silence as the devastating scene slowly became visible through the dark clouds. Nothing could have prepared them. Even Giffords, the tough Navy SEAL, was clearly finding it difficult to look at.

Between the East River and the Hudson River, the twenty square miles that once made up the totality of Manhattan Island was burning like a scene out of Dante's *Inferno*. Fires blazed out of control from ruptured gas and oil lines, and each flash of lightning lit up another grisly scene of total devastation.

There was no Times Square, no Central Park, no Rockefeller Center, no New York Stock Exchange, no United Nations building, no Museum of Natural History, no Theater District, no skyscrapers, and, of course, no people. In place of the Manhattan skyline were large remnants of buildings twisted into deformed metal and concrete skeletons that billowed smoke and fire into a dark canopy of ash and soot. In place of people was a mass graveyard that stretched for as far as the eye could see.

It was estimated that of the one hundred and fifty thousand who died in the blast, thousands had been buried, some possibly alive, beneath the ruble of the fallen buildings. Unfortunately, it was still deemed unsafe to begin recovery efforts.

Santini reflected back to his nightmare. The reality was much worse.

Giffords spotted the landing site adjacent to the Greenpoint National Guard post. The aircraft bucked and weaved in the relentless wind, and the passengers held on tightly as they made their descent. Ashen soot hung like a black shroud in the air and visibility was poor, but the skilled pilot deftly maneuvered his aircraft and set the bird gently down.

Salvo looked like he couldn't wait to get his feet on the ground.

"Sorry we couldn't get you any closer, sir," Giffords said to Santini, "but the erratic explosions sending fire plumes into the sky could prove devastating to a helicopter." He paused and shook his head. "I lost close friends in that crash at the Empire State Building."

"I'm sorry," Santini said. "They were very brave."

Giffords held out his hand. "These are strange times. I don't know why you're here, Detective, but I wish you success."

Santini nodded as he clasped the lieutenant's hand.

The three were then greeted by National Guard Commander Sheldon Deal. He looked tired, wet, and worn out.

"I've instructions from the White House to escort you and your friends to the Williamsburg Bridge," he said.

They followed the commander into his Jeep and rode in silence through the deserted neighborhood of Greenpoint, Brooklyn.

Santini sighed as he looked around, hints of recognition surfacing from his memories. "I was brought up here," he said. "On Bushwick Avenue and Frost Street. Life was simpler back then, at least for a time."

"Life, unfortunately, is even simpler now, Detective," Commander Deal said. "In fact, the only life at ground zero are the rats, come out of their subterranean holes, and even they're in pretty bad shape."

"The only thing I hate more than a rat," Salvo said, "is a bunch of rats."

After about ten minutes, the Jeep came to a stop next to a Hummer. It was painted Army camouflage.

Deal pointed at the vehicle. "Here's your transportation."

"What are the present radiation levels at ground zero?" Jordan asked.

"Hard to say exactly," Deal said. "It depends on where the readings are taken. Suffice it to say that exposure for just forty-five minutes would not be good for your health. More than forty-five minutes would slowly, and inevitably, be deadly. I suggest you take advantage of the hazmat suits in the back of the Hummer."

The three exited the Jeep, and Deal wished them luck and drove away.

They each pulled a suit out of the back of the Hummer. It was Level A hazmat gear, with a full face piece and a self-enclosed respirator designed for protection against radiation particles in the air. Luckily, both Salvo and Santini had some experience with hazmat gear.

"Why don't you two help me get this on first?" Santini said.

In just a few minutes, Santini was suited up.

"What kind of reception are you getting with your cell phone?" Santini asked.

Salvo checked. "Seems to be working at the moment."

"Good. Call Commander Deal and have him pick you up." He jumped into the front seat of the Hummer, cranked the engine, and peeled out onto the bridge.

## CHAPTER 52

Of the nine bridges and four tunnels that form the main arteries to the island of Manhattan, only the Williamsburg Bridge, crossing the East River from Brooklyn, was still relatively passable. But barely.

The cables supporting the old suspension bridge creaked and groaned as the cracked anchor terminals struggled to hold fast. The entire structure swayed precariously from side to side, the wind and rain continuing its assault, slashing relentlessly at the old damaged bridge.

Normally, the seven thousand three hundred-foot long structure carried more than one hundred and ten thousand cars each day, a commuter frenzy. On this night, however, only one solitary vehicle raced across the roadway.

Santini's adrenaline was pumping as the Hummer sped over the rough and broken pavement. Lightning bolts flashed all around him, and the howling wind threatened to cast the vehicle into the East River, now a roiling, tumultuous sea of blackness. He didn't know what the gates of hell looked like, but he was certain it couldn't be any worse than where he was headed.

He thought about his two friends. He didn't like what he'd done. They didn't deserve to be tricked that way. But he was damned if he was going to let them get anywhere near this dangerous area. Just because he was risking his life didn't mean they had to as well. They'd get over it.

The windshield wipers slammed furiously back and forth, struggling to keep the ashen rain from obscuring his vision. In the distance he could see fires interspersed across the horizon.

He pushed the accelerator to the floor and the Hummer lurched forward. It rattled and bounced, swerving over the cracked and pitted roadway, Santini holding tight to the steering wheel. Finally, after what seemed like an eternity, he made it to the other side of the bridge.

He stopped the Hummer and looked around. There were no street signs anywhere. In fact, there were no streets at all. He remembered that should be Delancey Street, but all he could see was smoldering concrete and twisted metal spread across the landscape. Explosions from broken gas lines filled the air with smoke that made it all the more difficult to see.

He knew the city—every street—but still he hesitated. There were no familiar landmarks. Finally, he chose a direction and maneuvered slowly through the fallen buildings, stopping often to navigate past piles of rubble and fires that erupted spontaneously.

After a few minutes, he once again brought the Hummer to a stop. He looked around hoping to see something recognizable. There was nothing. He looked back toward the direction from which he'd come to get his bearings, but the smoke-filled air made visibility impossible. He got out and managed to climb onto the roof of the vehicle.

From atop the Hummer, he slowly scanned the horizon in a 360-degree sweep, but all he could see were burning buildings and fires spewing smoke and flames.

On his third sweep, just before he was ready to get back into the Hummer, he stopped. In the distance, amid the rubble and hanging upside down from a twisted metal pole, was a street sign. He climbed back into the vehicle.

It took several minutes of maneuvering, but the Hummer finally came to a stop near the twisted pole. He got out and walked over piles of debris, losing his footing several times, until he reached the sign. He picked it up. The metal was partially melted and blackened. He rubbed away the black soot that covered the sign to reveal three letters, *Fif.* He stared at the letters and thought for a minute, and then it came to him: Fifth Avenue. The remnants of the building couldn't be too far off. He climbed back into the Hummer and continued in a northerly direction.

After several minutes of scouring the area in the vicinity of the sign, he spotted it.

The two hundred-foot spire of the Empire State Building lay on its side, broken and smoldering, the old edifice spread out in all directions from where it had collapsed.

He climbed out of the Hummer and walked over to the spire and then punched in the numbers that would signal to Whitaker and the president that he was ready. He prayed the signal would go through.

He retrieved his staff from the vehicle, and as he walked back toward the broken spire, an odor of gas caught his attention. He turned toward the smell and saw a sudden bright flash—the Hummer exploded. And then a fireball propelled him into the air. He landed face first on the ground, shrapnel from the truck shattering his leg and tearing through his hazmat suit.

Stunned, he tried to move, but his body didn't respond. He lay there, semi-conscious, dizzy, burned, and bleeding, with the hazmat suit smoldering. Finally, with great effort, he turned his head and gazed at the collapsed spire.

His only thought was of how beautiful the spire had been every Christmas, adorned in bright red and green lights.

He lay there for a long time, the ringing in his ears gradually subsiding. In the distance, he thought he could hear the sound of an approaching vehicle. The sound grew louder. Then the engine stopped.

"Well, look at you, Santini. That will teach you to leave your friends behind." Salvo gently turned his partner onto his back, and Santini saw the look of alarm on his face. "What the hell happened?"

"Gas line explosion," Santini said, his voice faltering.

"Quick, Salvo," Jordan ordered. "Help me get his suit off. The leg is bleeding badly. We need to tie it off."

Salvo used a knife to cut the hazmat suit open. Santini grimaced as they peeled it off his burned leg.

"How did you find me?" Santini said.

"Tracking device on the Hummer," Jordan said.

She rummaged through a first-aid kit for a tourniquet and cinched it at the top of his thigh. Then she placed ointment and bandages over the burned parts of his body and gave him three injections.

"Nothing to make me sleep, I hope," Santini said.

"Painkiller, antibiotics, and something to counter radiation poisoning," Jordan said. "Your respirator is damaged. You have about forty minutes before your lungs fry. If we leave right now, the exposure should be manageable. Your leg is shattered and you've already lost a lot of blood. Let's get him into the Hummer, Salvo."

Santini shook his head. "No!"

"If you want to save your leg and live," she said, "we need to get you out of here right now."

"My staff!"

Salvo found it in the rubble, undamaged.

"Help me stand," Santini demanded.

"Not a smart idea, Detective," Jordan said.

Santini looked at both of his friends and smiled. "Thank you for coming to my aid. And I'm sorry I tricked you like that. But my signal to the president has been sent. You can help me finish what I came here to do if you'd like. Otherwise, please hand me my staff."

Salvo and Jordan exchanged glances. The doctor shook her head, and Salvo placed the staff in Santini's hand.

"Okay, fine," Salvo said. "But can we just speed things up a bit?"

As they bent forward to help lift Santini, a sudden explosion sent them flying through the air.

Drakin loved grenades, and he'd become particularly skillful in throwing them accurately. He wasn't happy he had to come here to deal with this, but he didn't want to take any chances that Santini would interfere with his plans.

Drakin-Shahid walked over to Santini's body, now lying facedown in the rubble. Salvo and Jordan, who had been standing in front of him, had taken the impact of the blast. Drakin-Shahid flipped Santini's body around so he could see his adversary's face.

"Detective Santini," he said. "Still alive. So persistent."

With a swift powerful movement, he kicked Santini's leg. The detective's eyes fluttered and then flew open wide in obvious agony. He tried to move but dropped his head back down.

"What, no fight left? I was at least hoping for a little clever conversation before I kill you. It's kind of lonely out here. Just us and the hungry rats, who are eagerly anticipating nibbling away at your body."

Santini managed to lift his head. "It was you, wasn't it?"

Drakin-Shahid laughed. "You are quite slow. I was wondering how long it would take for the great detective to figure it out. It was nothing personal. But you looked so happy that day and I just couldn't stand it. Maybe if you hadn't been foaming with excitement I would have chosen someone else." Drakin-Shahid laughed again. "Your father's death was your fault, Detective."

Santini seethed. "You'll never succeed. People will never stop fighting back."

"Really, I'd have never thought of you as an optimist. But I know your kind better than you do. I've lived untold centuries inside their heads. I've listened to their hateful thoughts and felt the greed and anger swell in their hearts. They don't need prodding from me. I'm just a casual observer watching human destiny unfold."

"Not true," Santini said, his breath becoming more and more labored. "Only a few are like you and the puppets that dance to your tune."

Drakin-Shahid laughed. "Really? And you? I've seen your mind. The parts beyond your reach—your deepest fears, your hidden secrets, your pathetic weaknesses, your petty desires. If you had the chance, you would put a bullet right between the eyes of your daddy's killer. You've imagined it your entire life. You've dreamed about the moment."

Santini cried out as Drakin-Shahid kicked his leg.

"You're no different from the murderers you hunt." Drakin-Shahid pulled out a long sharp knife. "Unfortunately for you, Detective, I grow weary of this conversation. I have places to go, people to meet." Smiling, he ran a finger slowly across the blade and raised the knife high in the air.

Drakin was surprised when Santini slid the staff out from under his body and swung it around, striking him on the side of the head. Shahid's body went down with a thump. But Drakin's influence gave his host unusual strength, and in a flash he was up again, knife still in hand, as Santini struggled to hoist himself up.

"Be still, Detective. Better a quick death than to endure the slow gnawing of the rats."

Drakin watched with amusement as Santini once again brought his staff around, and his injured leg buckled, throwing him off balance. The missed swing left him lying exposed on the ground. Drakin-Shahid saw his opportunity and pounced. Grinning, he thrust the blade of the knife into his side. Santini grimaced in pain, and Drakin-Shahid pulled the knife loose and again raised it high in the air.

A stupendous crash of thunder and bolt of lightning lit up the wild-eyed face of Drakin-Shahid silhouetted against the black ashen sky, a triumphant cackle of laughter emerging from his twisted mouth.

Santini groped for his staff, but it was nowhere. Instead he felt a sharp object, a long shard of glass. He clasped it tightly, feeling the glass cutting deeply into the palm of his hand. Just before his assailant's knife came down, he plunged it into the throat of Josef Shahid.

Blood sprayed everywhere. Drakin-Shahid dropped to his knees, hands clutched at his throat in an attempt to stem the flow of blood.

Santini hoisted himself up and stood over Drakin-Shahid. He glanced at his two friends lying still and raised the staff high over his head. He let out a scream.

Summoning all his strength, Santini sank the end of the staff deep into the heart of Josef-Shahid. A fiery energy streamed through the end of the staff and blasted a gaping hole in his chest. Shahid looked up at Santini, a grimace of hatred forming on his twisted face just before he quivered, fell over, and died.

Santini limped to where his two friends lay facedown in the rubble. He turned Salvo's body over. He was unconscious but still had a faint pulse, and his respirator had been destroyed.

He then turned Jordan's body over. One side of her face was covered in blood, the hazmat suit melted and oozing, the respirator useless. He pulled off the damaged hazmat helmet, lifted her head, and called her name. Opening her one good eye, she smiled.

"It's gonna be okay," he stammered. He pulled out his cell phone, which was somehow still intact, and despite numbing fingers, managed to punch in the numbers for Lieutenant Giffords.

Jordan reached out her hand and he took hold of it. "It's okay, Detective. You must finish what you came here to do." She squeezed his hand weakly.

Santini crawled over to Jordan's medical bag, which had been tossed upside down. Four of the five remaining vials were shattered. Only one vial still contained the anti-radiation serum. He looked over at Salvo, hesitated, and crawled back over to Jordan. He ignored the searing pain in his bleeding hand and abdomen and injected the contents of the vial into Jordan's arm.

"Promise me you'll find my daughter and keep an eye on her."

"You're going to keep an eye on her yourself."

"Promise me."

"I promise," he stammered. Leaning forward, he kissed her on the lips. She smiled again and closed her eyes.

He felt for a pulse . . . Nothing.

Dazed, Santini stared off into the bleak landscape, the wind and ashen rain pelting his body, fires erupting all around him.

Finally, he hoisted himself into an upright position, using the staff as a crutch. The excruciating pain of his shattered leg and bleeding abdomen no longer seemed to register in his mind. Nor did the burning in his lungs, the radiation levels now starting to take their toll on his body.

Slowly, he dragged himself toward the splintered spire of the Empire State Building. He wanted to climb to the highest point of what was left of the skyscraper. He struggled and clawed his way, using the staff for leverage, and made it to the highest broken section of concrete near the spire, which even now felt hot from the explosion.

When he reached the top, he lay on his back for several minutes to catch his breath. The tourniquet Jordan had applied had loosened from the exertion, and he was beginning to lose blood again. He fought the dizziness that swept over him and gazed into the sky. Through the black ashen canopy, he couldn't see the swirling orb of stars that comprised the wormhole portal. But it was up there. It had to be. And he knew the aliens were about to break through.

He rolled onto his side and slowly, painfully maneuvered his broken body into a kneeling position. Then he clasped the staff in both hands.

As he held the staff, he could feel a slight tingling throughout its length. He tried to focus, but he couldn't help thinking about his two friends lying in the rubble. Everything he'd done to protect them had failed.

Santini watched the fires explode around him, and he could feel the poisoned smoke burning his lungs. As the blood continued to seep from his wounded leg and abdomen, an overwhelming loneliness washed over him. He looked around. His eyes burned and he was so very tired. Finally, pain and fatigue took over.

The last thoughts he had before falling over onto his side and closing his eyes were of his friends.

*"Darkness can only be scattered by light,
Hatred can only be conquered by love."*
—Pope John Paul II

# CHAPTER 53

President Tyler was glad to be back in the Oval Office. The familiarity of the furnishings—his desk, the soft leather chair, the bust of Lincoln, portraits of past presidents hanging on the walls—helped soothe the ache in his heart that had been lingering since the destruction of Manhattan Island.

He gazed into the eyes of George Washington, then Thomas Jefferson, James Madison, and the other great leaders donning his walls. He'd often taken solace in their company during the difficult times of his presidency, trying to see problems and solutions through the unique perspective of each.

Every one of the founding fathers and early presidents were men with weaknesses and flaws, but each seemed to have an inner strength and deep spiritual conviction that allowed them to weather any storm. Yet could they have weathered the storm he presently faced? Who could have foreseen the country, and the world, would be facing an enemy as powerful and ruthlessly evil as he now faced?

He tried not to think about his encounter with Drakin, but it was like a mental thorn festering in his mind that he couldn't dig out. He would not allow the memory of the event to cloud his thinking, though. He was back in control, and he was the president of the United States.

James Whitaker knocked and walked into the room. "Our technicians have been working 'round the clock, Mr. President, and in conjunction with other communications networks around the globe, they believe they have achieved optimum coverage for your address.

National and international feeds are up and ready. Fortunately, the unnatural electromagnetic storm we're experiencing is localized in the New England area and hasn't affected the rest of the Earth. We've also figured out a way to boost and maintain our signal, despite the disturbances created by the storm and the wormhole."

"And what is the approximate number of people I'll be speaking to, Whitaker?"

"Hard to say exactly, Mr. President. We've made it clear that listening to your address could have a direct bearing on their survival, so the motivation to tune in should be quite high. All the world's leaders are cooperating in synchronizing this event. If we include that part of the seven billion people on Earth that have cell phones with Internet capability, the number of potential listeners would be around five and a half billion people. As to how many will actually tune in to the live broadcast is unclear, given the variations in time zones, but we're confident this will indeed be a historic moment. You'll be speaking to close to five billion people, if not more."

"Thank you for your hard work, Whitaker."

"Certainly, Mr. President. Are you sure you don't want to reconsider broadcasting from within the Oval Office?"

"For the same reason I don't want a prepared speech or a teleprompter, Jim. I want to be able to look into the faces of my fellow Americans and all people. I want to speak to them directly from the heart. I can't do this from the Oval Office."

"Then tell me you at least have an outline of what you're going to say before you step in front of five billion people."

Tyler shook his head. "I'm going with my gut this time."

Whitaker sighed.

"What about the outside logistics?" Tyler asked.

"The same venue as your inaugural ceremony. We've sent the message out that you'll be giving a live address to the world from the west end of the capitol building and that it is open to the public. It was short notice. That coupled with the constant downpour and lightning makes it difficult to know how many will actually show up. Most people are still afraid to come out of their homes. Traveling is difficult. About ten thousand chairs have been hastily assembled. Your security teams are going crazy, but I assured them you couldn't be dissuaded. There were over a million people at your swearing-in ceremony, but on that day the sun was shining, there was no storm of the century, and there were no threats of terrorist attacks."

"They need to know the truth," Whitaker. "We need to let them know what's coming through that wormhole. We need to let them know what they're capable of. They need to be prepared. That's part of the reason for this address."

"Unfortunately, there will be some degree of panic, Mr. President."

And it will be my job to explain to them that fear is exactly what these creatures thrive on."

Whitaker nodded. "Unfortunately, we haven't yet heard from the detective."

"Their helicopter should soon be landing just outside of ground zero," Tyler said. "A team will be waiting with hazmat gear and a Hummer for them to use. As you know, Santini has a direct sat-com line to us when the time comes. Hopefully, we will hear from him shortly."

"I hope he knows what he's doing," Whitaker said. "Either way, we'll be ready to launch our warheads as soon as the aliens come through the portal and enter our airspace."

Tyler shook his head. "So much uncertainty, Whitaker. But let's you and I focus on the task at hand."

# CHAPTER 54

Chief of Staff James Whitaker walked into the Oval Office, where President Reginald Tyler sat lost in thought.

"It's time, Mr. President. We received a signal from Detective Santini just moments ago."

President Tyler smiled at his friend. "Walk with me, Whitaker."

The two strolled casually through the West Wing of the White House.

"How is the weather holding up, Whitaker?"

"A steady rain but no heavy downpour, Mr. President."

"I suppose that's the best we can hope for, considering how bad it's been."

Tyler had decided to do without the Honor Guard, so when they reached the French doors that led into the open area, it was just the president and Whitaker.

When Tyler stepped outside, he was amazed to see a sea of umbrellas that stretched as far as the eye could see.

"Thousands of Americans have come, Mr. President," Whitaker said. "Despite the rain and despite the danger of another nuclear attack. They came because they love their president and their country, and because they don't scare so easily. Even the entire Congress is here, and you know all too well what a bunch of wimps they are."

Tyler smiled and took hold of Whitaker's hand. "Thank you Jim."

Whitaker walked away and took a seat next to Vice President Sanchez.

When Tyler reached the podium, there was complete silence. Then the clapping began. Softly at first, but then it erupted into a crescendo that rivaled the loudest thunder the storm had yet offered.

After the applause died down, he began.

"I come before you today not just as president of the United States but as a citizen of the world. The leaders of your countries have granted me the opportunity to speak to you, and because of their help, today is a historic moment. Never before have so many gathered together, and never before has this coming together been more important to our survival than at this moment in time.

"You all know about the destruction of our city and the death of thousands of innocent men, women, and children. The entire world has grieved with us and demonstrated that when it comes to tragedy, there are no national borders that separate us.

"What I'm about to tell you concerning those responsible for this horrible crime might be difficult to believe, but I assure you, all of the facts I will present have been confirmed by scientists from all over the world.

"This was more than a terrorist attack. In fact, it was not orchestrated by anyone human. As we speak, there are alien vessels preparing to enter the Earth's atmosphere through a wormhole in space created by the nuclear explosion in New York City. These visitors have only one objective, the total domination and subjugation of the human race."

He paused. Through the mist of the rain he could see the stunned and fearful expressions on the faces of his fellow Americans, and he imagined that those same expressions were printed on the faces of all the unseen billions listening right now. But he had no choice but to continue.

"Unfortunately, one of these visitors has been living among us for a very long time. The old and the young, the rich and the poor, the black and the white, from the peoples of one continent to another, across the globe, he's moved without notice. His purpose has been simple: to create an atmosphere of suspicion and hatred between our peoples; to poison the human heart and mind with all that is negative and dark; to create chaos and violence; to pit one nation against another, one ethnicity against another, one religion against another, one man against another. This alien feeds off all the negative thoughts and emotions of humankind and instigates these tendencies whenever possible. This is how these aliens derive their power, and this is how they seek to destroy us.

"And this is where we take our leap of faith. If it is possible to open this portal with negative energy, then it stands to reason the opposite should hold true.

"People of Earth, if ever there was a time to lay aside your hatred, it is now. If ever there was a time to lay aside your weapons, your anger and your fear, it is now. If ever there was a time to embrace love and forgiveness, it is now. The major battle for Earth will be fought not with rockets and missiles but within the hearts and minds of mankind.

"I know we've made mistakes in the past, but I have faith in the human spirit. If we are to overcome these very powerful and evil adversaries, it is imperative we all focus our mental and emotional energies on what it means to be human. Love, compassion, forgiveness, courage—these are the virtues that bind us and define the human family. Look deep within yourselves. You know the truth of what I say.

"And so there is something we can do, and that we must all do together, right here and right now. Just as a magnifying glass will focus the scattered rays of the sun into a sharp beam of light, so must we use our minds to focus our thoughts and send an intense beam of positive energy into the heavens. This is how we will save ourselves. This is how we can re-create the world. This is the last great hope for humanity."

He paused.

"People of Earth, fear is what the enemy is banking on. Don't give in. In a few seconds, I'll close my eyes and concentrate on the profound love I have for my family, my friends, and for all of you, and I will send this ray of hope upward. I ask that you join me."

*"What lies behind us and what lies before us are tiny matters, compared to what lies within us."*
—Ralph Waldo Emerson

# CHAPTER 55

Santini opened his eyes and saw the sunlight spilling through the swaying branches of the willow. He smiled. He loved the old tree and the green grass surrounding it. It had a calming, soothing effect on him. Sitting up on the stone bench, he looked around. He recognized the place, of course.

The detective stretched out his legs and turned his face up toward the sunlight. He'd forgotten how much he missed the golden rays of sunshine. His whole body seemed to tingle with the warm energy as he fell into a wonderfully relaxed state of mind.

*If I could just stay here forever.*

As soon as that thought entered his mind, Santini heard footsteps. He stood up and saw a man walking slowly up the cobblestone pathway toward him. The man was smiling, and as he approached, Santini noticed he wore a blue uniform with a metal object affixed to his hat that sparkled in the sunlight. The man stopped before him.

"Hello, son."

Santini blinked. He tried to speak, but nothing could get by the lump in his throat. Tears filled his eyes. Then his father came closer and put his arms around him.

"I've missed you so much, Anthony. Please forgive me for leaving you."

It was as if a dam had broken and a flood of emotions cascaded from the heart of Anthony Santini. For several moments, he sobbed as his father held him. Finally, the sobs subsided.

"You didn't leave me," Anthony said. "It wasn't your fault."

"Please sit down, Anthony." Michael Santini motioned to the bench. "I want you to know how proud I am of you. Every son should be able to hear his father speak those words. I'm sorry it took so long." Then a concerned expression replaced his smile. "What are you doing here, Anthony?"

Santini's mind filled with confusion as he struggled to remember.

"Am I dead?"

"You're very close to death."

Santini concentrated. "There is something I must do, isn't there?"

His father nodded. "You still have a promise to fulfill."

Santini grimaced as he remembered something else. "Dr. Jordan is dead, isn't she? My partner barely alive."

His father put his hand on Santini's shoulder. "I know you tried to protect them, but it was because they loved you that they chose to follow you. It was not your fault."

Santini hung his head. "I wish I'd kissed her sooner."

"One of the most painful things for the human heart to bear is the loss of a loved one. We grieve the passing of those we lose so deeply only because we love them so deeply. This is what makes us human. This is what you must focus on. This is what will give you the strength to go back."

"I can't stay here, can I?"

"You know the answer to that question, son."

Santini stole one more glance at the old willow and turned his head up to feel the sun's rays one last time. He stood up and embraced his father.

"Good-bye, Father."

Santini's eyes slowly opened. Lying on his back, he could see the ashen sky and the black clouds of smoke from the fires that continued to burn out of control. His skin had been badly burned in the explosion, and the heat from the ground and the fires intensified his pain. Because of the radiation in the air, his breathing was labored and every inhalation set his chest on fire. He knew he would not last very much longer.

He rolled onto his side, and an immediate flash of agony lit up his entire body. The leg was useless, so again he used his staff to slowly prop himself up onto his knees. The effort made his body shake and his lungs burn. He placed his good leg forward and with all his strength, using the staff for leverage, managed to hoist his body into a standing position.

Balancing on one leg, he raised the staff high in the air with both hands. He knew that the orb of swirling stars that formed the portal to the wormhole was up there and that the alien ships were there, too. He hoped he was not too late.

He squeezed the staff tighter, and a tingling sensation began to flow through his hands. But at the same moment, he heard a buzzing inside his head and a painful squeezing pressure he recognized all too well. Then a deep voice emerged from inside Santini's mind.

"Give up, Detective. Your body is broken. You're dying. There's nothing you can do."

He tried to ignore the voice.

"The human race was always a flawed species. You know that. You've seen what they're capable of. Give up. Lie down and rest. It is time for new masters of the Earth."

Santini dropped his arms, the muscles too weak to hold them up.

"That's it, Detective. You're so tired. Tired of fighting. Tired of chasing the evil that's everywhere. Come. Lie down. You deserve to rest. To be at peace. Soon you'll be with your parents in a very beautiful place, where there are flowers and trees and sunny skies."

Santini recognized his own words as the voice inside his head laughed.

"I'm not one of your puppets," Santini shouted over the thunder and lightning. "And I'll never be."

Then he thought about what his father had said: *"We grieve the passing of those we lose so deeply only because we love them so deeply. This is what makes us human. This is what you must focus on."* So he took a deep breath, and ignoring the voice between his ears that had risen to a deafening volume and the searing pain in his leg, once again he raised the staff high into the air.

This time he reflected on his life and on all he held dear. He thought about the selfless love that his parents had for him. He invoked all the positive virtues of humanity—courage, compassion, sympathy, generosity, forgiveness. He concentrated on love, his love for Jordan and Salvo, his love for his parents, and the love all humanity shares.

Now his arms began to vibrate as a surge of energy shook the staff. He held on tight as a beam of light shot out from the end and began to blaze an opening through the soot and smoke of the black ashen sky. As he held fast, he could make out the swirling stars of the portal.

Instantly, Drakin's voice escalated into a thunderous rant of anger that made Santini's whole body tremble.

"Give up, Detective. You're too late. Just like you were too late to save New York. It was your fault, Detective. You let them all down. They're dead because of you."

Santini's head felt as if it were in a vise, the pressure mounting. Then he felt a snapping sensation, and a barrage of memories cascaded into his mind, creating a kaleidoscope of dark images. He saw himself standing over his murdered father. He saw himself weeping over the mangled body of Stephanie Winchester. He saw the faces of all the victims and their murderers. He saw himself defusing the fake bomb and the black mushroom cloud rising over New York. He saw Salvo and Jordan lying bloodied on the ground.

The images danced and swirled in his mind, and in the background he could hear Drakin's taunting laughter.

He lowered the staff. He felt dizzy. The beam of light weakened, and he struggled to concentrate and thought about Father O' Brian's words: "You cannot do this alone, Anthony. The staff is just a conduit. Its real power comes from all of us."

Then he remembered his signal to Whitaker. President Tyler was delivering his message. He closed his eyes and saw millions of people concentrating. He visualized their energy converging, and even through the nightmare images and Drakin's venomous voice, he focused their positive thoughts into his staff.

He raised the staff skyward.

"Help me!" he cried. "God, help me!"

At that instant, with the ground beneath him beginning to tremble, a deafening scream filled his head and the pressure in his brain released.

Holding the staff firmly and balancing on his good leg, he felt a powerful surge beginning in his feet and rising through his body. As the wave intensified, his hands began to glow with a dazzling white light, and out the end of the staff bolts of lightning shot toward the heavens.

He struggled to control the shaft of light. He wavered and faltered several times but finally was able to point the staff in the direction of the wormhole portal.

Then the storm joined the attack on Santini. The rain and wind intensified, and lightning bolts exploded all around him. The voices in the storm rising to a maddening crescendo, the ground beneath Santini's feet trembled as fires erupted all around him. But despite the assault and the excruciating pain, he found the strength to hold firm. With one last burst of effort, he let out a scream, and his staff sent out a blinding bolt of energy that exploded into the portal with the dazzling brightness of a hundred suns. The tremendous surge of energy slammed Santini onto the ground, and his world went black.

# CHAPTER 56

A cold rain pelted his face, and a faint whirring sound penetrated his awareness. He tried to open his eyes, but the lids would not respond.

"Santini!" Through the howling wind he could hear someone shouting his name. The whirring sound grew louder and seemed to be coming from all around him.

His eyes fluttered open. In the sky, through the ashen rain, he could make out the blur of rotating helicopter blades. He closed his eyes again.

"Let's go, sir. It's time to get out of here."

Santini opened his eyes. It was Lieutenant Giffords, with a ladder from the helicopter dangling behind him. "My friends—please, take them first."

"We already have them, Detective. Now just lie still and we'll be out of here in an instant."

Santini felt himself being strapped securely into a large basket. "Please, my staff."

Slowly, he rose into the sky. As he drifted, barely conscious, he looked toward the heavens. The shifting clouds and smoke coalesced, and for a moment he thought he could see the face of Stephanie Winchester. She was smiling happily. When her image faded, through the opening in the clouds, Santini could see that the swirling stars of the portal were gone. Then he lost consciousness again.

# CHAPTER 57

Santini slowly opened his eyes. He squinted at the brightness and quickly shut them. He took a deep breath and opened them again. It took a while, but his vision eventually cleared.

There was a woman standing over him. She smiled.

"Well, it's about time, Detective."

"Kelly? . . . Am I dreaming?"

She took his hand. "No. Fortunately for all of us, you are not dreaming."

He smiled, his eyes watering. "Salvo?"

"He's driving the nurses crazy. Insists he's well enough to get up to see you. But they won't budge. They've just about tied him down."

He wiped away a tear. "Where am I?"

"Every trauma center near Manhattan was already swamped. So the president had us flown here to John Hopkins."

He looked down at the cast and bandages on his leg and winced.

"You've been out for five days. They had to induce coma. Luckily, they were able to save your leg. It's going to take time, another surgery, and a lot of painful rehab, but you should be able to walk again. Though maybe with a limp."

"That's okay," he said. "I have a cool walking stick."

She smiled. "Apparently you do. Your abdominal wound didn't hit any vital organs or major arteries. Otherwise, you wouldn't be here today. The injuries to the rest of your body were superficial."

He stared at the bandage around her forehead.

"Severe concussion," she said. "But there should be no long-term effects. Some headaches. Lots of stitches. Same with Salvo. Burns and lacerations from the explosion. Although they got us out of there in time, we'll all need to be tested periodically for the next few years for any radiation effects. We were very lucky."

Jordan glanced at the staff standing in the corner of the room.

"When your strength returns and you feel up to it, Salvo and I want to know everything that happened."

He smiled. "You won't believe me."

She laughed. "I don't think there's much that could possibly surprise me anymore, Detective." Then she leaned over and kissed his lips. The kiss lingered, and Santini felt as if he were floating. "I'm going back to my room. We both need to rest. I'll check in on you later."

Santini lay there smiling and, in a few moments, closed his eyes.

# CHAPTER 58

*Three Months Later*

The makeshift 109th Precinct was an old warehouse just outside Long Island City. A third of the officers and personnel from the precinct had perished in the explosion. Before the attack, they'd been operating on a skeleton crew, with many lucky enough to have been helping with flood evacuations outside the blast area. A section of the warehouse had been turned into a memorial for those who had died.

When Santini limped into the station, he noticed everyone fell silent. Then a gradual round of applause escalated and a succession of tearful hugs followed.

"Welcome back, partner," Salvo said.

"I don't think I've ever seen you in a suit," Santini said.

"It's not every day you get to sit next to the president," Salvo said. "And you clean up pretty good yourself. How's the leg?"

"Rehab is over, thankfully. Doctors say there may still be improvement over time." Santini began limping around staring at the photos of the fallen. There was a photo of Captain Johnson and his family. There were fifteen similar photos of those who had died. Flowers and personal items were placed on the floor beneath them. He wiped his eyes.

"Are you ready?" Salvo asked.

"Yeah. I told Jordan we'd pick her up at eight. The memorial services begin at ten."

"Did you know O'Brian is giving the opening prayer before the ceremony?"

"Kelly mentioned it. I'm looking forward to seeing him again."

Salvo and Santini left the warehouse and got into the Crown Victoria, which Salvo had found still parked safely on the shoulder of the Long Island Expressway.

Memorial services were being held all over the world today. Flushing Meadow Park in Queens, the site of the 1939 World's Fair, was the focal point for the nation's services.

Of the four boroughs surrounding Manhattan Island, Queens had sustained the least damage from the explosion, so residents had been slowly returning to their homes.

Scientists and engineers from around the world were intensively researching radiation-contamination neutralization, and breakthroughs were being reported that could have Manhattan Island habitable in ten to fifteen years. Architects were already drawing up plans for the "New Manhattan," which included blueprints for a new Empire State Building, only this one, of course, would be taller than its predecessor.

Dignitaries from all over the world were present. At center stage, and surrounded by thousands of seats, was the world's largest global structure, the Unisphere, rising over 140 feet into the air. It was originally commissioned for the World's Fair in 1939 to celebrate global interdependence and the beginning of the Space Age.

The sun broke through the clouds as the prayers, speeches, songs, and tears began. When President Tyler gave his speech, he stressed the historic importance of what humanity had done by coming together to defeat the alien threat.

Salvo, Santini, Jordan, her daughter, and Father O'Brian sat in the row just behind where Tyler and his family were seated. When the memorial was over, Tyler turned and addressed them.

"You're all invited to the White House for dinner as my personal guests. There will be tokens of recognition for what you've done. Unfortunately, your part in all of this hasn't been made public."

"I was never one who enjoyed the spotlight, Mr. President," Santini said," but I think my partner might be disappointed."

Salvo smiled.

"Scientists can't explain what caused the explosion that destroyed the wormhole portal," Tyler said, "but I know what you did."

"We all played a part," Santini said. "Every human being."

Tyler extended his hand to each of them. "See you next Saturday night, if that works for all of you."

Salvo made as if he were seriously checking his appointment book until Jordan swatted him.

"Good." Tyler said. "I'll send a car around to pick you up."

As the crowds began to disperse, Santini, Salvo, Jordan, and O'Brian remained seated, basking in the sunlight.

"Do you think Drakin is dead?" Jordan said.

"I should think so," O'Brian said. "No storm, no voices, peaceful prayers and meditations. And from the energy surge Anthony described through his body and Drakin's subsequent scream, I would hope he was fried. You have all done well."

Santini took Jordan's hand. "Any plans for tonight? I know a cozy little family-owned Italian restaurant. The best baked clams in the world."

Jordan smiled. "Are you asking me out on a date, Detective?"

"How about you call me Tony?"

Jordon laughed. "Tony. I like the sound of that. I'm spending the rest of the day with Dayna. Pick me up at seven." She hugged Salvo and Father O'Brian. "I'll come see you before you leave, Father."

"Seven it is," Santini said. His grin expanded from ear to ear as Jordan and Dayna walked away.

"Before you leave?" Salvo said.

"I'm flying to the Vatican on Thursday," O'Brian said. "It seems retirement doesn't suit me after all. There is still much of God's work to do." He embraced Salvo and Santini. "Any time you would like to meet the pope, let me know. And God bless you both."

"God bless you, too, Father O'Brian," Santini said.

Salvo gave Santini a look of surprise. "What was that you said?"

"Shut up, Salvo. Let's go."

"Before I go back to the precinct, I have some unfinished police business to attend to," Salvo said. "Unlike you, I'm not on sabbatical."

"Wasn't it you that told me I needed to take a vacation?"

"Come on. It's on the way and won't take long. Then I'll drop you off."

"All right. But don't forget I have a date tonight."

"I won't forget . . . Tony." Salvo gave him a sly grin.

The Crown Victoria took off, and in twenty minutes they were parked outside an apartment building in the East Bronx.

"So what's this about?" Santini said.

His partner dropped a file folder on Santini's lap. Then he handed him a note.

"Remember this?"

Santini took the small piece of paper and looked at it. It said "a tattoo of a swats-sticker with the initials R and M on either side."

"Don't remind me," Santini said. "Drakin set me up and I fell for it." He crumpled up the note and tossed it out the window.

"It just so happens while you were rehabbing in the hospital, I had Marissa search the prison records for any inmates that might be in the system with this identifying mark. We got a hit on a Raymond Mancuso, sixty-seven years old. He served ten years for armed robbery and then another ten years for aggravated assault. I interviewed three of his five previous cellmates and they all confirmed he'd bragged about killing a cop. They're willing to testify." Salvo paused. "We've been keeping an eye on him until you got back."

Santini was speechless. He stared straight ahead as his heart pounded and a surge of adrenaline shot into his blood. Two patrol cars pulled up alongside the Crown Victoria.

"I thought it should be you that makes the arrest," Salvo said.

In five minutes, the detectives stood just outside the apartment door, guns drawn.

"Raymond Mancuso. NYPD. Open up," Salvo yelled.

The door unlatched and a bald man with a gray beard and black eyes stood there with an annoyed expression. "What the hell do you want?"

Santini pointed his gun at the man. For years he had imagined this moment. The moment when he would fulfill his promise and exact revenge on the man who had taken his father from him. He stood there staring into the man's eyes, years of frustration and pent-up rage boiling to the surface, his finger edging onto the trigger.

"Santini!" Salvo yelled.

Santini didn't move.

"Don't do it!"

His arm trembled.

Salvo put his hand on his shoulder. "Don't do it, Santini."

He lowered his gun. "You were wrong, Drakin. I'm nothing like you . . . Turn around, puppet."

"What's this about?" Mancuso said. "I didn't do anything."

Santini pushed him hard against the wall, and Salvo handed him a pair of handcuffs.

"Why am I not surprised that you're bald, asshole?" Santini said. "Raymond Mancuso, you're under arrest for the murder of Officer Michael Santini. You have the right to remain silent. Anything you say can and will be used against you in a court of law. You have the right to an attorney. If you can't afford an attorney, one will be appointed for you."

Santini took a deep breath and as he exhaled he felt a heavy weight lift from his soul. He turned to look at Salvo. "Thanks."

"Hey, that's what partners are for. Right, Santini?"

"Right, Salvo."

# EPILOGUE

It was a cold but sunny day, and the glistening icicles from yesterday's winter storm were beginning to slowly melt off the branches of the trees.

Twenty-two-year-old Thomas Hunt sat in the warmth of his 1982 Chevy Impala with the radio blasting, feeling sorry for himself. Yesterday, his girlfriend had called it off, saying he was too controlling and too angry.

What the hell did that mean?

She wouldn't say much more than that even though he'd pressed her to the point where she asked him to leave and never talk to her again.

He looked over at the building where she worked. He took out a cigarette, puffed on it a few times, tossed it out the window, and cranked up the radio even louder as he drummed on the dashboard to the rhythm of the music.

For nine months he'd put up with her crap. And for what? They were all the same, as far as he was concerned. Needy and whiny, always trying to change you and make you soft. He didn't need her. In fact, he didn't need anybody.

As that last thought lingered in his head, Thomas Hunt got out of his car and popped the hood of the trunk. He slipped on the vest with the two pistols in each pocket and grabbed the AK-47. Then he slid two magazine clips under his belt and strolled, whistling, toward the entrance of Dawson Elementary School.

Drakin's energy consciousness quivered within the brain of Thomas Hunt. His newest protégé was working out quite well. The young man was wired for violence. Another mind ripe for the picking.

Drakin thought about the portal. He was surprised at the entire chain of events. Santini, the interfering Astrolite, and the troublesome staff had been entirely unexpected. He knew the staff had power, but to destroy the wormhole portal?

He'd been badly weakened in the battle at ground zero and had to lie low for quite a while until his strength returned. But there was always plenty of negative energy to be had. Now he was back and, of course, he had a plan. In fact, he had several.

Throughout human history, he'd been a player behind the scenes. But what if he were to reveal himself to the world? There were many ways he could accomplish this. Then he could destroy their faith and religion by telling them the truth about their alien Astrolite messiahs. That should stir up quite an emotional frenzy. An explosion of sorts. Slowly, he would once again build up the negative energy required to destroy the barrier and create the wormhole.

And then there was the Middle East, where things were progressing quite nicely. The Iranians should be weaponized in just a matter of months, and Drakin wanted to be there so he could help orchestrate the fireworks.

Drakin curled Thomas Hunt's mouth into a smile.

This present escapade was, of course, a mere diversion. Something to attract the attention of his pal Anthony Santini. And the staff.

With his AK-47, Drakin-Hunt blasted the lock to the front doors of the elementary school and casually walked inside.

Santini bolted upright in his bed, droplets of sweat sliding down his temples. Kelly turned on the light and placed her hand on his shoulder.

"Drakin again?"

Santini nodded.

"I'll call Salvo while you get dressed."

Santini and Jordan waited in front of their house for a few minutes before Salvo pulled up in the driveway. The two quickly got in.

"Where to?" Salvo asked.

"Dawson Elementary School," Santini said as he slid the old staff out from the purple silk cloth. "And step on it."

Salvo slapped the siren onto the roof of the Crown Victoria and peeled out into the dark of the early morning.

# ABOUT THE AUTHOR

Dr. Richard Sparacino was born and raised in New York City, where he graduated with a degree in psychology. He has spent the last thirty-five years in Tucson, Arizona, raising four children with his wife, Mari, and maintaining a Chiropractic clinic.

Being from New York City, the events of 9-11 were particularly painful.

What causes people to commit evil acts? Is humanity wired for constant wars, hatred and violence? What if there was something out there influencing human behavior that we were not conscious of? And what if this entity fed off the negative energy produced by its influence? But most importantly, what can we do about it?"

These were the burning questions that eventually spawned the idea for the fiction novel, "Riders on the Storm," a good vs. evil story, with an unexpected twist.

Dr. Sparacino, novelist, singer, and songwriter, can usually be found hiking in the mountains of the beautiful Sonoran Desert of Tucson.

Made in the USA
San Bernardino, CA
09 January 2017